Morphine

The Rush World Series

SAM LYNN

Copyright 2022 © Sam Lynn

All rights reserved. This book or any portion thereof may not be reproduced or used in any manner whatsoever without the express written permission of the copyright owner except for the use of brief quotations in a book review. For more information, email authorsamlynn@gmail.com

This is a work of fiction. Names, characters, businesses, places, events, locales, and incidents are either the products of the author's imagination or used in a fictitious manner. Some organizations and tv shows names have been changed due to copyright. Any resemblance to actual persons, living or dead, is purely coincidental.

Person Cover Art: graphicescapist

Object Cover Art: TRC Designs

Proofread by Meg Woods

*To all the readers who want to become authors.
Write that story.*

Authors Note:

I wrote Maria Alejandra in the way you would read a male athlete. There may be times when you question her actions and her dislike for her team principal. But just know she is stubborn, hotheaded, very sure of herself and can be naïve. No matter her actions try to see her growth because it is something worth reading!

WARNING

Before going any further know that this book contains profanities, explicit content, and everything about this book is **18+**.

This is a contemporary romance with dark themes, keep that in mind while reading.

VOCABULARY

G Force (G's): The multiplication of the force of gravity during braking, cornering, or accelerating.

Grid: The area where cars are set into a grid formation in order to start the race.

Calendar: The racing schedules.

Formula One: An international form of auto racing, whose races are called Grand Prix.

Formula Two: In order to make it to Formula One, it is the level right under the main racing sport. It consists of smaller cars, lower budgets, and aspiring F1 drivers.

Overtake: Passing a driver from one position to the other.

Collisions: Two cars crashing into each other.

First Driver: The main player in any Formula One team, most likely the one with more experience and highest probability of winning the Drivers' Championship.

Second Driver: The driver that is seen as the support to the first driver.

Halo: The halo is a driver crash-protection system used in open-wheel racing series, which consists of a curved bar placed to protect the driver's head. It's a safety precaution.

Driver's Championship: The competition to see who wins first among all the racers, teams don't play into this whatsoever.

Constructors' Championship: The competition to see which is the best team. If both drivers are fast and the car delivers, it means that more points are scored. The team with the most points wins the trophy.

FOR MY FORMULA ONE FANS, NAMES—such as associations and shows—HAVE BEEN CHANGED DUE TO LEGAL PURPOSES.

PROLOGUE

Maria Alejandra - 10 Years old

"Papá!" I squealed as I ran, throwing myself into my father's arms. Wrapping my legs around his torso, I gave him the biggest hug I could muster.

"*Te extrañe tanto, princesa.*" He nuzzled his head in my neck while giving me a bear hug. I smiled at the gesture.

"I missed you more," I replied in English. I looked him straight in the eyes with a smile on my face, hoping he wouldn't ask me the question I had been dreading to hear. I had been struggling with my training. Everything was hurting and my dream of becoming an F1 driver seemed intangible.

"How's karting going, Ale?" I groaned inwardly. There it was. The question I didn't want to hear. Karting is the first level I needed to pass on my way to the big leagues—

Formula One. The cars are smaller, and they've helped me learn from a young age how to maneuver a vehicle similar to an F1 car. I sometimes felt like this was a pipe dream.

"I don't know if I want to keep going, it's hard. Tom has been making my neck exercises harder. Plus, he's slowly introducing me to G-force."

Rubbing my neck in discomfort, I tried to avoid looking at the disappointed expression plastered on *Papá's* face. I pouted as I feel the constant reminder of the physical exertion my trainer had caused. I offered him a small smile hoping to dissipate his look of disapproval, but he frowned even more, making my insides twist. I didn't like it when *Papá* disapproved of my behavior. I just wanted to make him proud.

"Let me tell you a secret, *princesa*." He paused. "Whatever it is you want to do with your life, I will always be here to support and love you. Whether you want to stop this journey and start a new one, I will be there with you every single step of the way. You do understand that, right?"

His stern eyes looked down at me while I tried to unpack his words.

"*Si, Papá*, I know," I reassured him with my hand on his shoulder, attempting to make him feel better.

"You are my child. My heart. My soul. You will never understand the love I have for you until you are a parent. When you were born, I knew that you had a purpose," his voice wavers trying to finish his statement.

"Do you remember that day when you pointed at the TV

while we were watching that championship race?" I nodded. Remembering it like it was yesterday, he continues, "I just knew by the twinkle in your eyes, that F1 was your purpose. The sport was made for you to change; then you got into a kart. The happiness on your face was above anything else I had ever felt in my entire life." He paused to look away like he was recalling the past. "Because that happiness—your happiness—is everything to me. I will say this once, and only once. You can quit whenever you want, but I refuse to let you quit when something gets hard. Because once something gets hard, that is when it will turn into something legendary."

A tear slipped down his face. He looked away trying to shield his emotion. One thing I know about *Papá*, he hates to show weakness even towards the ones he loves.

"It's okay, *Papá*, I won't quit." I hauled him into my arms giving him the biggest hug I could. *Well, I tried to, anyway.* I wanted my *Papá* to feel better, he was my world, and in that moment, I would have done anything to make that happen.

"Good. Now, let's get you competing. I think you're ready," he said with a small nod, smiling with sad eyes as a tear fell down his cheek.

"Let's go talk to your trainer before your session starts. You can tell him how you are feeling." He kissed the top of my head then lifted me off him and my feet touched the ground shortly after. Taking my small hand in his big one, he guided me through our hacienda.

Everything about the Castillo family was grand, my dad

loved it that way. The hacienda was inspired by Spanish architecture, one that only my dad would appreciate due to his travels.

Beige bricks were stacked onto one another creating the structure's shape. Blossoming green vines overlapped on the exterior of our home angling from the rooftops perch, showcasing plush colors that filled the dreadful house with life. The gardens sat at the back of the property—filled with every kind of flower imaginable—dominated by a large green maze.

After walking for a few minutes through the house and out the back door, we made it to the gardens, passing the lilies and daisies. My eyeline was met with the maze, its huge structure towering over me.

We entered the archway, signifying the beginning of the maze; our knowledge of the passageways guides us through swiftly.

We are met with the wall of roses, indicating that we've reached the middle. It was made as a memorial for my grandmother, her love for red was unmatched. The wall has vines enclosing the green leaves, each vine the color of muted brown. To the side of each ivy there are red roses placed adjacent to one another. The unique thing about the display is the black rose sitting right in the middle.

On the day of my grandmother's passing, I asked why the rose was placed there. I was six and utterly heartbroken. I remember that day perfectly as if it was just four years ago. *Everyone was dressed in black. It was weirdly sunny out. The sun* was blazing on us while we sat in black chairs placed in four rows lined up horizontally. We sat there in Sinaloa, mourning the light of our family.

My grandmother would have wanted it that way, her light shined ever so brightly, even in her death. My father sat right next to me with my mother on the other side, both looking straight ahead.

Mother wore a massive black droopy sun hat covering her face while her long dark brown hair reached her lap. She had a slim figure, with lace covering every inch, including black gloves that were tailored perfectly to her hands. Huge sunglasses covered her bright green eyes that would be glistening with the remnants of the tears that ran down her face. Her small sniffles were heard beside me.

Next to me, my father was sitting there in his black suit. No emotion ran across his face, he just looked straight ahead, lost in his thoughts. This was his way of showing affection towards his mother. I remember putting my hand on top of his, showing him the remorse he was trying to give with his loss of words.

Next thing I knew, I was asking why the rose was placed there. I remember my dad's words as if it was ingrained in my soul.

He turned back to face me, showing no emotion as he uttered something I would never forget for the rest of my existence.

"No matter how much you love the people in your life, death is inevitable. All the color you see around you is just the road that leads to La Muerte. We all turn into ash and become that one black rose. But all that vibrant color that we spread throughout *our lives, just like your Abuela, means more than our inevitable demise. The overflowing passion that we experience in this life means more than anything else. Because when we leave the people we love, when we finally reach the inevitable, we leave that one black rose and all the color that surrounds it. Because the impact that we left behind is the life that we lived."*

That's why the memorial was my favorite part of the gardens and it always had butterflies surrounding it.

We turned right and passed the wall which was far behind us. The opening to the maze exit was now in sight. Walking through it, we made our way across the field leading up to the back part of the acreage where my home grid was placed.

Seeing the shine of the gates made of silver wire around wooden stakes that surround the track, I always felt the rush filling me as if I was seeing it for the first time. I always got that feeling before going to practice.

My father had built this track for me on the *hacienda's* acreage. He had said it was practical as I could wake up and train.

Even though racing had its moments, this sport was my life, and I will be forever indebted to my father for the dedication and money he put into my passion.

We walked through the gates surrounding the whole track and then rushed towards the garage. As the smell of gas hit my nose, signaling the preparation of my kart, I couldn't help but smile. I saw my trainer already huddled over my vehicle, most likely fixing a comfort alteration I told him about the other day. Upon hearing us enter he turned around, giving us a beaming smile. As he rubbed his hands on a towel, trying to remove the grease, he greeted us a little too excitedly.

"Hi Maria Alejandra, are you ready for training today?" I let out a groan thinking about neck training. My dad gave me a playful whack on my side.

I replied with a quick yes, rapidly walking over to my locker where all my gear was, and started preparing for a few more hours of pain.

"Make sure everything is in order. I expect the best from you, she will only have the finest at her disposal. She has been complaining about her neck so make sure you push her, but not to the point where I will have to take her to the doctor for a neck strain, am I clear?" My dad said with his eyes blazing at Tom.

"Yes, Don Castillo. I am positive she will get the best training possible. I will try my best to stretch her more and give her ice after every exercise we do," my trainer said in a reassuring tone. I snorted, as if that was going to help.

My father glanced at me before he nodded at Tom. When he attempted to walk away, Tom said something to him that caught my full attention.

"I am so sorry for your loss." My father stopped dead in his tracks.

Turning around he gave Tom a murderous look then uttered the words, "thank you."

I remember thinking that it was incredibly odd.

My dad has never been a blunt man, he likes to be detailed and elaborate in his words. Making sure people receive his message clearly and precisely.

As soon as the presence of my father was gone my little voice echoed off the garage walls.

"What loss?" I questioned with curiosity.

Tom then turned around to face me. "You haven't heard?" he asked in a shocked voice, almost like he couldn't believe I didn't know the information he was about to tell me.

Taking a few seconds to think carefully about what he wanted to say he finally said six little words that carried so much meaning.

"Your mother was killed this morning."

Everything stopped. It was as if the world was no longer spinning. My reality completely paused in shock.

Make no mistake, no tears fell. *Not a single one.*

My mother was dead. No one had the thought or the courtesy to tell me. Not that I had much of a relationship with her. My dad had taken multiple mistresses, my mom being his legal wife. They met when they were young and fell in love long before my dad had power and money. I knew he loved her more than anyone else, but he had hurt her, and all that hurt turned into resentment towards me. Thus, resulting in our relationship being strained by both of my parents' actions.

I was in shock. Even though I didn't know her that well, she was still my mother. I would never have the chance to try to start a relationship with her once I got older. She wouldn't see me become an F1 legend or get married and have kids. None of that, because she's dead.

"Who killed her?" I uttered out.

He turned around, regret plastered all over his face. The regret of telling me that my own mother had died. That's when I knew he was a coward.

Understandably so.

He would have to face my father after all of this. Because my rage wasn't directed towards him, it was directed towards my *Papá*.

"That is information that you'll have to figure out on your own, Maria."

The anger I was feeling at being pushed away bubbled inside my gut. They saw me as a little girl who knew nothing, but I knew more than they thought.

I demanded he answer my question, repeatedly.

But he never did.

Even now, ten years later, I still haven't found out who killed my mother. I just accepted it, like absolutely nothing had ever happened. I had no image of my mother to honor and guard because I never really knew her.

The next day I woke up and got ready for her funeral.

Walking through the greenery of the maze wearing a black ruffled chiffon dress and a white ribbon holding my hair up, I made my way towards the square, eventually reaching the wall of roses that honored my grandmother. Something was different, the aura was utterly dreadful. It was a rainy day with dark clouds blocking out all traces of sunlight, perfect for *Mamá's* funeral. It represented the pain that she felt in this life.

Turning to my left, I was met with a flower display mimicking my grandmother's. It was different from the original; it had white lilies surrounding one black one. *My mother's favorite flower.*

Finding my seat right next to my father, I noticed León, my half-brother, sitting right beside him. His mother, Lillian, was sitting behind my dad, giving her condolences, her hand patting and slowly caressing his shoulder. As I sat there, I realized the filtered life I was living. The game that was being played before my eyes.

The two women in my life had just died, and without them, there would be no more sympathy, peace, and no more authenticity.

Looking straight ahead at my mother's memorial, I realized in that moment that the Castillo women all die in chaos. They stay in the remnants of the people who killed them.

I was sitting right next to the man who killed my mother.

I was an imposter just like the rest of them.

CHAPTER ONE

MARIA ALEJANDRA - 10 YEARS LATER

"Alejandra, how does it feel?!" a female reporter yells.

"What are your plans for next season?" shouts the next.

"Do you consider yourself ready for F1?"

This type of attention at a Formula Two press conference isn't normal. All the cameras flash around me as I bask in the attention.

I, quite literally, have just come back from one of the best moments of my life. "Many congratulations to the top three winners of the 2021 Formula Two driver's championship. In third place, Oliver Semenov, representing Russia. In second place, Elijah James, representing Great Britain. Then, finally, our Formula Two driver's champion, Maria Alejandra Castillo, representing Mexico," Jackson Owens exclaims in his staple British accent.

"Alejandra, that was a brilliant and stunning win from you." I nod and smile at his statement, muttering a brief "thank you" before he continues.

"How do you feel not only being the first Mexican driver in sixty years to have reached this achievement, but also the first woman?"

"It's surreal if I'm being honest. I remember growing up and just knowing that this was what I wanted to do for the rest of my life. I wanted to become a legend, and today I did what my six-year-old self dreamed of; I became that legend. That being said, I'm not only proud as a Mexican to have achieved this, but I'm even more damn proud to be a woman doing it. It's been long overdue for a female to reach this level in the sport, and I am so glad to have opened these doors for the future of racing. Because today, I proved that the future is female," I reply.

I *am* damn proud. I've worked my ass off to be here. Dealing with sexism and backhanded comments every single day is tiring. As are the constant sexual advances of my fellow drivers and team members.

The comments I get on social media telling me that racing is, and I quote, "a man's sport." On top of the pressure that a Formula driver has to deal with, I have the added fact that I'm a woman. It's plain and simple really, this industry is blatantly sexist. The men get the money, the sponsorships, and the attention.

"This being the most pivotal moment in your career so far as a driver, what would you describe this moment as?"

Jackson Owens interrupts my thoughts and I stop to think for a second.

"It's many things. So many adjectives. But I would describe this moment as reaching that point in your life where you finally know that it was all worth it. The tears, the anger, the hard work, and the discipline."

"So, what's next for the Formula Two Driver's Champion?" This is the question I have been dreading because I have absolutely no idea. I love dependability, but at this moment my career is far from dependable.

"Well, it depends on what answer you would like. The future I'm hoping for or the future that is more likely," pausing, the next sentence rolls off of my tongue.

"I'm hoping for the spot at Elektra that recently became vacant. Ever since Luke Davis announced his retirement, it hasn't been filled. I have shown consistency and talent, not to mention I'm a part of Elektra's Driver's Academy," I state bluntly before I continue. "But the option that is most likely is the renewal of my contract in Formula Two," I finish off.

"How do you feel about the arrival of Luca Donatello as the new team principal of Elektra?"

To be honest, I haven't really thought about the team principal change. The decision had been announced recently and hit the tabloids like Harry Styles announcing his next tour.

Luca Donatello is a world champion. He achieved this with Elektra Motorsports about twelve years ago and is pretty much their poster boy and god.

I know that he's a former Italian F1 driver who hasn't been seen for awhile in the public eye. After his retirement, he decided to quit all social media and completely go off the grid. I think he also got married to some model afterwards. They went on their honeymoon, and no one has heard from him since.

"I think it's an exciting change for Elektra as a team in general. With him, they may even have a chance to advance further. The change was a smart move on Elektra's part and if I were to be selected for the 2022 Formula One cycle, I would be honored to drive under his management." I smile, the kind of smile that is genuinely forced.

"Ok, one last question for the champion. If you were to become a Formula One driver next year, do you think you are fully ready for that responsibility?"

"I think that I work my ass off every single day to stay in this sport. If I were to have the opportunity to advance my career by going into F1 next year, I would not only give my blood, sweat, and tears to the team, I would also give them my every thought. If they don't pick me, well, that's their loss. They will never find a driver as dedicated as me. I have the drive, I have the fight, and most importantly, I have the ability to deliver the results that are needed. So, in that aspect, yes, I know that I am ready," I answer.

"Thank you, Alejandra, and congratulations on your win!" I give him a nod and a short "thank you".

"Now onto our second and third place winners, Elijah and Oliver."

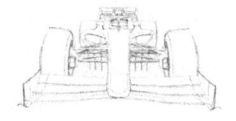

That was the longest press conference of my life.

After asking Oliver and Elijah about their podium standings, he then proceeded to let the other reporters ask questions. It went on for an hour and a half.

AN HOUR AND A FUCKING HALF!

Who wants to watch an hour and a half press conference asking the same questions over and over again?

Thankfully, it's over and I can't wait to get on the next flight back to Mexico City.

I want to see my family.

They planned to come, but my dad had a last-minute business deal.

I miss them, but I understand.

They don't want their business close to my career, that much I am thankful for.

Exiting the paddock, I see a figure standing ahead of me. His outline right in front of my training room. His arms are crossed and there are men flanked behind him. In an Armani suit and reflective glasses, I just know it's him by his signature look. That intimidating and powerful aura is very much evident to anyone in his vicinity.

"León, what are you doing here?!" I squeal, running towards my brother.

He turns around to face me, a smile adorning his

features. I jump into his arms, hugging him as tightly as possible.

"*¿Tú crees que me perdería este momento, princesa?*"

His brotherly admiration that I adore so much hits me, making me warm inside. I return his tight hold, his love for me taking me full force.

"I thought you had work?" My eyebrow raised in question.

"You don't have to worry. I have been here since yesterday. I wanted to surprise you before the race, but I didn't want to distract you. I am so proud of you, *princesa*," he says, his accent way thicker than mine.

I want to cry. I'm proud of myself too, but coming from León, it means so much more. This man has protected me through everything, and I am forever grateful. *El es mi hermano, sangre de mi sangre.* My dad always says that León loves me more than anyone else in the family.

Setting my eyes on León's men behind him, I frown. "Hello Sebastián," I pause then turn to his counterpart "Lucero," I acknowledge them with a look, annoyance visible in my tone. They are definitely not my favorite people.

Being the sons of Los Reyes de la *Muerte* de Sinaloa, of course they were deviant. They had to be. Inevitably, they were passed down to my brother within the bond of the cartel. León, being the heir to the Castillo name. For years, Los Castillos have owned Sinaloa. When the drug shortage happened in the sixties, my family was the first to jump on to the wave, resulting in us becoming the biggest cartel in all of Mexico. This information is unknown to most, which allows my brother to be seen as a businessman, helping him blend into society effortlessly.

León will be bearing the weight of an empire on his shoulders. He will own Mexico in its entirety and become extremely powerful. I'm frightened for him; he must sell his soul in return for his life.

"How long are you here for?" I question, laying back on the couch after we walk through the door to my training room. I start to take my shoes off and massage my toes, the ache spreading through my whole foot.

"I have to leave in about an hour to go back to Mexico City." I jump up at his response letting a smirk spread across my face.

"Did you charter your private plane?"

"Yes," he responds. Just as I hoped.

"Can I go back with you? I'm dreading having to fly commercial. It's double the time and so stuffy," I say, with pleading eyes.

"Don't you have more publicity to handle?"

"No, not really, I just finished the winners' press conference before I came back over here. The season is over, so the post-race brief isn't until we go back to headquarters in CDMX in a few days."

I really want to go home. Not only to see my family, but to be in my space. In my apartment that I absolutely adore and to finally see my best friend, Violetta.

"If your publicist says it's okay, then yes. You know you don't even have to ask, *princesa*, what's mine is yours."

He's my brother. My *hermano*. He might be my half-brother but my brother, nonetheless. He took care of me when *Mamá* died and he never involved me with business. He knows that my career comes first, and I would never allow something of that magnitude to affect it.

This sport is my world and so is my family. I would do anything to never have to live a life without racing. The thrill of the overtakes, the rush from the speed, and the adrenaline from the podiums. No one would give it up if they were in my position and if they did, they would be crazy.

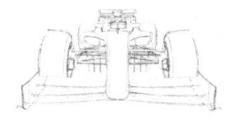

As I make my way down to the publicity office, I'm interrupted by Lauren, my publicist, or as I like to call her 'my savior.' Having gotten me out of so much, I will be forever indebted to her.

I'm currently on an "alcohol cleanse" ever since the last time I drank myself away. It was the night of the Monaco Grand Prix and I had won, so I decided that one drink wouldn't hurt. Just one.

I ended up having ten shots and my lightweight ass almost got alcohol poisoning. Somehow, I was able to sneak out, no idea how no one saw me. But my night didn't end there. By the end of the night, they ended up finding me completely naked on the sunroof of a private yacht doing the Scottish jig.

Don't drink kids, it's not worth the humiliation.

I shake in disgust from that memory. How did I end up in that state? I don't even know. But no alcohol will be entering my system for a long time.

"Lauren, I was just coming to talk to you."

"Good! I have something to tell you, let's go to the conference room. It's important," she seems frantic in her response.

"Okay."

Grabbing a hold of my arm, she drags me into the nearest conference room. As we walk up to the door, she opens it rather rapidly and pushes me inside. She shuts the blinds and locks the door behind her, turning on the noise canceling feature on the iPad that controls the rooms systems. I look at her in curiosity.

She's acting weird.

"I have news that I think you'll be excited about," she says calmly.

"Oooookayyy," I extend each syllable out as I speak.

Standing there for a minute she says rather quickly, "Lucia isn't here right now as you know, but Elektra just sent an offer and she told me to tell you." I freeze, registering her words.

Holy. Shit.

CHAPTER TWO

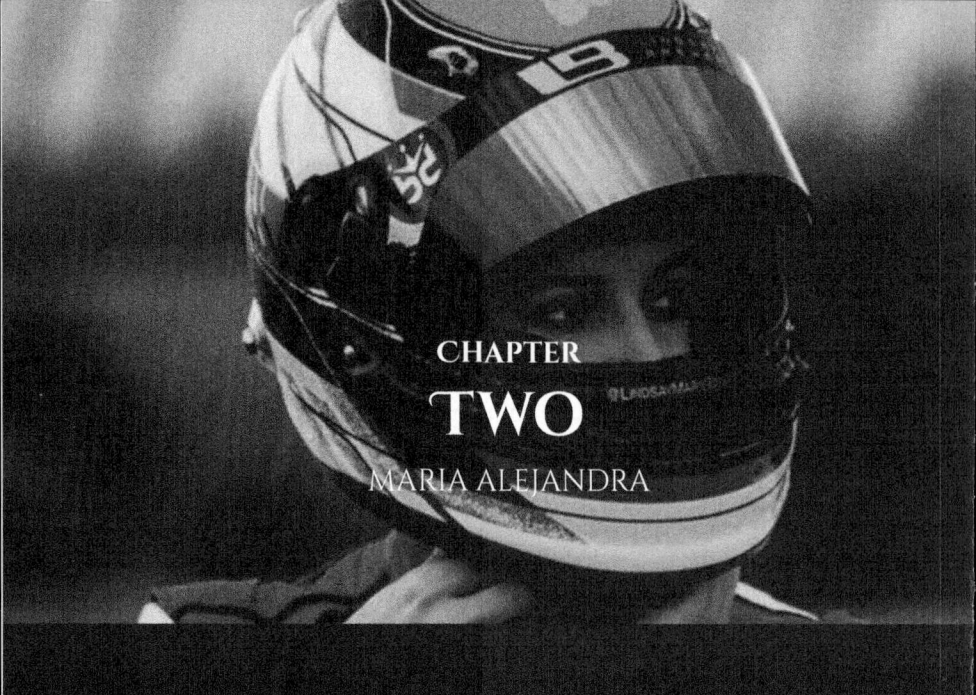

MARIA ALEJANDRA

"You've got to be shitting me right now." A single tear escapes, rolling down my cheek. *I never cry.* I have been taught my whole life that it shows weakness. Since I already have a disadvantage in this sport, I don't cry often. My only leverage is my talent, and damn have I worked hard for that.

One thing I've learned from my father and this sport: never show weakness. People feed off it, they use and abuse it for their own gain. Their own *success*.

All these years of hard work and dedication. All these years of begging my dad to give me a break because I was tired. Every single minute of that struggle was fucking worth it.

In about three days, I will be able to stand in front of those incompetent blood sucking reporters—the same ones who once told me that I would be nothing —and tell them that I'm a fucking Formula One driver. Not only that, but I also have a seat on the best Formula One team in the world.

It will be the biggest "fuck you" of my life. I can't help but smile at the thought.

"Why would I be shitting you when I have this?" She reaches into a folder laying on the table and holds up a piece of paper, waving it dauntingly in front of my face before playfully stepping back.

"No *mames*," I say in a whisper as I look at the contract she's holding.

But there is one more thing left to do.

Revise it.

The thing I hate more than anything in this world is revising a legal document. Hours and hours of sitting next to your lawyer, publicist, and manager to go over it word for word. Discussing every single detail that you, as an athlete, would be agreeing to. As a driver, you are an athlete. While others let their manager take care of it, I don't. I like to be hands on, especially after hearing so many horror stories.

At the end of every year, whether you're going to resign or stay, you have to revise your contract. It's a matter of your integrity and the respect that is given to you. Money has a big part in all of it, but it's not like I need it. My family is the biggest drug cartel in all of Mexico, and some would even argue all of North and South America. I could sponsor the team for however long I want with the money I have in my bank account.

I know I'm an expensive asset. I know my worth and my

capability. I can boost their social media numbers up to millions. The story would be covered not only in every sports tabloid, but also on every local news channel.

I can imagine it now ***"First ever female F1 driver has been signed with hopes of changing the sport forever."*** I can do that. And they need it. They need me.

If they try to offer me a low-ball number or anything remotely insulting to what I have to offer, there will be only one word coming out of my mouth.

No.

I know myself too well. If another team on the lower ranks of the grid offered me a spot in F1, I probably wouldn't take the position. Formula One fans are passionate, a little too passionate at times. They expect a rookie driver to deliver results for a team that not only lacks the budget required to make a championship-winning car, but lacks the engineers needed as well.

The best teams are lined up in the top three and I am going to be a driver for one of those organizations.

"Lauren, I can't believe this." I'm still in shock from the news.

"I can. You carried yourself perfectly at that press conference. You showed confidence and drive. Your words were concise and you showed who you were up there. Not to mention, you're a fucking amazing driver." I beam up at her before she continues. "This contract was sent via fax ten minutes after you finished your winners' press conference. Sent personally from Luca Donatello himself."

"We have to get my lawyer immediately," I tell her.

"Anastasia is waiting for us back at headquarters in Mexico City. Could you ask your brother for a lift on all our behalf? I know he chartered his jet to come here."

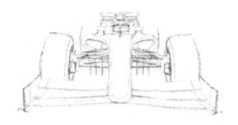

Five minutes later, I see León leaning against the door of his classic black Escalade, or as I like to call it the "narco car." It's a trademark in Mexico. Every head of a cartel owns one. They remind me too much of home.

I would never be ashamed of my family in any literal sense. I love them. But what they do is completely different from who they are. When I was fifteen years old, I told my father that if the family business had anything to do with sex trafficking, I would disown them myself.

They swore to me that day that it didn't. Drugs, I can handle. Money laundering, I can handle. But selling another human being against their will to be used every single day like a scrap of dirt, hell no.

I know what feeling helpless is like and I would never, and I mean never, let anyone else feel that way again.

He looks up as I walk toward him. "What did your publicist say, *princesa*?" He raises his eyebrow.

"Something kind of came up."

"*¿Que paso?*" he says in a worrying tone.

"Te juró que si él está en contacto contigo de nuevo, voy a cortarle su pinché verga de su cuerpo," he says, through gritted teeth.

"What? No! No. It's actually really good news." I set my hand on his shoulder trying to calm him down. Finally, he does.

"About twenty minutes ago, Lauren got a fax from Luca Donatello. He sent an offer for me to join Elektra next season. I need to fly back to Mexico City with you. And I need to ask you a big favor. I need you to let Lauren and Lucia come with us. Anastasia, my lawyer, is waiting for us at headquarters already, and we need to get there to rebut his offer," I finish, looking down at my feet hoping for a yes. I gasp, as my feet are no longer on the ground, but in the air.

"¡Alejandra no mames. ¿Es en serio? I am so happy! My baby sister is going to be an F1 driver." I try to stop him before he gets too excited.

Not like you're already planning the Instagram post announcing your seat.

"But the deal isn't settled yet so that's why I need this favor from you," I hush him while hiding a massive smile after his outburst of joy.

"There are no favors in our family. You, your publicist, and manager are welcome on the jet. I just have to get some things settled first." He hugs me again, nudging his face in my neck right next to my ear. "You always make me proud, *princesa*. Remember that."

"Stop, you're going to make me cry." I push him away,

playfully. "And you know how I feel about that, because you feel the same way," I say again.

He just looks at me. "This is an occasion where crying is necessary. I will bet you that once we get back home *Papá llorará, nuestros primos van a llorar, y yo probablemente voy a empezar a llorar.* This was your dream and you worked your ass off to make it a reality." He has both hands on either side of my shoulders. "You did it," he whispers with a proud look in his eyes.

Those three words break me.

I start crying. No, I start sobbing.

I end up wrapping my legs and arms around my brother. León carries me inside his car calling off his two minions in the process.

I end up crying in that car for what seems like a lifetime, but only an hour has passed.

He's the only man in my life that I trust completely, not even my father comes close to the trust I have for León.

Not like I have much trust in my father.

When I finally stop crying, he chuckles.

"So much for chartering the jet at 7:30," I laugh. "At least Lauren and Lucia had time to get ready. They're probably waiting for a response." Pulling out my phone, I see ten notifications from both of them.

I text them the location and the new charter time, then get out of the car and come face to face with my luggage in front of me. I spin around to face my brother.

"You let them touch my things," I say in a harsh tone.

"Did you want to take forever and not get to Mexico on time? *¿No verdad?*" He pulls me into his Escalade and calls out the location to the driver. Leaning back against the seat and sighing, I look out the window.

I know I'm ready. Ready for anything that wants to come my way. I'm in it, and I'm going to obliterate anyone who stands in my path.

Because I am Maria Alejandra Castillo, and I am going to be the first ever female F1 driver.

CHAPTER
THREE
MARIA ALEJANDRA

S tepping off my brother's jet, I feel the cool breeze of Mexico City rush against my face. I sweep my dark curls just an inch behind my shoulder stopping them from completely covering my features.

The obsidian curls on my head are my own personal statement.

Length wise they reach right above my breasts, the curls twisting and turning into an almost barbaric form. I love how untamed they look and how free they stand atop my head. These curls represent who I am and how I want the world to see me.

The media and the image that is presented to the public of who I am is reckless and untamable. Not like it's a bad thing, but people tend to perceive it in either two ways.

1. I'm a bitch.

or

2. I'm a whore.

I prefer the bitch notion if I'm being honest. The media likes to manipulate who I am into a single image. That image most likely falls in line with the notion of what a woman needs to be.

Sadly, F1 is way behind in the concept of equality. The sport is filled with old white men who want the world to adapt to their idea of what other people should be. I don't blame them. I blame the people who taught them to be this way.

Societal ideals, morals, and technology all need to advance with the passing of time. It's basic fucking science, but these men are still stuck in the 1800s spewing all their misogynistic bullshit.

Not only are women in sports seen as inferior, but they are also treated with the smallest margin of respect possible, while the men are given common decency and praise.

I'm wearing my usual attire. A black matching set consisting of a crop top and sweatpants, which makes me think of all of the comments made about what I wear. Men usually don't have to deal with sexualizing comments telling them that their skirt is too short or that not wearing a bra is asking for it. I've made those mistakes being a female athlete. But as a woman who is sitting in a car that reaches up to 110-degrees at times. How the fuck do you expect me to wear a bra with support?

That's literally the whole purpose of sports bras, and if my nipples show, well, that's not anyone's business. I don't go around pointing out my fellow drivers' boners. So all I have to say to those bloodsucking misogynistic asshole's is . . . free the nipple!

At this point in my career, I literally couldn't give less of a fuck. I wear whatever I want, when I want, and if someone says it's too revealing or not fit for a woman I tell them to fuck off. I think about that one little girl sitting in front of her TV watching me walk onto the grid's grounds aspiring to be confident and completely and irrevocably herself. That's what I want to show to the world. Not my "reckless" image or me being a badass. I want to inspire all those little girls out there and show them that they can be whoever they want to be, no matter the obstacles they may face. Because being able to be whoever you want is the most freeing feeling in the world.

Ultimately, I'm carving out a path for all the young girls that follow, and just thinking about that notion makes me proud as hell. Because I can sit here and tell you that I made a difference for the future of women in sports.

There's no point in denying the fact that I compete against men.

Not like it's more of a challenge.

As a female athlete I always felt like I have to be a certain way, to act in a certain manner. But then I realized.

Fuck it.

Me conforming to what someone else says would be completely against my morals, and I never go against my morals. As a woman, I have come so far, and I have learned a lot about who I am and who I want to be.

Looking out onto the field sitting right beside the runway, I see lavender plants adorning multiple spots within the field's property. The light purple ascends down the length of each flower. It's beautiful. I missed my home.

Mi tierra, mi casa, y mi fé.

The time went by so fast that when the flight attendant told us we had landed, I was surprised. Making my way down the steps, I look up seeing the sun setting. A light yellow mixed with a vibrant orange, a hint of pink cascading down the image of the horizon. The view capturing me in the moment. This scenery could be laid out as a painting.

The Mexico City private airport is one hundred and fifty thousand times better than the commercial airport. Far away from the heart of the city and sadly underfunded, the commercial international airport is just sad. Lights falling from the ceiling, unpainted walls, and worst of all, the smell.

Mexico in general has problems with its plumbing systems. Sewage portals have become lakes, and all the waste travels down toward the end of the city, ultimately ending up near the airport.

My country is beautiful, but there's no denying the fact that it's a third world country. Even so, Mexico is one of the best countries in the world.

Our vibrant oceans hold crystal clear turquoise water just down the coast. The miles and miles of jungle, has years of history filled with mystery and vibrant cultures of their natives. Then there's our cities, where our people ardently decorate them with our culture.

Walking towards the airport's entrance, I see my motorcycle parked out front.

In CDMX, it's almost impossible to get anywhere with a car on time. The hours and hours of traffic, the crashes, and the reckless driving is all a part of the Mexico City "experience."

With 8.8 million people and it being the twelfth largest city in the world, it's no wonder that traffic is the worst. Just imagine all those people going to work on a daily basis.

That's why I own my baby, a BMW S100RR with a matte black exterior. I'm able to speed down the streets of Mexico City, swerving in between cars as I make my way around this sinful *ciudad*.

I was introduced to the city early on in my life even though I had lived in Sinaloa for the first sixteen years of it. When León had been promoted to my dad's second hand he had to move from our estate to Mexico City to monitor the cocaine deliveries. My father had given me the decision to move out or stay in Sinaloa. I had chosen to leave, especially after what had happened prior to my brother's promotion.

I knew I had to leave with him because he was the only one I trusted in that moment of my life.

Now, I'm living my best life in an apartment that I designed myself. Being a Castillo, I had the opportunity to use the team of my choice. I have never regretted the smart move I made as an athlete.

When I first moved here, I also had the option to move in with my brother. That option was immediately ruled out when I realized that I could possibly hear him having sex.

That was a clear no on my part.

So, I decided to take some money out of my trust fund and find the perfect place to live. I ended up finding a building and designing my own living space, allowing me to live by myself since I was sixteen.

Walking up to my bike, I quickly turn around to see all the people who have accompanied me on this long and unamusing flight. A loud silence is heard among all of us while in each other's presence.

"Lauren and I will see you at your apartment in two hours to discuss the offer that Elektra sent," Lucia breaks the silence while giving me a serious expression. Her long brown hair cascades down her front as she looks at me with her soft brown eyes.

"Okay, make sure to bring donuts, red bulls, coffee, and tacos. I have a feeling it's going to be a long night," I respond with a quick nod, giving Lauren and Lucia a smirk. They simply nod in response and walk across the ashen street quickly hopping into their cars. Driving off with a clear friction in their tires, they slowly merge onto the enclosed highway.

"What about me, *princesa?*" I turn around to see my brother looking at me with his classic eyebrow raise.

I totally forgot about him. Oops.

"*¡Muchísimas gracias, hermano!*" I pull León into my

arms, squeezing him as tightly as possible. He changed his clothes while we were on the flight.

It isn't that big of an outfit change: the suit has gone from a gray tone to his signature all black. His reputation precedes him in every way. Ways that I don't even want to mention, but he is called *El Rey Del Hampa de México* for a reason.

"It's nothing. Now go and make those negotiators your bitch." He smirks.

"*Tú sabes.*" I give him a wink before walking away.

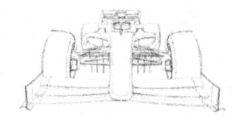

I finally reach my apartment complex in Polanco. The black reflective mirrors on the exterior of the building shine brightly. Holding up my card to the monitor, it flashes a purple and blue light over the barcode. The garage door opens, signifying the card's authenticity.

Inside, I'm met with the view of my own personal garage. Grabbing my phone, I press the open button and the shiny black titanium door opens, revealing my collection of cars. The black and white marble walls can be seen through the windows of all the vehicles.

Parking my motorcycle inside, I quickly pass by all my babies, briefly glancing at my favorite. My custom 2021

McLaren 720s with a matte black exterior and red leather interior.

My other two cars pale in comparison. To the left, my black Jeep with a custom gray interior and to the right is my black Buick Enclave with an orange interior. My cars are sexy, and I love them.

After reminiscing over my beautiful automobiles, I turn away and tuck a curl behind my ear while walking towards the elevator. Pressing the button, it lights up with a faint purple glow and a ding sounds. The doors separate pushing a cool breeze onto my face. I press the only button available on the panel and the elevator passes multiple floors until the view of the city is visible.

The elevator is encased by four rectangular panels of glass that forming the space. Looking out, white lights adorn every building in sight. Looking down, multiple restaurants are sitting in a straight line, filled with crowds of people talking and laughing, Polanco's lifestyle shining.

Lost in thought, I barely hear the elevator ding signifying my arrival. Snapping out of it, I step into my apartment and the smell of L'homme from Prada is revealed to my senses.

I smile. I'm home.

Walking onto my smokey gray wood floors, I'm met with my living room. Bending down I take off my sneakers before I walk into my primary living space. From the high ceilings to the multi-level floor leading to my spacious black couch. My feet are met by my traditional hand woven black and gray carpet. Looking up, the view of the city is right in front of me.

Moving my toes back and forth against the carpet, I finally fall back onto my couch. Sinking into its consuming warmth. I'm greeted with the sight of the TV hung against a gray concrete wall. Staring into nothing, I come to my senses and notice my housekeeper, Nieves.

She's fifty-six years old and still looking like she's in her forties. She greets me with her adorable smile. Her stick-straight long black hair flows beautifully around her five-foot one body.

"*¿Hola señorita, quieres algo?*" She motions towards the kitchen as she talks.

"*Pues . . . voy a tener visitas como en una hora. Si puedes preparar agua de Jamaica y unos platos listos para tacos, porfa?*" I smile at her lazily. She smiles and nods walking towards the kitchen.

I quickly stand, making my way through the main spaces of my house. I walk up my spiral staircase and my eyes are met with the first two bedrooms, taking a right I'm able to see my bedroom just hidden slightly in the corner of the hall.

Striding towards my space, I rub my eyes.

Damn, I'm tired.

Opening my black steel door, I walk into my bedroom. The black curtains are closed, and my nightstand light is shining brightly. I turn towards my closet, walking in and stripping off my clothes, tossing them in the hamper. I walk to the other side of my bathroom and turn on my gray and black tiled waterfall shower.

After I get the shower started, I step back and pick my clothing of choice. I land on a black sweatshirt that says "fuck off" across the chest, some black leggings, and my grey fuzzy socks.

I walk into the shower, cleaning myself of a championship race and an eighteen-hour flight.

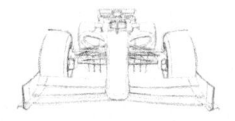

Drifting out of sleep, I hear my ringtone go off. I slap my hand over my phone and groan in the process as I hit the answer button.

"Hello?" I say groggily as I rub my eyes.

"We're on our way towards your apartment," Lauren says. I hear a plastic bag rustling in the background, which I assume is food. My stomach growls at the sound, I can almost smell the Al Pastor from here.

"Okay, just tell me when you get here so I can open the garage door." Slowly rising out of my bed with a groan, I snatch my laptop and a highlighter, making my way out the door as she proceeds to speak into the phone.

"Okay. But before you hang up, I have something to tell you." Lauren pauses, as I am skipping slowly down the steps.

Then, a statement I thought I would never hear flies out of her mouth. "Luca Donatello is coming to your house right now to discuss your pending contract." I stop dead in my tracks.

"What?!?" Just as those words come out of my mouth a knock is heard at the front door.

Shit.

CHAPTER FOUR

MARIA ALEJANDRA

I watch in shock from my place on the stairs as Nieves walks into the living room. She looks up at me as I peer down at her.

"¿Quien lo dejó entrar?" I tell her, Nieves doesn't even take a second to respond.

"Yo señorita, tú me dijiste que ibas a tener unas personas de tú trabajo y me dijeron que un trabajador de Elektra estaba abajo."

Nodding, I go to open my front door. As I walk through the main entrance area, the sleek white lighting beams down on the gray concrete cut out in the wall. It is about 12 inches wide creating a curve with enough space to place a few items inside. I have a few things placed neatly along the opening, mostly trinkets that I have accumulated over my years of traveling. I own a few Mayan and Aztec artifacts that I won in an auction, as well as some traditional indigenous South American tablets.

As a history freak, it was a no brainer on my part. All I can remember from my childhood was the idea of the history of my homeland. Every year during the Mexican Grand Prix, I take a trip around Mexico to see the historical sights again. Being able to learn my own culture and the history of others is a privilege. The fact that you can retrace the steps of some of the most important events in our history is enthralling and provides a sense of adrenaline.

Continuing down the hall toward the door, I turn the black lock, reach for the doorknob, and turn it slowly.

As the door passes my view, it folds towards the wall, and I'm met with hazel eyes. My breath catches as I try to form a sentence.

Reaching out my hand to shake his, I say, "Hi, I'm Maria Alejandra, it's nice to meet you." I smile and give a friendly nod. He returns the gesture with a smile that doesn't reach his eyes, signifying that it isn't genuine. I don't really care if it's genuine or not, as long as he isn't a dickwad.

"Hello, Miss Castillo, I have heard great things." His tight lipped smile still plastered on his face and even though its emotion is nowhere to be found, it still takes over his face. His thick Italian accent is prominent in every syllable of his pronunciation.

I drop my eyes, trailing my gaze anywhere else but his stare. To say that he's beautiful would be an understatement. His face is rugged, with stubble adorning his jaw. His jawline is sharp; clenching while he's looking me up and down, which I don't like, despite him being gorgeous. But I can't complain, I'm checking him out too.

He places his sunglasses in his hands, his fingers curling around them. His tall frame is styled with perfectly tailored Hugo Boss hugging every single muscle and crevice.

A black sweater displays every muscle on his chest and his thick thighs strain against the slacks he's wearing. It's a weird combination, but it works very well on him. A little too well. God definitely took his time on him. I look up as he looks behind me, expressing his demand to enter my apartment.

I move to the side, welcoming him into my home, and as he passes, I see his watch. It's a DATEJUST 36 Rolex. It's what a man with expensive taste would wear, which fits exquisitely with his facade.

Not only do I know he probably has a whole collection of them in his closet, but I also know that this man makes bank. Which I don't doubt, not even for a second.

Walking down the hall, I trail slowly behind him as he takes in his surroundings. So far, my first impression is that he doesn't have the best manners. He didn't introduce himself and he also walked past me, like a damn bullet, into my home acting like he owns the place. He knows who he is, that much is clear.

Following him further through my apartment, I examine his backside. I don't like the man, but his butt is really nice. It's literally like a melo—

Alejandra, stop!

"Your apartment is very sleek. I like how untraditional it is." His compliment shocks me. Because I was not expecting a comment, much less a compliment to come out of his mouth.

Well, at least I think it's a compliment.

"Thank you, I designed the layouts myself." He turns around and just stares at me.

What's his problem?

I literally just met the man, and I already know I don't like him. I shoot him a questioning look, trying to say, "*What are you staring at?*"

"I know I came last minute, but that sweatshirt probably isn't the best choice to meet your new boss."

Oh my god.

Eyes bulging out of my head, I mutter a quick sorry. As I meet Nieves's eyes, I give her a *"mantenlo ocupado mientras no estoy"* stare.

I jog up the stairs and hear a deep chuckle release from his lips as I turn the corner rushing to my room. Opening the door and closing it behind me I take a deep breath. I cannot believe I just met my future boss while wearing a "fuck off" sweatshirt and some fuzzy socks.

Walking towards my closet, I slide open the black and gray ombré glass doors. Finally deciding on a pair of black washed-out mom jeans and a leather crop top, I slip them on. Striding towards my vanity mirror, I just stare at my reflection. The man who could quite literally determine my contract saw me like this. My hair in a messy bun and my face has a pillow indent displayed across my cheek.

Holy shit! How did I not check myself in the mirror before I went downstairs?

Well, because no one told you that your boss was coming over, and it's just your luck that on the day you meet him you have the best sleep of your life since the start of the 2020 season.

A groan leaves my lips as I attempt to fix my complexion.

Personal Reminder: *Make sure to tell Nieves to inform you if you look like death before meeting absolutely anyone at the front door.*

Taking a makeup wipe, I quickly wipe off all the residue on my face. Grabbing the hair tie and yanking it out of my curls, I grab a brush off the counter. Vigorously bringing the brush down my hair, I yank as fast as possible. I don't remember my curls being this knotted. I turn on the sink and let the water fall onto my hands, rubbing both together as I let the water transfer from one hand to the other.

Sweeping my hands through my hair, I let the dampness of the water soak up. Scrunching up my curls as I look in the mirror.

I apply a little bit of concealer, mascara, and lip gloss to try to look more professional.

Like that's going to help, I already fucked my first impression up.

Reaching for my jewelry box, I grab a silver chain necklace, some hoop earrings, and a few rings. Gliding the rings onto my fingers, I walk towards my perfume display.

MORPHINE

I have a thing for men's cologne, I don't know why, but they just smell better. My hands go for the black square bottle that I always use, Bleu De Chanel. It's one of my favorites. My brother thinks I'm weird for using cologne, but I don't care. At least I smell good, that's all that matters.

When I finally look somewhat presentable, I grab my phone and look at the time.

Good, I've only been up here for ten minutes.

Making my way down the stairs, I count each step, dreading coming face to face with him again. Especially considering the circumstances that happened just ten minutes ago.

My feet meet the final step and I groan internally.

I walk towards the dining room where my black square marble table sits. I see him sitting in one of the black quilted seats that are spread around the table. I had this seating arrangement custom made by a local granite shop because I wanted it to sit all my family at once. All my decor and seating arrangements are Mexican made.

He's holding a black Talavera mug in his hand, it's from my favorite set that I bought in the outer regions close to El Zocalo.

I would have never considered him to be a coffee kind of guy.

He's looking at the big floor-to-ceiling windows showcasing the skyline of Mexico City. This specific window has a balcony, my favorite view from my apartment.

"The skyline is one of my favorite things about my home." He turns around and looks at me.

"Nothing I haven't seen before," he says arrogantly.

Hunch confirmed, we definitely don't like this guy.

I grimace at him. "Then what would you say is better?" I challenge him, taking a seat on the other side of the table.

He smirks. "It depends on what you're looking for. All cities have the same boring skylines filled with the ideals of people who don't want responsibility. Cities don't have anything unique about them, they're just a bunch of flashing lights. But I would argue that my city is the best. Not only is it the ruins of an empire so big it took over a large area of the world in its time period, but it is also the mecca for intense people filled with life."

"I'm guessing you're talking about the Roman Empire?"

"Of course I am." His pride is dripping off of him. Not that it's a bad thing, but I don't like arrogance and this man is the exact definition of it.

"Rome is absolutely incredible and unique,I concede, "so in that sense, I agree with you. Ardent people grace every part of the world, fully embracing their own passions. Mexico City is one of those places. Food that is world renowned, people who are known for their kindness and service towards others. This city was built on the soil of one of the most intricate civilizations known to man. It is a mix of culture and modernism that combines two opposite cultures into one."

"I wasn't talking about Rome; I'm talking about

Florence. And Mexico was built off of the enslavement of Aztecans," he challenges.

"The Roman Empire was built similarly, but instead of one group of people, they enslaved people from all of the places they conquered." Like children, we keep going.

"Our food is better."

"I disagree. Have you ever had mole poblano?"

"Our language is prettier." He sounds like a little girl; I'm thoroughly enjoying this.

"Spanish spreads over a whole continent and has people who speak it in Europe and North America. It's been used as an advantage against old horny white women for generations."

"Italians are better looking." I'm not blind. I've seen Damiano David from Manéskin. So, he's not completely wrong.

"You really don't like to lose, do you? I think that's going to be a quality I hate and like about you for the future of this arrangement. But to respond to your previous statement," I pause. "Salma Hayek, Selena Gomez, Eiza González, Belinda, Luis Miguel, Alejandro Fernandez, Danna Paola, and I could go on. Would you like my name on the list too?" I smirk, suddenly hearing my phone ring in the distance.

Alejandra: 1 Mr. Donatello: 0

Picking it up without even looking at the caller ID, I answer.

"Hello?"

"Ale, we're downstairs." Knowing it's Lauren from the

sound of her voice my whole body begins to relax. "Okay, perfect. I'll tell Nieves to let you up," I reply, ending the call.

"Nieves," I call out. A few seconds later I hear her faint voice call out *"Si, señorita?"* Her head pops out of the kitchen doorway.

"Porfa deje a Lauren y las personas con ella subir." She nods and presses the button, a long buzz sounds.

A weird feeling runs through me, the buzz stirring my brain for a second.

Looking up, my gaze meets Mr. Donatello's eerie smirk. I have a feeling this man is going to make my life a living hell. "Now let's see who wins this." He just sits there looking at me.

That's when I know the saying "hell on earth" is my reality.

CHAPTER FIVE
LUCA DONATELLO

She's a spitfire. I don't necessarily like it, nor do I hate it, but the way she snaps back at me is annoying. She reminds me of a spoiled brat fighting with her parents to get everything she desires.

At the same time that's what I'm doing... fighting with a child.

I'm thirty-eight for Christ's sake and she's freshly twenty. Why am I trying to argue with her about something that she isn't informed on?

I don't like to be challenged and that's exactly what she's doing. Sooner or later, she will realize this isn't a fair fight and I will win.

Miss Castillo and I both know that I'm the sole person who could determine her dream, her future, and her place for the next Formula One calendar. Whether that is going to be on the F1 grid or back where she was in F2, is her choice.

Looking at her renewal contract on my phone ready to be printed off, I smirk at the thought.

Don't get me wrong, the girl has talent. That's why I picked her as my first choice for second driver. After watching her press conference, I liked the way she carried herself. The way she delivered her words clearly and confidently. Then I looked up her accolades. She has a solid consistent record of wins and overtakes.

She possesses an impressive quality when it comes to her technicality. All her drives are clean. Meaning her overtakes are swift, she doesn't have any collisions on her record, and she drives really fucking fast.

Miss Castillo holds the passion that we need, and if she needs to piss some people off along the way, she does it without thinking about the repercussions. In the long run that's something that I can only see as a benefit because I was the same way.

But every athlete has a downfall and hers is the mere fact that she's a woman. I don't mean that in the way most would assume, I could care less that she has two X chromosomes and something different between her legs.

The main problem here is the fact that *she* still sees it as a disadvantage. Even though there are people around her who see it that way and make their opinion very clear, her talent speaks for itself. She can beat almost any driver at their own game.

Male or female it doesn't matter because she is a driver and that's all it should be to her. Regardless of gender, they should just be people to beat. It's true whether she wants to admit it or not.

But I won't tell her that right now. Once I have her contract in hand that's when all hell will break loose.

She hasn't seen anything yet.

Just as I finish my thought, she walks in with her legal team trailing slowly behind her. I notice a weariness in their eyes.

Good.

Looking up, I notice the scowl she is attempting to mask. The smiles and nonchalant nods, the "thank you's" that aren't even close to genuine, and most importantly, the look of annoyance in her eyes. Behind her stand three women looking anywhere but my gaze. It seems like they're intimidated by my presence.

"Mr. Donatello, this is my team." She gestures her hand towards her colleagues.

I nod, standing up as she introduces them to me.

"This is Lucia, my manager." A woman with brown hair looks at me with a faint smile.

"This is Lauren, my publicist." Her hair contrasting that of her peers, a blonde woman with gray eyes shakes my hand firmly.

"And finally, this is my lawyer, Anastasia. She's Italian so if you have difficulty communicating throughout our meeting, she is here to help." I look up at the black-haired woman. Her round face is framed by her stick straight black hair and her curtain bangs leave space to see her big brown eyes.

"It's nice to meet you all." I nod, gazing at the gigantic black marble table I was just sitting at while dealing with an immature young woman.

They all follow my movements as I sit down ready to negotiate.

Let the games begin.

CHAPTER SIX
MARIA ALEJANDRA

I want to die.

The cause: the man sitting right in front of me. His stupidly smug looks and dominating smiles make my blood boil. My acrylics indent markings into my palms. After three hours of basic agreement clauses, we are finally getting to the important part. My pay.

No matter how rich an F1 driver may be, being paid a low-ball number is insulting. It's not like you can hide the contract after signing it. Eventually every news outlet becomes curious, which results in every little detail of your agreement being plastered all over every sports channel known to man. The most important part of any driver's contract are three basic things.

-Your pay.

-How many seasons you will be driving for them.

-When can you renegotiate and reevaluate terms.

Looking down onto the table, I see him take his pen out and quickly scribble something down onto his bright yellow sticky note.

Slowly but surely, with a steady hand, he takes the sticky note and slides it across the table, landing in the empty space between my arms.

Looking down at the small square piece of paper right in front of me, I quickly look back up and quirk an eyebrow, challenging him. Reaching for the bright yellow sticky note I unfold it slowly, making sure to never once break eye contact.

The slight change in his demeanor shows me his annoyance.

Finally unfolding the last crease, I look down, but I don't let my eyes focus on the number just yet. I need to mentally prepare myself for this life changing moment that is going to determine my future and even my pride.

Taking every single ounce of courage that my body and mind can muster, I finally look down and focus intently on the number.

HELL. FUCKING. NO.

Shooting out of my seat, my chair slides backwards away from my body abruptly. I notice Lauren, Lucia, and Anastasia flinch at my sudden movement which leads to Lucia grabbing that fucking piece of paper. Slowly, I raise my gaze to meet his. One thing is absolutely fucking clear, he wants to intimidate me.

MORPHINE

He may terrify other people, but there's one thing he'll soon understand.

I grew up with wolves.

I watched people I loved die right in front of me. I have fought every single day of my life to get where I am right now and if he thinks he can break that all down with a simple low-ball number he is sorely mistaken.

Fuck that.

"1.2 million euros," I scoff.

In any other situation, this would be a Godsend to some, but to an F1 driver who has more than enough potential, it's an insult.

"It's more than enough for a rookie driver. I'd remember that if I were you." He's trying to put me in my place. I roll my eyes to the back of my head and let out a strangled breath.

"That's where you are wrong. Xavier Valente was offered 5.5 million euros his rookie season with an extended two-year clause. Then you upped his salary to 70 million euros in his new five-year contract. My stats are just as good, if not better than his were when he entered the F1 calendar."

"Is that the way you think you can talk to the man who has your future in his hands? Your future boss? One thing I'll tell you, Miss Castillo, is that I will never let you disrespect me. You can speak freely, but don't question my intelligence."

"Then don't question mine!" I shout, furthering my statement. "Elektra Motorsports was first in the Constructors' last year, and you have the current World Champion under your contract. But the one thing that Elektra doesn't have is a solid second driver. They chose for an older driver by enlisting Luke Davis to take the empty seat. Whether any older driver wants to admit it or not, we all burn out. But just as we all burn out, we all have our glory years and the fact that you can't even admit the potential that I will provide is an insult to my intelligence.

"So, here's how this will go. I will be able to benefit you in more ways than one, and you will be able to benefit me in other ways as well. But one thing that needs to be clear here is that this is an equal exchange. I have been at the top of F2 for all three years that I have been competing. Even though you need a second driver, I can assure you that, in time, I will most definitely become your first. I am the future, and you cannot deny that."

I shove myself into my chair and glare at him. He scoffs, and finally speaks after what seems like hours of silence.

"I will up your contract to 2 million euros, which is eight hundred thousand euros more. That is as high as I will go."

"We both know that this isn't just about the money, Mr. Donatello. I could do without all of it and I would be perfectly fine. This is about proving myself as a driver in F1 and at Elektra. 5.5 million and we're getting somewhere," I fire back.

He lets out a long deep breath.

"Okay, deal. But I'm changing your contract to a season-by-season basis. If you don't deliver what you have assured me, we will question your contract and place at Elektra. Am I clear?"

"Crystal," I bite back.

I don't think I've ever in my life disliked anyone more than this man . Well, that isn't completely true. All I know is that this is going to be an eventful season, not only for me, but for Mr. Donatello.

Waiting for Anastasia to finish editing the contract and updating the clauses we have just negotiated, me and Mr. Donatello's heated gaze goes on until we hear the printer make a beeping noise, signifying that the contract is almost ready to sign.

Anastasia reaches for the papers and staples them together, doing a final flip through to make sure there are no errors. Handing the contract over to Mr. Donatello, she quickly looks over at me with a proud expression.

Yanking his pen off the table, he signs on the dotted line, then shoves the papers towards me.

With a steadying breath, I take my pen and sign. I grab the corner of the last page and flip it over to the front and drop it in front of him. Extending my hand to shake his, he takes it with a firm grip.

"Congratulations, Miss Castillo. I hope what you just agreed to will be everything you're hoping for." He smirks again with that narcissistic expression. Have I mentioned how much I hate it?

He walks away abruptly, striding to the door across the living room and down the hall. I know he's left when the door slams shut. Looking out at the Mexico City skyline, I smirk at the thought of the havoc I'm about to wreak on not only F1, but also on Mr. Donatello's life.

The game has only just begun.

CHAPTER
SEVEN
MARIA ALEJANDRA

The sound of tools dropping onto the floor and the smell of fuel sends me to an all-time high. After announcing my entrance into Elektra Motorsports at a press conference on Friday night, everything has gone full speed. The press conference was eventful; hundreds of reporters lined up for the special announcement of my recruitment as second driver to the current reigning world champion. Thousands of cameras streamed live on almost every sports channel known to man. Tons of F1 influencers and commentators went live on their Instagrams while Elektra's social media and PR team filmed every second to catch each reaction.

Whether the press's reaction was good or bad, it's still good content. As the first female Latinx driver to hit the sport, I'm out of the norm when it comes to appearances in

F1, which is why they use every single video or picture they can get.

After the news was announced, everyone went into a frenzy, or should I say, Twitter did. Millions of Facebook F1 groups rioted over a female being in F1. Old white men with crippled dicks express their "rage" while others support and even encourage my entrance.

All over Sky Sports, the commentators praise the new change and even congratulate Elektra for taking the plunge. It's been a good but stressful week, and I'm grateful for everything that has happened.

Walking through the garage, I make my way to the corporate offices at Elektra HQ. The large, black, reflective building stands in the middle of a busy street just blocks away from La Reforma. Since the company that funds the Elektra F1 Team is known as a banking empire, the levels that don't have anything to do with administration are on the first five floors. When you enter the building, the sleek black marble interior catches the eye and would make anyone's jaw drop.

Elektra has been in the game for ten years, but in a sport that has been alive for seventy-two this makes them relatively new. I still remember when they took over an old team that was burning out.

Their funding gives them the best engineers and cars to date. F1 is all about money and fame, so whoever has the biggest budget has the fastest cars. The teams with the fastest cars get the best drivers. And we all know what that means: winning.

It's all a game. If you know how to play it, you'll succeed.

Nearing the end of the garage, I finally make it to the office part of the building. The gray cubicles line the way to the conference room. Walking towards the end of the cubicles, I see in bold letters **SOCIAL MEDIA MEETINGS IN SESSION.**

So, this is where I have to go for the PR debrief.

I peek my head through the door and see about five people in seats surrounding a shiny table. Lucia stands at the other end of the conference room drinking water out of a Styrofoam cup, while listening to a social media strategy being spewed out by a redhead at the other end of the table. Feeling like I can enter without interrupting anyone, I open the door wide and put one foot in the door. I let my combat boots take me forward until I am in full view of everyone. Lucia greets me with a wide smile, as do the other people in the room who are about to start the meeting.

"Hi, I'm Maria Alejandra," I say while walking up to the other end of the long table. Going up to them and shaking hands, I give each of them my warmest smile. Once I am done greeting, I sit down in the closest vacant seat.

"So, what are the PR rules and appearances I have to make for Elektra?" I raise my eyebrow. This whole social media situation makes me nervous. I'm fully on Instagram, but I do it myself. I'm able to express myself freely on there without any control from the companies I have worked with.

"Well, we don't ask for much company-wise. You can control your social media how you want, but there are a few prerequisites to what you post while racing, on and off the track. We also have some suggestions that you don't have to take, but overall, we have an audience that is very diverse. So, we have to see what fan base you're going to be catering to when you post or make appearances on social media," a guy with brown shaggy hair says while turning on his projector and connecting to screen mirroring. Looking at the screen, he pulls up my Instagram.

"Overall, your feed in the new era's POV is trendy. You have a solid, consistent feed that can be seen as relatable to the youth." I nod my head.

"But F1 is not only an audience of kids, teenagers, and twenty-somethings who appreciate a good feed. Who do you think brought the new generation's attention to the sport? The sport is not only known for its conservative fan base, but also for the people who have been watching F1 religiously since day one. I'm not talking about 80-year olds who just sit on their couch and watch races. I'm talking about the 40-year olds who were taught by their fathers."

I attempt to listen and not roll my eyes. He then scrolls and clicks on a post, attempting to give me an example of what I am doing wrong.

"This photo for example, is a picture of you in a bikini,

but to other men it could mean you want to... attract attention." He's very careful about the last two words he says.

The photo is taken from an angle that is facing downwards towards my body and the ocean that surrounds me. My body is clad in a white bikini, showcasing the marvelous tan from my vacation in the Maldives. The bright blue ocean contrasts the color that overlaps it with a tiny shark circling the boat dock that I'm on. I love that photo because it was my first vacation that I paid for myself and also because I look damn good in it.

I look at him. "Can I see your computer?" I ask casually. Confused, he hands the computer over to me. I quickly take it out of his hands and start typing.

"What's your name?" I ask him

"Troy." I almost laugh. Troy is a name for registered assholes.

"Troy. Like the city of Troy or as in High School Musical's Troy Bolton?" I look up making eye contact with him. He then responds with the boring answer, "Like the city of Troy."

I laugh a little. "I bet Mr. Donatello loves you then," I say in a mocking tone.

Looking back down at the task in front of me, I finish my scroll through the social media page I searched for. Pressing on the post I want, I slowly push the laptop away from me.

I look over and point at the screen with the most sarcastic face I can muster, and turn my head back in Mr.

Troy Bolton's direction. I finish off the "lost puppy" facade with a little head tilt. "Does he want to attract attention?"

The picture on the screen is of my fellow teammate, Xavier Valente, after a "tiring" workout session. The pose shows him exhaustedly looking up at the ceiling. Shirtless, might I add. The caption reads: **THEXAVIERVALENTE**: *Working for that second world championship title.*

He stays silent.

"You see, there are only two differences between me and Mr. Valente in the two pictures that have been presented to all of us today. One, he is completely shirtless with his titties out, whereas I happened to have all my assets covered. Two, one picture is intended for the female gaze while the other is for the male. While both objectifying, one is drawing only good attention while the other is receiving both good and bad. Which one of the two do you think it is, Mr. City of Troy?" I lean down and grab a pretzel from the bowl in the middle of the table. Leaning back against my chair, I pop it in my mouth while maintaining eye contact with him.

He looks at me, not wanting to say anything because he knows it'll get him in trouble. "That's what I thought. So, here's what I think is best for everyone. I will post the prerequisite posts that you require, if they are F1 based. I don't need anyone running my socials like a lot of drivers do. I'm a big girl, so don't worry."

After a second of silence passes, he quickly smiles then passes the laptop to a girl with an impressive set of braids. She looks at me with a proud smile that fits her so perfectly.

MORPHINE

Her white smile accentuates her dark skin. I like her already, and she hasn't even started talking yet. She presses a few buttons which projects a PR schedule onto the white screen.

"Firstly, I just want to say hi, and welcome to Elektra. We are incredibly happy to have you on the team. My name is Abigail. I'm the head of social media and PR here, so if you have any questions about photoshoots or anything, I'm here to help. What you see here is a schedule of all the pre-season photoshoots and interviews that have been scheduled for the months entering pre-season testing as well as the first race of the season. In two days, we have the big photoshoot for all the F1 promotion, such as candids of you in your racing suit as well as your pre-season F1 YouTube clips that will eventually be put into a compilation on the sport's official channel featuring all the other drivers." She takes a breath. "In two weeks, you have your first interview with Netflix for 'Drive for Your Life,' as they have offered an in-depth episode on your journey into F1 as well as how you advance during the season. They want you to be a frequently shown driver throughout the fifth season. You can decide whether you want to be featured or not, but it is a part of your contract that you are obligated to at least be shown twice. After those two appearances, you obviously have the choice of whether you want them to go in depth or not. There are some more things here and there that you will learn about along the way. I'll give your schedule to Lucia, and she will keep you up to date on all the interviews and social media promotions you will have to do." Finishing up her explanation, she looks over at me with a warm smile. I return it. Then I hear the door open and none other than the devil himself walks through.

Mr. Donatello greets everyone.

"Hello," he says in his deep Italian accent. "I came in here to see if you were done with the meeting because I would like to steal the rookie for a moment."

It takes everything in me not to roll my eyes when he says "rookie." I wouldn't mind the word if it came from anyone but him.

Before I can say anything, the marvelous Troy Bolton answers, "We just finished with her, Mr. Donatello." I almost groan out in frustration before Mr. Donatello speaks again.

"Perfect. Thank you everyone. I'll be taking her for a tour around the building." Standing up, I politely say, "thank you" and "goodbye" to everyone as I slowly and painfully walk towards Mr. Donatello. I step out of the conference room past him. After managing to walk out, he then gives a nod to someone in the conference room and says a brief "Thank you, Troy," while shutting the door.

I knew it.

Mr. Donatello slowly catches up to my strides and meets me at my side. There is a silence between us while we make our way around the room. Once we reach an area that looks like a garage, he breaks the silence.

Kill me now, oh dear Lord, I beg of you.

"This is where they will be fitting the car to your accommodations such as, your height, weight, and body shape. You will be here most days when you visit. As you know, it's important to keep in shape and also maintain your weight. You'll be assigned a nutritionist to help you."

"You know I have my own nutritionist, right? I have been a driver my whole life. I think I know how to stay in shape."

He scoffs. "I've been informed of that, Miss Castillo. Remember, I'm not incompetent. I know everything and everyone that has been involved in your career so far. That's my job."

"I've been informed of that as well. It's common sense that you know how to do your job. Because if you didn't, you wouldn't be here, right?" I reaffirm sarcastically.

"Miss Castillo, pay attention." I roll my eyes replaying that whole sentence in a mocking baby voice to at least give myself some serotonin from this draining experience.

"Oh, Mr. Donatello, I didn't know you were so needy." My eyes twinkle in mischief.

"I didn't know you were so childish." I just laugh.

"Very funny, old man."

"I'm only 38. I wouldn't count that as old yet, *ragazza*."

"Well, it's old. You're eighteen years older than me. That pretty much means you're *The Godfather* to my *House of Gucci*."

"What I got out of that sentence is that I'm a classic and you're an Italian film that only got press because Lady Gaga plays a murderer."

"Aw, did I hurt your little Italian ego, Mr. Corleone?"

"No, you didn't, Ms. Reggani." He leans close to my ear. So close that I can feel his breath. "You gave it a little boost." I can feel his pompous egotistical smirk against my ear. It makes me want to gag.

Ale: 1 Luca: 1

CHAPTER EIGHT

MARIA ALEJANDRA

It's photoshoot time.

We are officially in pre-season. My schedule is full of PR appearances for the F1 social media platforms, as well as pre-season testing. My ass has been measured a few hundred times to get my car fit to me and my body weight.

The car's unveiling was five days ago. A few hundred people gathered around the HB13 2022 Elektra Formula One Racing Car in awe. The classic black and white colors spread through the exterior as the lines intertwine in the front creating each driver's number. My number is nine, and my fellow teammate Xavier's is the famous number three.

The overall lines and cool graphic design inspiration fits perfectly with the team's investors logo plastered on the sides of the exterior. It's not a classic, predictable F1 car design, but it's interesting considering the basic lines and layout. It's not anything anyone has seen on the track before.

It's one thing to appreciate being an F1 driver, and another to really appreciate the car you're driving.

The next day, after attending the unveiling, my team and I hopped onto the next flight to Barcelona where the initial three-day testing will take place.

Before every season, two official pre-season testing dates are held where each team is able to test out their cars for the first time. The pre-season testing dates are held a few weeks apart the first test which is only three weeks from the first race of the season. Each year, a new grid is chosen for said testing, and this year's grid will be the Circuit de Barcelona-Catalunya. The second pre-season testing site will be held two weeks after, at the Bahrain International Circuit where the first race of the year will be held.

The thought that I'll be starting off my inaugural season as an F1 driver is surreal. I'm extremely excited yet nervous. The pressure and the buzz can be nerve wracking, but that's what F1 is, right? The adrenaline of it all.

Since we're three weeks out from the first race, we're finally getting the official F1 promo done. That's what I'm here for anyway.

The photoshoot is being held just a few blocks away from the grid in Barcelona. When I walk into this gray concrete building, I begin to worry my publicist has led me to a place where I might be kidnapped. I quickly realize that isn't the case when Abigail, Elektra's social media manager, walks in to greet me.

Saying our hellos, she proceeds to lead me down a long hallway and into a big space with five large triangle windows up ahead. A white backdrop is hung up on a rod that sits in the middle of the room. A camera is facing right in the center of the backdrop, which is surrounded by big blinding white lights facing the same direction as the lens.

So here I am, sitting in a makeup chair being assaulted by makeup brushes that aggressively caress my face with basic, muted tones. I stare at my reflection wanting to tear the makeup brush out of the artist's hand and apply some real ass pigment.

I stop myself. Everything about this photoshoot is planned. The makeup, the racing suits, and the backdrop have been meticulously chosen by the F1 PR team to convey the image of the sport. I can't always be in control of everything. Especially when I'm an underdog in all departments, except driving.

That I'm good at, but driving isn't all that Formula One is about.

Even though I would love to tell this girl to put a real ass lash on my face while contouring the fuck out of my cheek bones. I don't think the F1 crowd would take nicely to a full beat. I'll just keep my bomb makeup skills to myself.

Just when she's finished fixing my complexion, I hear laughter coming from the hallways leading up to this room. It's none other than my teammate, Xavier Valente, who walks in with his quirky and colorful signature street style. His hands are in his pockets with his face tilted back from the laughter echoing out of his mouth.

To his right, the devil, doing the unthinkable.

Laughing.

Swearing to all things holy, Luca Donatello, the arrogant stoic faced asshole, is laughing. Am I in a different dimension? Did I transport myself to the multiverse? Because right in front of me, I'm literally witnessing the impossible.

I must admit, after my first encounter with Mr. Donatello, I googled him.

I know, I know. I hate the guy, but knowing more information about someone you don't like gives you leverage. I love leverage in all situations.

Anyways, the moral of the story is curiosity killed the cat.

While sitting at my computer for hours searching things like:

Photos of Luca Donatello's World Championship Podium.
Why was Luca Donatello Elektra Motorsports first choice for team principal?
Why is Luca Donatello such a dick? (Showed me way too many dick pics).
And last, but certainly not least:
Photos of Luca Donatello's wedding.

It's not a surprise that there are hardly any photos

considering he completely went off the grid just months after his wedding, but the weird thing I noticed about all of his pictures is that he never smiled. This man never fucking smiles, he just smirks. A goddamn annoying smirk.

The only recorded photo of Luca Donatello smiling is when he won his world championship. His smile is so apparent throughout the whole ceremony, there's not one picture where he wasn't. On the other hand, you can't find a single picture where he's smiling at his wedding. Not like there were many photos to go off of, but it was a grand wedding. One made for kings and queens.

I don't think anything makes him happier than F1 does. I'm not one to judge. Racing is my drug, and it appears to be his too.

While falling into the rabbit hole that is google, I ended up seeing how nasty his divorce with his ex-wife was. Adèle Manon is a supermodel and the daughter of world-renowned fashion designer and owner of Adèle fashion house *André Manon*.

Obviously, it was named after her. She's her father's pride and joy. Her beautiful, long silky blonde hair and signature tooth gap are the poster child for the brand. As a socialite, her luxurious and glamorous lifestyle started at the young age of sixteen years old, which led her to marry Luca Donatello at the age of twenty-eight.

That's what male F1 drivers typically go for, the model or the heiress. Mr. Donatello went for both. Not that I can blame him, most male F1 drivers are surrounded by the best looking women in the world.

Luca and Adèle were married for two years and ended up divorcing in 2018. She sued him for over 6.3 million euros and claimed she was pregnant throughout the whole trial. She was, but not with Mr. Donatello's baby. That's the only public thing about his entire relationship with Adèle and the fallout of their divorce.

I've always said to myself that if I ever married or dated someone in F1, it would never be anyone who saw the sport as more important than me. I know it's selfish because for years I've been doing that to my family, but even if this sport is my life right now, it won't be forever.

As the laughter dissipates, both men look in my direction. I just stare, not initiating any conversation.

My teammate smiles when he notices my presence. This one is just going to be a ball of sunshine—I already like him.

"It's the rookie!" he announces while looking at me, his smile taking over his face.

"Well, hello there to you, Mr. Valente." I get out of my chair and walk up to him. I stretch my hand out and he takes it.

"It's nice to meet you, Ale, just call me Xavier so I can give you a nickname. It's a thing I do with the team, right Luc?" He looks over at him and Mr. Donatello, or should I say Luc, gives a brief nod with visible annoyance. I like it.

Interrupting our conversation, Laura quickly walks over to us and gives us a brief rundown of the schedule. I smile at her, giving her a reassuring nod to show I understand what she's saying. Which I do, but I don't think I like the arrangement of it all. First, we take candids, then we take teammate photos, and lastly (my least favorite of them all), we take photos with Mr. Donatello. That means I have to get close to him. I don't like it. It's already an uncomfortable situation when we're five feet apart. That's the perfect distance to keep calm, I feel like if I get any closer to the man, I'll punch him in the face.

"Let's start with Maria Alejandra first since she was here before the others," I hear Laura yell.

After taking what feels like a million photos, it's time to take teammate candids with Xavier. The photographer yells out different poses such as us facing each other with our arms crossed over our chest. Holding that stance I can't help but laugh while looking into Xavier's eyes. Trying to hold in our laughter just made us laugh harder.

The photographer yells at us to be serious and do the stance again. We try, but fail and burst out laughing again.

My head falls back as I'm wheezing and Xavier topples over trying to contain his laughter, but it isn't working.

You can hear the barely audible gasping statements that we make consisting of "you" *insert snort* "we have to be profession—" while another wheeze comes out. I already like him more than Mr. Donatello. Interacting with people can be dreadful, but interacting with him is delightful.

After making our way through all of the shots rather slowly, it's finally time for the candids with the team principal. I can tell he doesn't want to be photographed, but he's going to have to deal with it.

Just like we've been doing this whole time.

He walks over to us and looks over at the photographer in question. Well, we all do, me looking more lost than the others.

"*Allez*," the French photographer says while clapping his hands. "I'm going to need Mr. Donatello in the middle, while the other two drivers are at his side, holding their helmets in their hands and facing away from him." He pauses, releasing a dramatic breath.

"Mr. Donatello, if you could take off your jacket and cross your arms in the middle while doing a power stance that would be great," he finishes. Looking over, I see Mr. Donatello take off his Elektra Motorsports zip up, showing his black tee underneath.

Holy fuck. I can't think what I'm thinking right now, it goes against everything I stand for. But shit, his arms are other worldly. From all the times I've seen him in photos and the encounters we've had, he's always had sleeves covering his arms.

But to see underneath all of that, wow. His tattoos go down his entire bicep, while some scatter his fingers. He's definitely gotten bigger since his retirement. F1 drivers have to maintain a certain weight because it affects how the car performs, so most male F1 drivers—including Mr. Donatello when he was racing—are on the slimmer side.

But now he's far from that physique, he's built. The ink caresses his skin so effortlessly, like his tattoos were made for him.

STOP. You despise this man.

But he *is* hot as fuck. It's science and nothing more. Grabbing my helmet, I try to take my gaze off the eye candy because I refuse to ever let it slip that I think he is attractive.

My attraction to him changes nothing, I still loathe the man.

He walks back to the center and crosses his arms. Holy fuck! How are they so fucking nice looking? I swear to God, I hate myself right now.

Composing myself, I finally move into the pose that the photographer asked me to get into. He snaps a few shots before saying we're done for the day.

Thank God.

Xavier slowly walks away while taking off his racing suit. He suddenly turns as he pulls his shirt over his head and faces me.

"Bye, Ale. I'll see you tomorrow for practice." He waves, a massive grin on his face, and walks out the door.

As I take my eyes off Xavier, my gaze reaches the outline of Mr. Donatello's back. It's not fair to the world that such an asshole has a body like that.

Putting his zip up hoodie back on, he freezes as he feels my eyes on him. Before he turns around, I make sure to switch my gaze from "you're so fucking hot" to "I despise you." I think it works because he returns the look.

He catches me off guard by stepping closer to me. Inch by inch, his long strides devour the floor beneath him. They are long, slow, and calculated. Then he's only inches away from my face, and I can feel his breath brush against my ear.

He is so close. *Too close.*

"Don't look too long at me with distaste, *ragazza*. It doesn't matter if you stare at me like I'm the devil incarnate. Those pretty sea green eyes won't forget when I really do make your life harder. You're in the big leagues now, so buckle up, *tesoro*, because I don't particularly like you either."

As he walks off, he calls for his team with the wave of a finger. Before he leaves the room, he looks back at me with his sadistic smirk that I hate so much. To say I see red is an understatement.

The only thing I notice before he walks out the door are his hands. Those large, tattooed hands, with an array of rings on them. It's so effortless, but so fucking hot.

Ale, get yourself together. You hate the guy; he's a narcissistic jerk who wants to make you work harder than you already have.

The pep talk didn't help me at all. I still think he's hot as fuck.

CHAPTER NINE
MARIA ALEJANDRA

"Your car should be aerodynamically correct to your weight and height. We tried to make it as easy as possible for you to become accustomed to the car early on," one of my engineers says to me.

"Okay, sounds good. I'm going to try and adapt as fast as possible today so that I can go faster in quali in a few weeks."

It's time to finally get into the car. Ever since the photoshoot yesterday I've been dying to drive again.

The first practice session is going to be underway in about thirty minutes. I'm nervous and excited, but at the same time I just want to get it over with.

Every time a driver gets into their car for the first time, it can go one of two ways. One, they acclimate lap by lap, or two, they crash and can't get the hang of the car for the rest of the season. Since every driver—rookie or veteran—has never driven their car before, it's fair game out there. It's really a test to see who's the best.

Testing is where we can really feel the car, how fast it can go, how grip is, and what it's like G-force-wise at turns and even the pull going down a straight.

For me, I try to analyze every single detail that can possibly help strategically. At the end of the day, I am the second driver. I'm meant to get second. I hate it with every inch of my being, but it's the reality of it all. All I can do is stay consistent and get as many points as possible in the Drivers' and Constructors' championships to stand my ground. I can be a team player and I will be, but at the beginning of the season, it's not about sacrifice. Once we get closer to closing out the season and fighting for Constructors' and Driver's Championships, that's when sacrifice truly begins.

Zipping up my suit and putting on my helmet, I jump into the car. My engineer grabs my halo and puts it overhead. The seating is good; not great, but good for my first test run.

Once my feet reach all the way inside the car, I'm handed my steering component and lock it on.

Turning on the engine, I let the car heat up a little bit. Hearing the go ahead from my main engineer, I begin at a low-speed and efficiently pull out of the pit lane. I drive until I reach the end, finally accelerating to medium speed. I try to find my pace; I reach the first curve, feeling the pull and overall push I can give. I'm happy with it. The car is nice aerodynamically, and now, it's time to push the hell out of it.

I can't help but smirk, it's time to fuck some shit up.

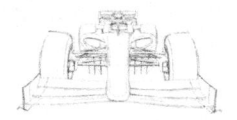

It's almost the end of practice and I feel good. The car is going at a moderate speed and the overall feel is stable. Since we have one more practice before the race, I think during this last lap I'll try to keep it steady.

Sometimes it's more important to go at a moderate pace than to go faster. Even though I'm not going at high speed, I'm also not racing. Feeling good in the car first is more important than speed and that's the secret to driving without any anxiety.

I want to push the hell out of myself and the car, but now is not the time.

"Miss Castillo," I hear in my ear.

"Yes."

"Donatello speaking, go faster for the love of God."

"Are you really in my ear telling me to go faster? In practice? Oh god, I don't want to see what it's like in races," I sigh.

"You're going slower than Xavier at the moment, we need to see the car's capabilities rather than the driver's, so go faster," he yells.

I stay silent, I'm not going to give him the satisfaction of a response.

I go slower making sure no one is on my tail. I don't fucking care. He can tell me to go faster over and over again, I won't. I slowly pull into the pit lane without telling anyone beforehand.

I let the engineers take over once I hop out. Taking my helmet off, then the suit piece that covers my head from the heat. I take my hair out of my scrunchie and shake my curls out with my fingers. Yanking out my earpiece, I shove it into my helmet as well as the cloth that was previously covering my head underneath the protection. I see Mr. Donatello in my peripheral vision and turn around. Walking up to him, I shove the helmet into his chest, then look up at him and smile.

Then, I just walk away, like nothing ever happened.

I walk away calmly. I feel good about that practice, and he is not going to take that away from me. Making my way out of the paddock and into my cubicle, I grab a water bottle and a straw. I open it up and slowly take a long sip. Hopping onto the couch, I grab out my phone and start scrolling through TikTok.

I hear the door open.

Looking up, I see him walking in with anger lingering over his features. I love it when he's angry, especially at me. The thought alone makes me smile.

"What the fuck was that, Miss Castillo?"

"That, Mr. Donatello, was me telling you to fuck off." I

flip him off causally without a sign of anger or frustration. He throws the helmet to my right and I look over as it plops next to me on the cushion. Bringing my gaze back up to him, I take a sip of my water keeping eye contact.

"Do you know what you just did, little girl? Not only did you do that to me, but you also did that in front of cameras. What did I say about disrespect? You're just a brat who wants attention, and that's what all those cameras saw out there. So, what do you want the world to see, huh?" he scoffs.

I scoff right back. "Don't call me a little girl, old man. I didn't disrespect you. I actually did everything I could not to. If I wanted to disrespect you, I would have given you a nice long monologue in front of all the cameras."

"You don't call that disrespect? I guess you were educated poorly, because to me, that was the definition of disrespect. You don't even know what you've walked into, do you? This is a lion's den, and you're just a mere kitten who has never had to suffer the consequences of your actions. Well, here, at the sport you love so much, you can't act like a five-year-old having a hissy fit with her father."

"You want to talk about disrespect? You not trusting my judgment or even asking me why I wasn't going fast before telling me to go faster shows your disrespect loud and clear."

"You talk about trusting judgment, but you don't even trust mine. What you ask for, you never give back, and that's the problem here. You simply have no idea what you've gotten yourself into. You don't know the massive weight on everyone's shoulders to make that car perform. Apparently, that's something your pretty little head can't grasp."

I just stare at him for a while, so I don't say something I'll regret.

"You call me a little girl, then come up to me and tell me that I don't understand this game. I know this game better than you, that much is clear. When the car needs to truly perform is when we race, not practice. When I race, I'll get you podiums and points. Me feeling comfortable and confident in that car lets you keep that enormous salary you love so much. It also gets me a title. It gives me a future in this sport that I work for every day. So, if that means pissing you off, that's fine by me." I shrug.

Lucia walks in just as I finish my sentence.

"Sorry to interrupt, but you're scheduled for an after-practice interview for Elektra's YouTube channel."

Nodding at her, I grab a hoodie, throw it over my head and put on a cap. I look up at him with disapproval.

"The seating needs adjusting, maybe an inch or so, so I can sit more comfortably. Nash can probably make it a little wider for overall comfort."

I turn around, open the door, and shut it behind me.

CHAPTER TEN

MARIA ALEJANDRA

It's race day, and I don't know how to feel.

I love the buzz and electricity that runs through me as I get ready to walk through the paddock., but this morning that feeling was not present. I woke up in a horrible mood, as always. I am not a morning person. I feel like I'm always tired no matter how much sleep I get.

I've never loved the sun, I'm sure that's a weird statement coming from a Mexican, but I only like the sun when I am thoroughly prepared for it. That's why I love the rain so much, I guess. It keeps me calm.

That can even be applied to my career as a racer.

When conditions aren't considered great on the grid is when I drive the fastest. Which is weird to most, but there's no point in lying that I dominate in the rain. I prefer it as such. It can be difficult to control at times, but the thrill of racing through the water and having it perfect at every turn keeps me calm. When precise control needs to happen, you lose yourself a little in the perfection of it all. The rush of possibility of spinning out at any second gives you a reckless nature.

That might be the hothead in me. I like the feeling of being out of control. It's freeing in a way. To feel like you don't need to be in control releases you from expectations. It releases you from the control society has on your life and doesn't cage you anymore.

I'm not saying that control isn't needed, it is. Especially in this sport, but sometimes just saying fuck it can take you farther than saying fight it.

You can't control an engine malfunction or a tire slashing on the last corner of a race, but you can control how much you give every single day. That's the control needed from every hard-working bad bitch out there.

That's what I try to project even on a day like today. Where pressure is the definition of my sorrows.

I take a deep breath before opening the door to my black Mercedes GTR. I can already hear the shutter clicks from the cameras being held by F1 publicity. Closing the door behind me, I start to walk through the crowd wearing one of my best outfits.

I've always thought that even though I'm a part of a sport that's considered relatively conservative, it doesn't mean I can't wear what I want to work.

I walk through the paddock verification gate in my custom, all black Doc Martens and black ripped shorts gracing the bottom half of my body. On my upper half is my custom Elektra hoodie that I had made by my best friend Violetta's little sisters, Chanel and Cleo. The team's black and white colors adorn it, while the word ELEKTRA reaches from the front to the back of the hoodie. The large graffiti font letters give it a street style look and my black sunglasses cover my face. Jet-black curls sprawl everywhere around me as I hold my phone in my hand.

I wave at the cameramen as I walk past them.

Finding the team building is easy enough as it's the first building on the walkway. Making my way through the automatic glass doors, I walk into my future for the next few months. Imagining a time where I might be able to fight for the Drivers' Championship.

The chair I'm sitting in is highly uncomfortable. I keep shifting my weight back and forth as the bright light blares against my skin.

The cameras ahead of me are placed in a straight diagonal line behind the black barrier. The biggest camera faces the middle of the backdrop, giving a wide angle in order to see all three chairs lined up. Hearing footsteps beside me, I turn to see Xavier walk in with his friendly confidence. It's the first press conference of the season and

I'm looking forward to talking to him about our future as teammates.

All that dissipates quickly when I remember that the devil himself will grace us with his presence throughout this press conference. I know I'm going to have to keep it together, but I want to punch the man in the face for even smirking in my direction.

Standing up, I greet Xavier with a warm smile and give him a hug.

"How are you doing? I heard you butted heads with the big boss," Xavier chuckles with his famous cheesy grin.

"Yeah, he told me to go faster during practice, and I basically told him to fuck off." I smile at the memory.

"He can be intense at times, but overall, he'll be able to push us in a way that nobody can even fathom, even if it's unconventional."

"I guess. I mean, he took a chance on me which I can appreciate, but I don't like to deal with narcissistic assho—"

"Are we talking about me? I'm flattered, *ragazza*," a deep Italian voice sounds behind me. I can already feel the annoyed, disingenuous smile that spreads across my face.

Xavier begins choking on the water he was drinking, but it isn't a successful task as he spits out all of it before he starts dying of audible laughter. I give him a glare and he shrugs. Then he walks away, cleaning off his chin while still laughing to himself.

I feel a tap on my shoulder and I slowly turn on my feet before meeting the Italian *demonio's* eyes. He just smirks down at me, waiting for a word to come out of my mouth. Refusing to give him any sort of satisfaction, I look up at him with my eyebrows raised.

"Are you going to finish that sentence to my face, Miss Castillo, or are you going to let that statement stay up in the air?"

"What I was saying, before you cut me off, is that you're a narcissistic asshole that has no thought for the people around you and you only care about your own well-being." I return that stupid smirk mockingly as I turn around.

He catches my wrist while I'm in the process of turning. His grip is tight, and it lingers there for a few seconds before he turns me back completely, keeping us at arms length.

He lets go of me, the feel of his hand still lingering in their absence. He slowly starts walking beside me, but stops briefly at my side.

"And you think your actions don't exude disrespect?" He plops into the seat farthest from my chair, at a distance where he can hear my voice faintly.

"I don't act disrespectfully towards you. I just say what I think." I wink playfully like nothing happened. Turning my head, I finally face the noise of my first Formula One interview.

After ten minutes of basic questions from a Sky Sports reporter, the rest of the session goes out to the interviewers in the small crowd in front of us. Fox Sports, ESPN, and all the other channels wait their turn to be called by the moderator.

"We saw the events of what happened between you, Miss Castillo, and your team principal at pre-season testing in Barcelona. Why was that a decision made on your part as a driver, and how did that make you feel as a team principal, Luca?" asks a male interviewer from I don't even know where at this point.

We stay silent for a bit looking at each other waiting for the other to respond. After a few moments, Mr. Donatello responds, saving the awkward silence from becoming a black hole enveloping everyone in the room.

Including myself.

"As team principal, it was sort of a disappointing occurrence from our rookie driver over here. I think when people come into this sport, it can be a lot at times. Unprofessional decisions are made and things get out of hand. But what happened a few weeks ago, I think, was a fault of judgment on both parts," he finishes his vague response. Leaning over to face him directly, I look at him for a second, dumbfounded.

"What do you mean by 'fault of judgment on both parts?'" I raise an eyebrow at him waiting for him to answer my question.

"Like I said, it was a fault of judgment on both our parts."

I hum in response looking back at the cameras. Everyone stays looking at me as I sit there in silence not wanting to answer the question.

I sigh knowing answering is inevitable.

"What happened in Barcelona was something that simply happened. I think it was a misunderstanding on some parts, but not what was important at the time. Being that this is my first year in the sport, as well as being recruited to a top team, means that there is pressure involved, which isn't something that bothers me. But, it does push me to do things that I don't like to do at times. A prime example of that was pre-season testing."

"Thank you for your responses, Alejandra, Luca, and Xavier. We look forward to seeing you out at the race tonight."

All of us nod our heads as we stand up from our seats and we make our way out of the room, shaking hands with a few publicity people before heading for the stairs. Xavier and Mr. Donatello are ahead of me as we descend down a few flights. Even though I was in the chair closest to the door, Xavier flew out of that room as fast as he could. Most likely trying to avoid the hateful vibes that our boss and I are expelling towards each other.

Xavier is all about good vibes and trying to stay positive. From the fan perspective, his presence in Formula One has always been a joy to watch. I don't think that man has ever had anyone not find him incredibly charismatic and funny. Not even me, and I'm kind of hard to make a lasting impression on. I get annoyed very easily.

Exhibit A: Mr. Donatello.

Speaking of whom, he's not so far ahead of me. Sprinting down the flight of stairs, I slow down my pace when I reach him. Our shoulders touch abruptly.

"A misunderstanding, huh? I guess you're already regretting recruiting me then." He rolls his eyes.

"I never said that, Miss Castillo. What I meant by misunderstanding is that you think I'm your age with the same thoughts as you. I'm not saying I haven't experienced the same things in my career. I have, especially since I started out around the same age, but don't forget, I'm eighteen years older, which means that I think more in the moment and about the consequences of my actions. I'm not the hothead I used to be, which is fine, but don't make it sound like we have the same thinking strategy, because it is clear that we don't. I am neither your friend nor your enemy; I'm your boss. To me, the thing that I'm most interested in from you is driving. Nothing more, nothing less. Do what you're best at. Drive that car as fast as you fucking can."

CHAPTER
ELEVEN
MARIA ALEJANDRA

Bahrain is a successful first race of the year.

I ended up in P2 alongside Xavier in P1.

I know what my abilities are, which means I know I'm faster than Xavier, but I can always do better, train harder, and ultimately be more consistent.

I walk into what I like to call the strategy room. The space is shaped into a rectangle that sits on the top floor just below the terrace of Elektra's paddock building. Multiple tables are lined up horizontally against the wall and in the middle of the room to form a square. On each individual table, the computers sit on the desks with their own separate keyboards and mouse just below the monitor.

The strategy room is where everyone that plays a big part in the team's dynamic comes together to go over each grid before racing.

Once the race is over, we come in here to see what can be

done to improve. We learn from our mistakes and ensure that they don't happen again.

Sitting down in the chair, I wait for the rest of the team to join me. Looking down at my phone, I realize I'm fifteen minutes early. Shrugging, I start scrolling through Instagram and decide to post a picture that was taken of me on the podium about an hour ago. I think about the caption for a minute and land on:

"An amazing way to start off the season. A one, two for Elektra at our first race of the calendar. Already fighting for that championship, baby."

I hit post and repost on my stories, deciding to post a separate story in the strategy room. With a smirk on my face, I take the photo, test some filters out and put text on top.

"Strategy Time."

Smiling to myself, I find a song to put over the pic. Deciding on "Yo Perreo Sola" by Bad Bunny, I click post and put my phone down just as Xavier walks in. I smile at him, and he returns it, plopping down in the chair next to me.

"That was quite the race, wasn't it?" he questions.

"Yeah. That's a one, two, baby." Both our faces are overtaken by massive smiles and we high five in bliss.

"You know, we should make a hand shake so that every time we achieve something, we have a ritual." Xavier says an expression of realization spreads across his face, giving his gaze a hint of mischief along with it.

"I'm down. After we're done with this meeting, we can figure it out." I reply.

"I have so many ideas. This is going to sound cheesy, but at this point I don't care. My last teammate was extremely competitive and we never really spoke. Not often anyway, that man was a grump. I'm ready for a banging handshake, so you better keep that promise." He points at me with a smile, and I chuckle at him.

"What critiques do you think they're going to have? After all, we did get first and second today."

"They always have critiques because there's always something that can be done to get better. I slid on a curve out there, so I think it's going to be cool to see Luca's take. I mean we also have to look at Dupuis and Sansui's progress on track. Amir looked really fast and so did Ren. Looking at their weaknesses will help." He tells me.

"Having Mr. Donatello in the room will make us realize our mistakes. That being said, I don't think he will let go of any of them." I tell him and then frown up at him.

"I don't understand why you guys don't like each other to be honest. Luca has been through a lot, especially in F1. For one thing, he is a part of a wealthy family who basically gave him never ending pressure to be the best. And it's not like he didn't have that already stemming from himself, we know how it is. Imagine also being forced into a marriage and then having to carry such a weight like F1 on your back." He shrugs.

Forced? What the fuck does he mean by forced? Like

obligated, mandatory, required to be in a marriage with someone?

"What do you mean by forced?" I raise my eyebrows in confusion.

"You don't know?"

"What do you mean by 'you don't know'?" I respond with curiosity.

"I forgot you haven't been in F1 long enough. I only found out recently when he became our team principal. It will never be put out on the internet, but Luca is a part of a generational Italian name. The Donatellos are known for their hatred of organized crime. During previous generations, they were the only families with status in Italy who were not involved in the mafia. It's not something you see often. Even Gucci had connections to the mafia at some point.

"Basically, when he and Adèle got together, they were lost in one another. They would never be seen apart, so to speak. People remark that he smiled more with her than he had in his life. Let me tell you, it's hard to make that man smile. Even I can't do it that often, let alone every day. He was whipped, basically. His family saw it as leverage, especially since the Manon family is incredibly well known in the fashion world. Thus—"

"The rest of the Italian mafia fashion corporations having connections with them," I finish his sentence for him.

"Exactly. Apparently, the mafia made his family's lives a

living hell. So, they kind of wanted revenge of some sort. During his engagement, he saw a deal breaker in Adèle. No one knows what it was even to this day. But eventually, he was forced into a marriage with her in order to get his family leverage," he sighs.

"How do you know so much about this?"

"People in F1 have known him for a long time and it's come down through the grapevine, I guess. When he was announced as team principal, it became a big thing around here." My eyebrows furrow as I think for a second.

"I personally don't see it as a problem. He's a legend, and he knows how to drive better than any other team principal in the sport. We have a lot to learn from him," he finishes off before he turns around and hits the power button on his computer.

Swiveling away from him in my chair, I can't help but think about the endless problems that can occur from this recent information.

In light of my thoughts, Mr. Donatello walks through the door with his other engineers. All of our colleagues rush to take their seats. Once everyone is settled, he claps his hands together and announces, "What a great team result today. Everyone in here has done a wonderful job, but right now, it's time to focus on the things we can fix and what the other cars are doing out there." He walks over to the computer right across from Xavier and starts sharing his screen with the others.

I can't pay attention to what he is saying right now, let

alone pitch into the conversation. After zoning out for a few minutes, I hear Mr. Donatello say my name.

"Miss Castillo, did you hear anything that I've been saying for the last twenty minutes?" He grimaces.

"Sorry, what?"

He gives me a dirty look, telling me to pay attention without even saying a word. "I said that you need to get more speed around the corners. You're losing traction and tire longevity by hitting the curve slower than Xavier." I nod.

"Yeah, I agree. I was feeling a little more force than usual. I can fix it by the next race." He nods with shock evident in his expression.

All I can think about are two things.

One: Did I just agree with the words that came out of Mr. Donatello's mouth?

Two: I can't let him ever know that I was born into the biggest organized crime family in Mexico, because if he finds out...

I'm fucked.

CHAPTER TWELVE
LUCA DONATELLO

Imola is one of my two home races of the season, and I don't know how to feel about it. Not being a driver anymore means that I can't do anything out there to deliver a good result. That's what makes me feel out of control.

I hate it.

Being in control is one of the things that I pride myself most on. No good comes out of losing control.

When I was in my early days of F1, I always lost control and had a bad temper, but now I have more authority over my actions, which I'm grateful for.

But the temper, that still needs a little work.

I play with the rings on my fingers, attempting to maintain control over my anxiousness. Cheering erupts outside of the car and I realize that we're arriving at the grid. I see some fans cheering as we drive by.

We head to the entrance of the paddock, and I make sure everything is in order before I get out of the car. Taking my sensor card out of my pocket, I open the car door, waving at the shouting fans. I stride through the security detector while scanning my ID on the barcode sensor. I keep walking until I greet some officials, FODA directors and such.

Looking to my left, I notice Xavier talking to Amir Zikraan. The classic black look that he wears tries to give the bad boy motorcycle vibe. His tattoos spread everywhere across his skin, from his neck all the way down to his ankles.

The man can drive, and I know that everyone is rooting for him, including me, to a certain extent. I know the story of his journey to F1 and it's impressive. Coming all the way from Egypt and driving for an Arab F1 team doesn't really give him a good first impression with Formula One executives—considering Formula One's years of racist commentators and fans. Younger audiences are attracted to the sport now that it's owned by an American company. Which means, as a whole, the sport is moving in the right direction. The boy drives fast, and that's all that should matter.

Seeing them both wave at me from across the walkway, I nod my head at them in acknowledgement, finally arriving at the building. Walking in, I mentally prepare myself to give an extensive speech to both drivers about how important this Grand Prix is.

Especially a certain girl who needs to get back in her lane.

MORPHINE

Neither of them got a podium.

"You know we did our best right? You can't just walk away from us in anger," I hear her aggravating Spanish accent from behind me.

I frown. "I'm not angry, I'm just disappointed."

"Oh my god, you sound just like my father," she mocks me.

"Well, I am closer to his age than yours, *ragazza*, so deal with it." I continue walking, but she follows behind me, resembling a pup following its mother. But in this case, the pup is throwing a fit.

"That doesn't mean you can treat me like a little girl, *estupido*. I'm a grown ass woman!"

"You're not even twenty-one." I throw my hands up in frustration walking through the paddock to get to a place without a camera in sight.

"You pulling out the age card every two seconds makes you seem even more immature than me. I could always pull out the 'you're too old to do this job card.'" In my peripheral view, I see her trying to keep up with my pace, cocking her head in frustration. Finally, when we reach a secluded area without cameras, I stop my strides abruptly, which ends up with her face planting into my back. I turn around and look down at her.

"I have said this before and I will say it again, you don't take into consideration the consequences of your actions. As you were telling me off on our way out of the team garage, cameras were following our every move."

"You know what's sad?" she questions. "The fact that you, a grown man," she uses her fingers to point at my chest applying pressure, "care about cameras seeing us argue. Here's what I think about that, *me vale Madre!*" She yells in frustration.

"I'm here at my home race and if you think that this type of behavior is okay, that's your own problem. My problem is having to go home tomorrow to a P10 and a P11 result IN ITALY!"

"I don't get why you care so much. You have two home races. I only have one. You still have Monza, so calm the fuck down."

Rolling my eyes, I can't believe the words that are coming out of her mouth.

"You told us how important this race is to you two hours ago and then you punched a wall in the garage. You don't think that says something? At least you hit a wall instead of a person, you should be proud of yourself for that." She pats me on the back like it's an achievement.

"Because I have control, which you lack."

"I have control, but knowing when to use it and when not to is more important. You are always in control and that's truly your downfall. Plus, I don't think punching a wall exhibits very good control." Scoffing, she walks out. Thinking for a second, I decide to follow her.

Grabbing her wrist I turn her around, pulling her into me while still leaving a small distance between us.

"You will not disrespect me again Do you understand me?"

Laughing in my face, she tugs herself out of my grip. With a menacing look, she slowly turns around and walks down the hallway. Before she reaches the end, she twirls around and glares at me. "I only give my respect to those who truly deserve it." She curtsies and then reaches for the doorknob, slamming the door behind her as she walks out.

Putting my hands over my face, I sigh into them, extremely drained from that interaction. Everything she does drains me.

That girl needs to be put in her place, that's something I'm quite certain of. And I'm going to be the one to do it.

CHAPTER THIRTEEN
LUCA DONATELLO

I feel the Florida humidity hit me as I walk off the Elektra private jet. To say that Xavier is jumping for joy right next to me would be an understatement. He's not just happy, he's literally shining brighter than the fucking sun.

It's Wednesday, which means that we're about a day and a half from the race. We have some time before the actual event to at least look around or, as I would like to do, rest. It's not going to be an easy task since F1 fans will have invaded Miami by Friday morning. Most of them are probably already here.

I walk down the stairs that lead to a long black carpet at the Miami private airport. I turn around and see Miss Castillo walking out in tiny shorts and a leather top that looks like a bra. My eye notices the huge circular hat that is on top of her head with large obsidian-colored sunglasses that cover her whole face. She's dressed head to toe in the same color, which I know by now is her signature.

But the thing that catches my eye almost instantly after ogling her gigantic hat, is her skin. The deep tan that she has year-round. The way it glows when the sun hits it. Those plump lips, creased in an unimpressed expression.

Her fashion sense is classy and chic with a modern twist. It's one of the only things I like about her, other than her challenging temper. Yes, I might get annoyed with her almost every day during the season, but that doesn't mean I hate the girl. I just think she's incredibly immature.

Xavier walks beside me, clad in a blinding neon outfit. It's incredibly funny to me how different Alejandra is from Xavier. They differ from each other in almost every sense, except for the way they interact in a friendly manner. At this point it's like they're best friends.

That relationship is something I would bet my money on.

"Hey boss, would you like to come on a sightseeing trip with me and the rookie? We want to go around today before we get into our racing mindset, you know?" He snaps me out of my thoughts while giving me a cheeky grin.

Miss Castillo gives him a glare telling him with just a look, *are you serious?*

Yes, Miss Castillo, he is serious.

"I would love to. I've never been to Miami before and it sounds interesting."

"Yeah, I bet you would just love the Versace mansion,"

Miss Castillo says as she walks past me. I hold in my scoff, not wanting to give her any validation. She walks ahead of me with confidence, carrying her two Louis Vuitton bags. As she makes her way towards the airport exit, I can't help but think that this is going to be interesting.

Peering around at our over-the-top hotel, which is walking distance to the track, the lobby is shaped in a circle with marble floors and murals of beaches on the ceiling. The inspiration is clearly that of the Vatican, but it's executed in such a tacky manner.

I will admit that I can be judgmental, but this is the epitome of trying to extract inspiration from something and having it go extremely wrong. Once at the front desk, I say the team's name, and immediately they give us all the information, handing it to our travel accommodations manager. She takes it carefully out of my hands and nods.

Turning around, she ushers all of us up the stairs leading to the silver elevators. Going up a few floors, we reach the lounge, which is on the eighth floor out of thirty-four.

"Now that I have all of you here, I will tell you which floors you will be on for the remaining time that you will be at this Grand Prix. The entire social media team will be on the eleventh floor, as well as all the engineers. Here are your key cards." She hands out the cards as she calls out names, each person coming up and taking them out of her hand and going up to their rooms to get situated.

Once most of the team is gone, she turns her head towards us.

"As for the two drivers, you will be on the floor below your team principal, which is the thirty-third floor. You'll be in rooms right next to each other." She hands them their key cards and then faces me. "And for you, Mr. Donatello, as requested, you will be in the penthouse suite on the thirty-fourth floor." She smiles and I give her a grateful look as I grab my things out of her hands.

"Everything should be in your suites ready to go. If you need anything, feel free to call me. My phone number is on a sticky note right next to the room's landline."

"Thanks, Nancy," Miss Castillo says as she smiles and walks towards the elevator with her bag.

"No problem. Any time." She waves before she walks off. Xavier looks at me before he steps into the elevator, standing right next to Miss Castillo. I walk in behind him. Pressing our own floor numbers, we stand in silence while the cheesy elevator jazz music plays in the background. I can feel the tension as I watch the numbers go by.

Once the number hits thirty-three, I step aside as Xavier and Miss Castillo walk past me. Xavier stops in the middle of the door before it closes.

"We're going to change before we go around and

explore. I already told Nancy, and she has transportation scheduled for five o'clock." Looking down at my watch, I see it's four on the dot. "We'll meet you down there in fifty minutes, Luc." Turning back, he makes his way out of the elevator and then turns around again before the doors close.

"Also, make sure to bring a swimsuit," he says with a smile taking up his whole face. I nod as he walks out and catches up to Miss Castillo.

Letting out an abrupt sigh, I wait for the elevator to get to my floor. After inserting my card into the reader, both doors open, allowing me to pass through.

As I walk out of the elevator, I realize that I don't have a swimsuit.

CHAPTER
FOURTEEN
MARIA ALEJANDRA

At five sharp, Xavier and I are down in the lobby. Just minutes ago, Xavier came to my door, practically banging down my door. Finally, when I opened it, he was smiling up at me, his expression dripping with excitement. The whole elevator ride down, he was talking about how excited he was to be able to walk around Miami for the first time.

Currently, we're waiting for Mr. Donatello to come down. Right next to me sits a nervous Xavier. His leg is bouncing up and down on the beige couch in the lobby.

"There he is." Xavier points at the gift shop.

I turn my head towards that direction and see a Mr. Donatello holding a gift shop bag. I thought our renowned team principal only shopped at Tom Ford.

"Sorry I'm late." He looks down at his watch before continuing his speech. "There was a weird woman in there trying to get a discount on everything in the store." I wonder what he bought. As if he reads my mind, he lifts the bag to eye level. "I forgot swim trunks, so I went to go buy some."

Now that makes more sense.

"I'm surprised you didn't get your assistant to go down to the luxury shops and get you some fancy swim trunks," I retort.

"Okay, let's calm down, kids. The car is here so we should get going," Xavier says.

I nod my head in agreement as we make our way to the Elektra SUV, which is custom made and available to any driver or worker with the F1 team.

Getting into the back seat, I sink into the leather. I feel the air conditioning blast onto my skin, taking me away from the Floridian humidity. Xavier goes to the driver's side while Mr. Donatello makes his way to the passenger seat of the car. Connecting my phone to the Bluetooth, we set the Waze app for our estimated location. Turning on the voice command mode, we get going on this long, excruciating *adventure*.

So far, the trip has been bearable. The three of us make our way to Lincoln Road, which is five minutes away from the beach. Xavier and I walk around, people-watching while I also go into some shops. One thing I will say about the shops in Miami is that there is a large variety of things that you won't be able to find in Mexico. Walking out of my last shop, I see Mr. Donatello sitting outside on the phone.

Looking over at Xavier, I mutter, "I'm done with the shopping, should we go to the beach now?"

"Finally," Xavier drags out the word until he sounds out of breath. I roll my eyes at his antics and look over at Mr. Donatello. After ending his call, he walks towards us.

"So, where are we going next?"

"The beach." He nods his head as we start walking towards the car on the other side of the mall. After an hour of walking, we make it back to the car.

Xavier turns on the engine, and I feel it start rumbling as I look out the window. So many people are living their lives without a care in the world. Some are laying on the beach with friends, while others longboard with a freeness to them. Miami seems to be a place where people live without stress.

Changing the song, I decide on "Hymn for the Weekend" by Coldplay.

"Can you take the top of the car off?" I ask Xavier.

He smiles and nods. I turn the stereo knob to full volume and take my seatbelt off, standing up and letting the air take my hair back. The song plays in the background.

As the music drops, I close my eyes while feeling the adrenaline course through me. Extending my arms out, I breathe out and laugh. I don't know how I feel, but the one thing I do know is that I'm free.

For the rest of our drive over to the beach, Mr. Donatello and I argued about which part of Miami Beach we should visit. Finally, we land on the side where the Versace Mansion is. I know he hates it, which is one of the reasons I want to go.

Well, not only that, it's also a landmark. The infamous spot where Giovanni Versace was killed by a psychopathic stalker. What used to be a house but is now a hotel is one of the most visited places in Miami, and I'm not missing my chance to see it.

Xander scores a parking spot closest to the beach and the hotel, I jump out and breathe in the fresh sea air. Someone comes rushing past me riding a bicycle on the sidewalk closest to the beach. Looking around, I see a café in front of the lot where we parked.

"What do you think they're talking about?" I hear his Italian accent drip off my skin as he points at the café across the street.

"It's obvious." I quirk an eyebrow at him, pointing at a couple on the farthest side of the sitting area.

"They're on a Tinder date. The awkwardness and

fidgeting shows, but also the fact that she keeps looking down at her phone. She's either texting her friend good or bad news or looking at Tinder to check if it's actually the guy she swiped right on."

I point my finger at the friends on the other side of the café. "You see her laughing? She's laughing at her friend's joke in hopes that she won't offend her. It's not that funny, but she wants her friend to be happy." I shrug up as I turn around and look at him.

"Shocking. You said exactly what I was thinking. That within itself is scary."

"It's not scary, Mr. Donatello, it's common sense. It's the viewpoint from people who are perceptive, which just so happens to be all of us." I wave my finger in a circle, reiterating that Luca and Xavier are both perceptive in their own ways.

Brushing past him, I catch up with Xavier. I set down the beach bag I was carrying and take out the towels that Xavier insisted I shove into my bag. The sand kind of scares me because the bag is Dior, but it was made for the beach after all, so I guess I don't see the harm.

Laying the towels down, I sit on one of them and take off my shoes. Xavier is already out of his clothes, except his swim trunks. I don't plan on witnessing or cooperating in any skinny dipping anytime soon. Although, Xavier is the exact person I could see doing it.

Walking past, he makes his way through the tan sand and dives into a wave, then starts floating in the ocean. I just sit there and take in my surroundings for a bit. Looking over I see Mr. Donatello coming back after changing. In Miami, restaurants don't let anyone change inside bathrooms when they're near the beach. He had to make his way to an outdoor bathroom by the sidewalk across from the lifeguard stand. I bet that was a pleasant experience for him, and I can't help but smile at the image of him struggling to take off his suit pants in a tiny bathroom stall. The smell is most likely pungent with the lack of plumbing inside. The image of bugs and him knocking into the dividers, cursing, graces my imagination. That would be a great thing to witness.

He's now in swim trunks that are far from his taste.

The man has pink swim shorts on with a little dolphin pattern adorning the entirety of the fabric. Mr. Donatello is in the most basic beach boy swim trunks. This is the best day of my life.

"I don't appreciate the laughing, Miss Castillo. I'm still your boss, just to remind you of my status in this power exchange."

"Not laughing would be a crime in this instance. You're wearing the exact opposite of what you would pick. Damn, I love Miami. Plus, you look adorable."

"I do not look adorable. What a dreadful word choice."

"I beg to differ, you're absolutely adorable."

"It was this or something even worse." He waves over his swim shorts.

"There can't be anything worse than those."

"Oh yes there is, imagine me in a bright yellow speedo.

My cousin Leonardo wears them every chance he gets, so I would rather not be like my imbecile of a cousin. I will never understand why people have a lack of taste when it comes to swimwear. It's a disgrace to society."

I laugh to the point that I can barely breathe. I lay down on my blanket, not able to get a full breath into my lungs.

"I am imagining you—" laugh, "in a tiny little speedo —" laugh. "Please do that at least once in your lifetime. I want a picture and a moment to witness it for myself."

"You laugh now, wait until you see things that you shouldn't see. You would be such a scared little girl, just like the women who take it for fun." I freeze. He did not just make a reference about his dick.

"That's the most dickhead comment I have ever heard."

"But it's the truth, and you know I always say what's on my mind," with that he takes his shirt off.

Look away, Ale. Do it now, before you think he's hot again. Yeah, no, you did not look away and that is all your fault.

I could stare at him all day.

Nope, Ale, you could not, because he repulses you.

But he also has a six-pack and a back that you would love to grab onto.

Stop staring, Ale, or he's going to notice you're drooling.

But his skin is glistening, it makes me want to lick it.

Nope, his good looks do not make up for his horrible personality.

Snapping out of my trance, I see Xavier run up towards

us to one of the beach towels after getting out of the waves for a little break.

"Ale, you have to get in, the water is amazing." He reaches up and shakes out his hair.

"Okay," I reply. "Give me a second."

He nods and jogs back in, making a splash as he dives.

Getting up, I take off my hat and glasses, dropping them carefully onto the towel. I pick up my bag taking my sunscreen out so I can reapply. I'm not about to look like a raisin at the mere age of twenty.

Pulling my shirt off reveals a simple black bikini top. I then sweep my shorts off, showing the G-string bottoms.

I take the sunscreen and start applying it all over. My face, stomach, legs, arms, shoulders, and even my ass. Trying to reach my back I reach over as much as possible, clearly struggling in the process.

"Your stubbornness is really showing, *ragazza*. Let me help," I hear the devil say from behind me. He takes the sunscreen bottle out of my grip and opens the lid, squeezing the liquid onto his palm. Turning back around, I look at the ocean, trying to concentrate on the waves and the breeze that the ocean creates. I feel his large, warm hands start applying sunscreen to my back. When the cold liquid in his hands hits my skin, I jump a little.

He starts from the middle of my back, moving to the top of my bathing suit bottom. Applying it meticulously, his hands feel like they're melting into my skin. Grabbing more sunscreen, he goes over my shoulders and rubs it in like it's a damn massage. The tension in my neck and shoulders quickly fades. His fingers go deep into my previously tense muscles, and damn does it feel good. He starts massaging the sunscreen so deeply into my skin that I moan out loud.

He stops, brings his lips to my ear, and says, *"Fatto."* He steps away slowly.

Holy fuck, did I just moan?

I start praying to whatever God is above.

God, please take me off this earth. I can't bear the thought of moaning at the hands of this asshole. Please erase this experience from my mind immediately, or I can't bear living. Please, I beg of you, God.

"Care to return the favor, Miss Castillo?" I hear Mr. Donatello say behind me.

I nod hesitantly as I reach for my sunscreen.

"You won't be needing that. I bought some spray-on sunscreen while I was in the gift shop." He smirks up at me.

This motherfucker.

CHAPTER
FIFTEEN
LUCA DONATELLO

"I am not going into that tacky murder house."

"This has been a place on my bucket list since forever and I need to see it. So, if you'll excuse me, I will be going in with or without you."

"Um, I'm going with her. The pictures will be insane." Xavier scurries after a very excited Miss Castillo.

I sigh, contemplating my morals, but I decide to go in. Peer pressure does things to you. I catch up to them and walk swiftly behind as we pass the famous gates on the outside. As I make my way into the lobby, I wonder whether we can go inside if we're not guests.

Walking up to the receptionist, Miss Castillo proceeds to tell her that she just wants to look around, and the lady, as I suspected, proceeds to tell her that we have to be guests to enter.

Without even a fight, she retreats, a look of defeat on her

features. I don't like seeing that look on her face, because she never goes down without a fight. Walking up behind Ale, I make my way to the front desk.

"Ma'am? Hi, I'm Luca Donatello, Elektra's team principal, and these are the two drivers for the reigning Formula One World Championship team. Is there anything you can do?" Her face lights up in recognition.

"That's why you guys look so familiar! I am so sorry I can't do anything. Unless you're a guest at the hotel, I can't let you in. It's protocol." I grunt at the receptionist's words.

"What if I book a room?" I quirk my eyebrow.

"I don't think we have a room available. We're often booked for months on end." She looks down at the screen in front of her, looking for an available room.

"Actually, we just had an opening for the Empire Suite, but it's one thousand six—" I cut her off.

"We'll take it." I reach for my card, dropping it on the marble counter.

She seems surprised, but she reaches for the card and proceeds to run it.

"Okay, this is your key card for your accommodations. Thank you for choosing The Villa Casa Casuarina." By the way she butchers the word *Casuarina*, I'm guessing she's Latin in some way, not Italian. I nod, grabbing the card and handing it to Miss Castillo.

The main restaurant is the first thing visible from the front desk. I look over at Xavier and Miss Castillo who seem to be in shock after that whole ordeal.

"So, where do you want to go first, Miss Castillo?" I ask.

"Um, can we go to the pool? I've always wanted to see the tile."

"Lead the way." I follow as she walks past me.

I see her whole stance change as we reach the *piscina*. She gasps, turning around to face me and Xavier. I can see that fire in her eyes again, just as I like it. Throwing her clothes off, like she did at the beach, she stumbles a bit before dropping her stuff on a pool chair.

She reaches for her phone and unlocks it before handing it to Xavier.

"Take pictures," she says while giving him a stern look. I almost laugh.

Almost.

She dives into the pool, letting her wild curls straighten in the process. Standing in the pool, she begins to direct Xavier on how to take her pictures. I just watch as this all takes place in front of me.

After taking photos in every corner, we finally make it to the observatory, which is currently empty. It's finally dark outside after spending hours looking around Miami and then finally being in the Versace Mansion. Yet again, I watch as Miss Castillo walks in and gasps in awe. It tends to be a recurring sound that comes out of her mouth, along with her famous scoff of disapproval. The ceiling is painted in a royal blue with gold eclectic pieces stuck to it.

The observatory is obviously open so that the stars can be seen. She's looking up at them with such fascination.

"They are so beautiful. I've always thought the stars were lost souls that didn't make it to Earth. They look down on us when we go through our hardest times, but continue to shine. As a little girl, they were my saving grace, along with my mother's gardens," she says, and I follow, telling her my thoughts.

"There are about 100 billion stars in the sky. Every now and then, we can see the Milky Way galaxy that carries billions of those celestial bodies that are composed of hydrogen and helium. Stars are just luminous balls of gas; it's that simple. Some people think the view of the stars means something spiritual or symbolic, like their loved ones. I see them for what they are. Just little, bright balls of gas in the sky."

"You always like to ruin things, don't you?"

I tsk at her.

"No, I just always give science the benefit of the doubt. I can't deny it though, they are pretty to look at." She frowns, turning towards Xavier for her bag, which he's been holding this whole trip around the mansion.

She takes out a flowy piece of fabric that looks like a dress.

"Thank God I brought this." She takes off her shirt, shorts, and sneakers before pulling the dress over her bathing suit. It isn't a dress; it looks more like a sarong draping her body that is shaped like a dress. The shoulder straps have gold cuffs that only cover the middle of the strap. It's completely backless and made of mesh. Xavier starts taking photo after photo, and each time she poses, she looks stunning.

Her delicate features meet her wild, curly hair like fire and ice.

She stands there like a statue made by Antonio Lombardo. The way her body curves as if the wind moves with her. I've never seen anyone glow like that before. She's haunting in a way that will stay with you for life. It's the type of aura a man would kill for.

Now I know why Helena started a war.

After the most intense photoshoot of the century, we decided to sit down and eat at the hotel restaurant to take a break from the tiring day. It's comfortably silent as we all eat like we haven't eaten in days. Let's just say we haven't taken a food break once today.

"This is the best pasta I have ever had," I hear Xavier say beside me.

Miss Castillo nods in agreement. "I'm currently having a food orgasm."

They both hum in agreement as they devour every piece of pasta left on their plates.

"I was thinking, since we already paid for a night in the nice suite, why don't we stay here until morning? That way, you guys can have the whole experience."

"Oh my god. Did Mr. Donatello actually think about someone other than himself for a change?"

I shake my head at her. "I would love to see the rooms here as well. They all have a story specifically picked by Gianni himself." Miss Castillo nods at my statement.

"What about you, Xavier?" He stops shoving bread into his mouth.

"I don't mind," he says.

"Okay, it's settled then." I wave the waiter over and ask him for the check. He nods, then quickly walks over to get us the bill.

A few minutes later, he returns with the check in hand. Grabbing it, I check it over. I'm dropping my Amex onto the table when Miss Castillo stops me with her hand.

"You're not going to pay every bill here. Remember, we make almost as much money as you do." She quickly picks my card up off the table and throws it to the side, placing her card on top of the receipt and handing it to the waiter.

I sit in shock. I would have told her no, but I don't want

her to be offended. I know she feels strongly about equality. Everything should be the same between men and women, and I agree, but that doesn't stop me from feeling bad that she paid. He swiftly returns with the black leather checkbook, and she signs her signature on the small piece of paper and gives them a tip.

Getting up out of my chair, the others do so as well. We make sure we place the chairs back where they were when we arrived, and then head to the lobby towards the elevator.

Finally making it to the gold elevator, we take it up to the second floor. Walking down the hallway, we see a door at the end of the hall. In sizable letters across the door, it says, "Empire Suite." Putting my key card in, I open the door to a massive room adorned in maroons and light blues, an odd color match, but very Versace.

One massive bed sits in the middle of the room, which means one of us will have to sleep on the floor. That person will most likely be me.

Miss Castillo walks through the room in an extremely attentive state. Running her fingers down the curtains and murals on the walls, you can see the fascination in her eyes. "This used to be his room. Gianni's," she says out loud, catching me off guard with her words.

"Doesn't that seem creepy to you in any way?"

"No, not really. It's actually a cool experience."

"Sleeping in a dead man's room is a cool experience for you?"

"That's not the point; it's his legacy that captivates me.

This is where he thought, created, ate, slept, and lived. This is an experience to honor the legend's legacy." She shrugs.

Absolutely not. As an Italian, I disagree, but it might also be due to my family's bias throughout my life.

"We have to figure out this sleeping arrangement," Xavier blurts out as he lays on the bed that he jumped on as soon as we walked in.

"Well, I'm not sleeping on the floor," Miss Castillo says, her snarky comment taking me in a completely different direction from my original thoughts. All I want to do is get a reaction out of her now.

"Well, I'm not sleeping on the floor either."

"Well, I guess I'm sleeping on the floor then," Xavier says as he starts getting up from the bed, sighing. Realization runs through me while I look into Miss Castillo's eyes. If he sleeps on the floor, that means . . . Miss Castillo and I would have to sleep in the same bed.

Fuck. No.

Realization hits Miss Castillo a few seconds after me. "NO!" we both yell in unison at Xavier. He just sits there in shock at our abrupt outburst.

"I'll sleep on the floor," I say.

"No, you won't. I'll sleep on the floor. You're an old man, you might get back problems."

"Well, you're still a growing child, so you should sleep on the bed."

"I don't know why this is such a big problem, you two

just sleep on the bed. I'll sleep on the floor without a problem." I sigh in frustration at Xavier's words.

Suddenly, a knock sounds at the door, and I go to open it to see one of Elektra's workers with three bags in hand containing all our stuff. I told them to bring us some things from our hotel.

I nod a thank you at her while closing the door. Dropping them on the bed, they both rush for their sleepwear and toothbrushes and run into the bathroom.

All I can think about is that one of my worst nightmares is coming true.

Miss Castillo and I will have to sleep in the same bed. Our stubbornness finally bit us in the ass for the first time since we met each other.

CHAPTER
SIXTEEN
MARIA ALEJANDRA

I wake up to warmth, a peculiar warmth at that.

I slowly open my eyes and take in my surroundings. Realizing that we're still in the mansion, all the memories come flooding back to me. I look up and see all the antique art surrounding us. I can't help but smile. The intricate details embellish the walls around us as well as the super eclectic decor.

Us.

Looking over to my side, I see something that I never thought I would see in my lifetime, nor did I ever want to experience. Mr. Donatello is cuddling up at my side. I shriek and then silence it with my hand, attempting not to wake him up.

Questioning my existence, I lay motionless, eyes open, staring at the ceiling. I feel like a dead body, which seems appropriate given that my pride is deceased at this very moment.

What the fuck do I do?

Looking up in front of me, I see a smiling Xavier. *Asshole.*

I slowly get up, not wanting to wake the man right next to me. I quickly hop off the bed and run into the bathroom.

Looking in the mirror, I take in my appearance, trying to breathe in and out. Xavier walks up behind me, popping grapes in his mouth. The fruit basket that welcomed us on the tiny table invaded by his hunger.

His smile, as always, takes up his whole face, and his arms are crossed.

"What did I miss, Rookie?"

"Absolutely nothing."

"He was definitely feeling you up. That's something I'll keep engraved on my brain for the rest of my life. The beginning of a beautiful love story." He sighs dreamily, mocking me. Turning around, I give him a nudge, and he laughs at my poor attempt at pushing him backwards.

Standing up taller, I point my finger in his face. "We will never speak of this again." He throws up in hands in defeat.

"Comprende," he says just before Mr. Donatello walks in.

"What are we not speaking of?" he asks. He's still in his sleep clothes, a black shirt and gray sweatpants, with his bed head completing the look.

"Nothing. It's a secret," Xavier says in a hushed voice.

Mr. Donatello gives us a raised eyebrow, letting the topic

rest. Reaching over for his toothbrush, he pushes me aside while applying toothpaste to the brush.

I walk out of the bathroom and fall onto the bed with my arms out, letting the fabric and mattress consume me. I try convincing myself he did it unconsciously.

But why did it feel good to be engulfed in his strong arms? I felt like I was in a vice grip, but with biceps, and I kind of liked it.

No. No. No. I did not like it. It was a mere coincidence, and I shouldn't even be thinking about it.

But you still liked it.

I hit my head a few times trying to get the thought out of my brain. Standing up, I gather some clothes out of the suitcase that was brought over.

Setting it down on the bed, I stride out and wait for the boys to finish in the bathroom. I walk out onto the famous patio where Gianni Versace would sit and say hello to people walking past his marvelous mansion.

Breathing in the air of an early morning in Miami, I linger outside until I hear the bathroom door open. Spinning around, I see Mr. Donatello walk out in his casual suit attire. Xavier is right next to him in beige khaki shorts and a shirt with blue, red, and yellow graphic designs in random patterns across the fabric. But the best part about the look is the bucket hat the same color as his shorts with strings hanging down on both sides of his face.

It's all very Xavier.

Picking my clothes up off the bed, I walk past the guys and close the bathroom door behind me.

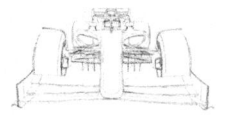

Eventually, we make our way back to our original hotel. Xavier parks and we hop out of the car, and walk into the incredible air conditioning. I sigh in bliss as I feel it spread across my skin.

In Mexico, we don't have air conditioning in most situations. It doesn't need to be used often, especially in a rainy city like CDMX, but in places like Cancun, it's essential. I like the heat, but only when I have air conditioning or something cold to jump into.

"I'll see you both later. Make sure to get all your PR stuff done today, and Miss Castillo, Netflix needs your interview for *Drive for Your Life*." Mr. Donatelo says. I nod in agreement and Mr. Donatello walks away into the elevator. Feeling a hand on my shoulder, I can already sense Xavier's mischievous smile behind me.

"Well, that was eventful."

"Yep. But remember, we will never speak of that incident ever again."

He smiles. "I wasn't even thinking about it, Ale. Until you brought it up."

"Liar."

His impish grin crawls up my skin like maggots decomposing a body. This man isn't going to be able to keep his mouth shut, is he? I sigh.

"I'm sorry, but it's not every day you see two people that absolutely despise each other as much as you two do, cuddling."

"I wasn't cuddling him. He was cuddling me. There's an extreme difference."

"It takes two to cuddle." He holds up two digits in front of my face, trying to get his point across. It irks me even more.

"I would never cuddle with that man on purpose. He is the definition of arrogant."

"You mean a man who knows his worth. Ale, I think it scares you to see someone who is just as confident in himself as you are."

"Nope, because I have all odds against me, and he is praised for coming back to F1. Again, big difference."

"Whatever you say." He walks toward the elevator like Mr. Donatello did just minutes ago.

I dislike Mr. Donatello because he's an asshole, nothing more, nothing less. It's not an obligation to like someone who treats people like shit. He can't even smile at someone or say a basic thank you. That shows how much of a prick he is. End of story.

CHAPTER SEVENTEEN
MARIA ALEJANDRA

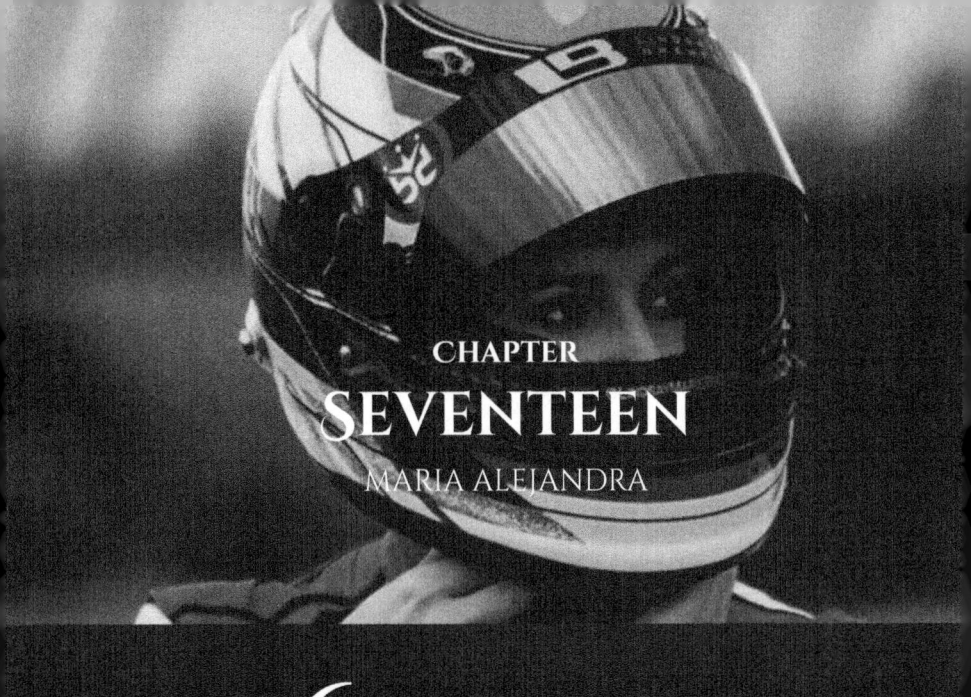

We're back in Barcelona, for the second time. This time not for pre-season testing, but for the actual race. I qualified second and Xavier qualified fifth. When I got out of the car, I knew that I could beat Ren, who was currently on pole position.

He's in a Sansui, which is the second fastest car on the track this season. But all things considered, Elektra is the quickest and most strategic. Even with all the regulation changes that happened last year, we're still at the top of the food chain.

I feel the win on my fingertips. Once I qualified second, I felt a thrill run through my veins. Now's not the time to talk about my place on the grid; it could be taken at any second, but I won't let that happen. All I can do is try and avoid any driver behind me, including Xavier. He's known for being able to overtake, even from the back of the grid. I love him, but he's not taking that grid place from me. The only overtaking that will happen is me going from second to first.

I know I can do it; I believe it to my core. I just have to put it into action. I can manifest all I want, but saying things isn't the same as doing them.

Putting my AirPods in, I press play on my pre-race playlist and "Friction" by Imagine Dragons starts blaring in my ears. I love to put it on full volume so that my whole body can feel the vibration of the music.

Jumping up and down, I shake out my limbs, trying to let the circulation run through my body. Getting into a Formula One car is like the pre-wave effects of a drug; you feel the rush about to hit. But once you start the race, that's when you get the hit of morphine coursing through every part of your body.

I walk out onto the pit lane after grabbing all my gear and sliding it on. Striding past the narrow road, I reach the starting straight, where all the engineers are checking out the car's diagnostics. Before every race, they make sure all of the parts are working correctly.

These precautions even apply to the drivers. Standing right next to me is my trainer who is holding a black umbrella over my head. Keeping my body at a certain temperature is crucial before jumping into a Formula One car.

Ever since *Race For Your Life* debuted on Netflix, the sport has had an influx of fans all around the world. Girls fawn over drivers like Xavier and even Mr. Donatello. When you look out into the crowd, you notice all the signs with affectionate messages towards us. But I usually see more signs for Xavier than anyone else.

Even the girls who genuinely love the sport can't help but find someone like Xavier Valente attractive. I mean, he is the heartthrob of the sport and is going for his second world championship. His personality, from his humor all the way to his massive grin, has swayed everyone.

Just a few years ago, it seemed like he was at the height of his career. Everyone called him the future of the sport and a potential legend. Until he made the "wrong" decision by leaving a team that was higher up on the grid.

Most teams on the grid fight for survival. Every season, the new car depends on how good the team is. Most of the time, the new car isn't as good as the last since the FODA likes to change the rules every year.

Xavier left his old team because he was frustrated that he was being overshadowed by his teammate, which resulted in a fractured ego. After a few years on the grid, he kept working for teams that weren't delivering good cars.

When he finally got the contract with Elektra, little did he know that they would return him to his former glory. He deserved it after staying in the sport through years of people telling him he would never go back to what he was. He is the current reigning world champion, and he might even obtain that title again this year. At thirty years old, Xavier Valente is one of the most well-known drivers in the sport, and for good reason.

For me to be a world champion as a woman during my rookie season is practically impossible. But that isn't my goal this year. I want to win the Constructors' again for the team, and at the very least be in the top three of the Drivers' championship.

All in all, I'll be happy with that, but next year, I'm coming for blood.

Hopefully with Elektra, but that all depends on Satan being the team principal, which can affect what's to come for my career. That's daunting in itself.

Directing my mini handheld fan on my face, I wait for the go ahead.

Finally getting the signal, I put my earpieces in and my helmet on, jumping into the boiling car. It's not like I'm not used to this temperature, but this is just the first laps of the race. The heat will only intensify with time.

Due to the physical exertion, because of the warmth and pressure experienced while driving, a driver can lose up to three kilos every race.

Hearing the formation lap go-ahead, I press the throttle and start accelerating. I'm going at a moderate speed, catching up to Aoki ahead of me.

Once I make the full lap around, I get into position, making sure I'm in between the lines. If I were to go ahead of the line in front of me a little bit, I would get a penalty. If I stay behind the line by an inch, I might not get a good enough start for momentum.

Sitting there while the suspense starts building up, I see the five lights in front of me. Breathing in, I see the first light turn red.

You can do this, Ale. Let the adrenaline run through you.

The second red light flashes.

Overtaking Aoki is easy.

The third light flashes.

All you have to do is focus.

The fourth light flashes.

You're a badass.

The final light flashes.

Breathe.

I can feel the rush. It's like something is seeping out of my skin. I'm internally shaking.

Then, all the lights go out.

I press the throttle and see that Aoki is ahead of me. In my ear my engineer is warning me that Amir is behind me and that he already passed James. He's heading straight at my car, aiming for my position.

Not today, buddy.

I hit the throttle, speeding ahead of Amir by an inch, solidifying my position. Focusing on Aoki, I press the highest speed possible and get to the side of his car.

We're wheel-to-wheel. He accelerates more and I catch up. I think he's forgotten that I'm in a faster car and I'll do anything to get past him.

Except for crashing, of course.

Catching up to the top of his car I push and push until I overtake him.

Fuck yes.

Now, I just have sixty-six laps to go.

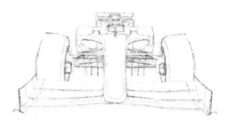

I can feel my tires losing grip by the second and I know I'm losing my position. We are on lap thirty-three, which is halfway through, and it means it's time for a pit stop. Originally, the plan was three pit stops until the safety car went out. One of the drivers hit a barrier when hitting curve three. The debris flew everywhere.

"I need to go into the pits, the grip on the medium is almost done. I can feel the tire puncture from here."

"Go into pits. Pit we have the go ahead," Alan, my race guide says to me. Reaching the end of the lap, I see the pit lane. I slow down and pull in, making it to Elektra's designated area, which is the second garage on the lane. Pit stops are always scary because of three simple facts: machines don't always work, engineers aren't always ready, and sometimes the tires just don't want to be screwed on.

They start changing the tire from medium to soft. Medium makes the car heavier which makes the car go slower. Having the soft tires on my car could help me win the race by a second. The advantage being that it's *lighter*. I can feel the tension inside of me at the sound of them taking the tires off.

One second.

Two seconds.

Looking at the engineer in front for the thumbs up, they pull off the rotators, which attach the tires to the car. A second later, I get the thumbs up.

I immediately accelerate and I breathe out as I pull the throttle.

"You have Aoki at the front, no one has passed you since. He's still driving on aging tires"

"Copy."

Now all I have to do is pass him on soft tires, this might be one of the easiest things I've ever done.

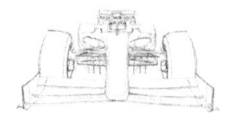

It is definitely *not* the easiest thing I've ever done.

Sansui is on a one stop strategy. The medium tires on Aoki's car are slowly withering, but he's still ahead of me. The tires that I pitted for helped close a five-second gap between us within a thirty-lap time frame.

I'm on his tail, and I'm ready to overtake. Currently, I'm pushing the car past its capabilities.

Every time I get closer to overtake, Aoki closes the gap

between us by defending quite swiftly. Ren Aoki isn't known for his speed or recklessness; he's known for how well he defends when someone is trying to pass him. He does extremely well when it comes to that part of driving. It's almost impossible to get in front of him. Only a few times has a person been able to rush past, and I'm going to be one of them.

I get closer.

Two more laps to go.

I get closer and closer.

Last lap.

Getting to the side of his car as fast as I can, I block him from shutting me out. At this moment, he's in an impossible situation. It's inevitable, I'm going to pass him.

I gain one more inch on his car. We get to the last curve side by side. Now it's time for the last straight. I press the throttle as hard as I can. I gain an inch.

Another inch.

And then another inch.

I get past his front wing. I can see the checkered flag wave now that I'm completely in front of him.

Holy shit.

"Ale, you just won the Spanish Grand Prix," says one of my engineers in my ear.

I yell and laugh out loud.

"Oh my god. Thank you so much, this is unreal." I almost cry but I don't. I'll save that for my first world championship.

"Miss Castillo. Donatello speaking, what a race! I'm so proud of you. Great job! You pushed until the very end."

Did Mr. Donatello just congratulate me? Am I in the Matrix? I swear to God. I don't respond, I can't. I'm speechless. Not only about my win, but also about how nice he was to me.

I just won a Grand Prix in my rookie season!

Driving up to the winner's lane, I stop right in front of the first-place sign. Getting out, I take the halo off and jump on top of the car. I raise my hands in the air, cheering.

I yank my helmet off as I yell in celebration. I see everyone clapping and there are smiles all around.

Aoki is to my right, raising his hands in respect as he claps up at me. I smile down at him before jumping off of the car. I give him the greeting that most men give each other, clapping our hands together, pulling each other into a one-handed embrace, then patting each other on the back.

Turning around, I jump onto my team, and they lift me up in cheers.

We just did that.

I turn and am met with a smiling Xavier. I hug him and he hugs me back as tight as possible. One thing Xavier is good at is giving congratulations. Even though he got third overall, he's still happy for me.

"Great job, Rookie, you did an amazing job out there."

"Thank you," I tell him genuinely.

Walking back into the weighing part of the dock, I step on the scale. Before and after every race, it is important to weigh each driver, ensuring that we haven't lost too much weight. This helps avoid any concerns one may have about our health. Once they're done weighing me, I get the go ahead, and I basically bolt to the winner's podium. Finally, I'm where I was always meant to be.

CHAPTER
EIGHTEEN
MARIA ALEJANDRA

I've been on a high since the events of the race.

I mean, who wouldn't be? I just won my first race, and it's only my first season. In celebration of this amazing moment in my life, I'm breaking my alcohol ban. Sometimes you just have to live your life, and that's exactly what I am doing.

In other words, I am getting shitfaced.

I already called Xavier, Ren, and Amir. Amir, in particular, was surprisingly hard to contact. I decided we are all going out to a club tonight in celebration. After all, I deserve it for winning my first Grand Prix.

While I'm getting shitfaced, I also plan on getting absolutely railed tonight. You may ask why, Ale? Well, because I haven't had sex in three years. After my extremely long and horrible break up a few years ago, I decided to say no to men for a while.

But now, in my surge of adrenaline, I've decided it's the perfect time. From my experience, all men ever want is a one-night stand, so why not use that to my advantage while blessing them with my presence.

I only have three rules for tonight, and they are incredibly simple:

1. Don't hook up with any of the drivers (that would end horribly).

2. Use a condom (even though you may be shitfaced, you don't want syphilis, or worse, a child).

3. Have fun and don't worry.

I know I have an image to uphold, but a lot of the drivers do this daily, so why can't I? Is it because I'm a woman?

I deserve some pleasure once and awhile. Preferably with an incredibly hot man who knows his way around a woman's body.

I will admit, I'm incredibly picky when it comes to guys. I like them a certain way. I'm known for loving blondes, but tonight I plan on going for a dark-haired man, thank you very much.

I head out of my hotel room and walk towards the elevator. I hop in and press the ground floor button. A few seconds later, I hear the ding as the elevator doors open. I see all three guys standing in the lobby, all looking good, incredibly good.

Ale, remember rule number one. It's vital to your existence.

Ren is in a cut-off t-shirt showing all his tattoos and his toned arms. He's seen as the Korean heartthrob all over the world, and I understand the appeal. Xavier is in beige pants and a baggy t-shirt with a cool street style graphic on the front. He also has tattoos, but they're more spread out. His favorite one is on his leg. It's his favorite cartoon character, Homer Simpson. He told me about it a while ago.

Finally, the hunk of a man that everyone calls Amir Zikraan stands there in a leather jacket and black ripped jeans. There's a chain from his jacket to his pants giving off a rugged appearance and it enhances his bright gray eyes.

Why do they all have to be so attractive? It's not fair to the world and most teenage girls' hearts.

"Look at you guys all ready to go out." I smile at them.

"Yes, ma'am, you don't look so bad yourself," Xavier says to me.

"Thank you. I wanted to go for an edgy look today."

I'm wearing a matching set of a leather long sleeve crop top and leather pants in my signature obsidian color. My feet are graced with black combat boots, finishing off the outfit. Wanting to enhance my eye color, I decided on a black smokey eye, which I paired with a nude lip. I straightened my hair and pulled it up into a sleek ponytail. I look like Catwoman, and I'm living for it.

"Let's go. There's a car outside waiting for us." I wave them over.

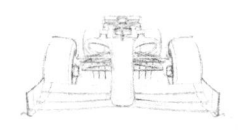

We make it to the club, and I can hear the music blasting from outside. I had asked one of the interns, who I knew was from Spain, and she told me this was the best place to go. On the side of a medieval-esque building, the word "Paciencia" shines down on us in bright, glowing red letters.

Seeing the huge line to enter the club, I walk up to the bouncer, and he let us in immediately. I give him a smile as I walk past the rope that he unlatches for us.

I can feel the whole club vibrating from the bass, and I see the lights flashing. Making my way through the little passageway, we step into the club. It's a vast space overflowing with people. The bar is to the right and the tables are on each side of the dance floor, where everyone moves their bodies skillfully. Before we are allowed inside, they take our phones and put them under our names, meaning I can do anything I want without being filmed.

Jackpot.

Thankfully, I had a reservation for a table, which I can see is empty from across the room. Pulling Xavier with me, we make our way through sweaty bodies to the table we reserved. "Lose Control" by Meduza, Becky Hill, and Goodboys starts playing in the background.

Waving the waiter over, I ask for ten tequila shots for the table. They arrive as another song starts playing, and I hand a shot to each of the boys.

Holding up our shots in the air, we all take them back in one swift motion. I can feel the burn, which is exactly what I needed. Looking at Xavier, he's shaking his head in disgust and sticking his tongue out of his mouth. I laugh when he looks at me disapprovingly. I shrug. That's what you get for being a sucker.

The music echoes off the walls and fades into a song I recognize.

"Without You" by Avicii and Sandro Cavazza starts playing, that's when I know it's time to dance. I throw back another shot and hold my hand out for Xavier, dragging him to the dance floor. We start singing obnoxiously and scream the words in each other's faces. Once the drop comes, I swiftly move my body with the beat and lose myself to the alcohol burning in my veins.

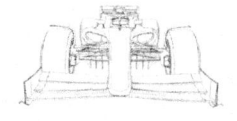

Two hours and about six shots later, I'm incredibly fucked up. I love it. Everyone seems to be having fun, and Xavier is stone cold sober.

Looking in the direction of my table, I see another figure talking to Amir. His arms are spread out on the couch. From here, I can't see his face, only his hands, and instantly I think I've just found my one-night stand. Making my way to the table casually, I fill up my cup with water. I don't want to sober up, but I also don't want to blackout. Once, when I was seventeen, I went out with my cousins to a club and ended up not remembering anything the next morning.

Apparently, I had thrown up all over myself and cracked a kid's skull open by accident. He was my cousin's friend and, let me tell you, he wasn't very happy about that the next morning. I never got to apologize, but I hope all is forgiven. I'm not letting that happen ever again.

Xavier is behind me telling me to drink more water after we leave the dance floor. I take the water and slam it back while I look up at the mysterious man at the table. My face drops. I was interested a few minutes ago, but now, not so much.

Definitely not fucking him tonight or ever.

Mr. Donatello is here.

"Who invited him?" I yell out over the music.

"I did. I was bored and wanted to talk to someone, so I sent him my location. He showed up ten minutes later," Amir says casually.

"What a buzzkill." I put my hand up dramatically in my drunken haze. Mr. Donatello seems amused. I hate when he's amused.

"Don't look at me like that, old man. I didn't come here to hang out with a senior citizen."

"I am far from a senior citizen, *ragazza*." I give him an *are you serious* look.

"Prove it then." I glance at the shot in front of me and lift it up for him to take. He shakes his head and declines the tequila I almost handed to him.

"See? I told you, he's a total buzzkill," I say in an exasperated tone. All of them laugh at me while I pout.

"It's not that I don't want to drink it, I can't," He responds.

"How come, grandpa?"

"It's a long story, and not one that I'd like to explain today or ever, especially to you."

I just shrug as Xavier drags me away swiftly.

I start dancing again until the DJ stops playing the music. I groan in disappointment.

Luca Donatello

"Is everyone having a good time?" the DJ shouts out to the crowd. Everyone screams out in excitement as a response. Initially, when Amir called me to come to the club, I didn't want to. That's until he told me who he was with.

I knew at that moment when he said Ms. Castillo's name that I would have to babysit her. Her track record for drinking has never been great, so in order to save the team's public image, I've simply come to make sure she doesn't fuck up.

The DJ continues speaking, "Good! Here at Paciencia, we honor special guests, and today, we have the winner of the Spanish Grand Prix in the house!" His gaze trails to Ms. Castillo as he looks at her with a smirk. She gives him a thumbs up in response. His voice booms through the speakers once again, "So, in honor of her Latino heritage, I can't help but play the icon and legend, Bad Bunny." She yells out in cheers as "Safaera" plays.

That's when I get up and walk over to where she stands beaming. I refuse to let her dance on anyone she doesn't know. No one, not even her, needs a social media rampage of someone telling the story of how Maria Alejandra Castillo grinded on a stranger.

Going through a mass mob of people is harder than expected when everyone is so entranced with the idea of fucking one another. Finally, reaching Ms. Castillo, she looks around dumbfoundedly until she makes eye contact with me.

"Alejandra, you can pick anyone on the dance floor and when you find them, dance on them. It's tradition here at Paciencia." The DJ yells into his microphone. Then a tropical beat comes kicking in. Tilting her head in question, a smirk spreads across her face as she walks towards me. Swaying her body to the rhythm, she does the unthinkable.

Dragging a finger down my chest, her body starts dancing against me. The beat changes up, and instead of swaying against my body again, she steps back, putting her hands in her hair seductively. This goes on for minutes until the beat drops and her ass is swaying against my groin.

That's when I lose control. I tug her wrist, turning her to face me. Her greenish-blue eyes become alert in a matter of seconds. Pulling her into me, I run my nose down the base of her neck slowly, and I trail back up to her ear. I take in her scent. It's clean, but smells of cologne. I don't like the fact that she smells of other men. It sends a shock of annoyance down my spine.

The music is still playing in the background, and everything stops for a moment as I say, "you want me to do bad things to you, Miss Castillo, don't you?" I run a finger down her chest and make my way down to her stomach.

"If you classify staying as far away from me as possible as a bad thing, then yes." I smirk.

"You're a little liar, *ragazza*, and you know it," I whisper against her ear. A look of shock spreads across her face as I walk away swiftly.

After three more shots, Miss Castillo is barely holding on.

A few minutes ago, she fell flat on her face, having tripped over air. That's when I knew her celebration time was done. When I picked her up and threw her over my shoulder from the depths of the grimy club floor, she started kicking and yelling at me to put her down. I didn't.

When we are finally out of the club, she implores me once again to put her down again. Tired of her flailing and carrying on, I placed her on the sidewalk next to me. Seconds after her feet reach the ground, she runs away, hiding behind a palm tree. I walk towards her giggling state as she starts talking to herself.

"He can't see me because I'm invisible," she snickers.

Who knew that Ms. Castillo was not only bratty while drunk, but also incredibly dumb?

Much to her distaste, I pull her into my arms and drag her to the car parked in front of us. Making it into the back seat, she keeps going on about how *10 Things I Hate About You* is the best romcom in history. I have no idea what she's talking about.

In the middle of her sentence, she giggles and then stops abruptly. "I was supposed to have sex with a random person tonight," she groans as I go still, along with Ren, Xavier, and Amir in the car. She continues speaking freely as if her colleagues and boss aren't around her.

"So, which one of you is going to ravage me tonight because your girl hasn't had sex in three years and her pussy is as dry as the Sahara Desert." We stay silent, staring at her after her outburst.

I swear to all things holy, she is crazy.

She continues speaking, "You guys are no fun. But I respect your decisions. It goes completely against my rules anyway. You're all too complicated." She yawns and closes her eyes, then passes out shortly after.

Pulling up to the hotel a few seconds later, I throw her over my shoulder again and carry her into the lobby. The boys follow behind me.

"I'm going to take her up to her room so she can rest." They all nod.

"We'll see you later," Xavier says, and waves goodbye. Letting out a sigh, I walk towards the elevator. Pressing her floor number, the elevator closes and reopens at her floor. I make my way through the hallway until I reach the front of her door.

Remembering to look for her room card, I reach into her pocket and fish it out. I open the door and carry her through as it closes behind me.

Seeing the bed, I gently place her on the comforter. She says something unintelligible, but she's still fast asleep. I lift her head up and gently place it on a pillow. I untuck the comforter from beneath her and tuck her under. Walking into her bathroom, I grab a bottle of Advil and put it next to her bed.

Looking in the mini fridge, I grab a cold water bottle and put it right next to the pills. Feeling satisfied that she's safe, I exit the room.

Hearing the click behind me, I start walking down the hall yet again. Pulling my phone out of my pocket I open my messages.

Landing on Xavier's contact, I start typing.

Me: If she asks, you were the one who took her up to her suite. She would feel uncomfortable otherwise.

Seconds after, he responds.

Xavier: Okay, boss. Just know that if you took something out of the mini fridge, she will never believe me. That little ice box is a scam.

I laugh.

Turning my phone off, I enter the elevator and press the penthouse button. Rubbing my hands over my face in exhaustion.

CHAPTER NINETEEN

MARIA ALEJANDRA

I feel my brain pounding against my skull, and the sound of Elektra's private jet isn't helping. I blacked out last night and don't remember anything that happened after the whole dancing on Mr. Donatello thing. All I know is that I woke up with a massive hangover and a bottle of Advil next to a cold bottle of water at my side. I wonder who dropped me off in my hotel room last night. It definitely wasn't Xavier because he wouldn't have taken anything out of the mini fridge. It could've been Ren. I know him better than Amir, so that's the only plausible option.

Walking into the all-black interior of Elektra's jet, I see the sheer curtains that open up into the bed area of the plane. Mr. Donatello is the one who prefers to go back there, so I never do.

I take a seat in one of the black leather seats designated for Xavier and me. I keep my huge sunglasses on as well as my black Yankees cap. If I look at the light for too long, I feel like someone is giving me laser eye surgery. At this point in my hangover, I want to pull a Cristina Yang, and scream, "Somebody sedate me!"

I pulled my hair back after taking a shower this morning. No vomit was in sight which gave me a sense of relief. The dinging flight noise goes off before the attendant starts talking.

She talks for what seems like hours. Blah, blah about the safety protocol that I hear every time I go on a plane. Blah, blah, if we crash and land in the water, the life jackets are under your seat. Blah, blah, our destination is Monte Carlo, Monaco, which is going to be an hour flight with no turbulence.

She's done talking, thank God.

Monaco. The race that's known for its glitz and glamour. This race is a part of the Formula One legacy. It will always be a race location for as long as Formula One keeps going. It's that iconic.

I, for one, hate this race. It is challenging in more ways than one, and if you win, it is definitely one of the highest honors. I've never seen the point, though. Yes, most people love Monaco, but there's literally nothing to do there. You can hike, see the coastline, and gamble at the only casino in practically the whole country. It's so small, and there are only one or two clubs. I always feel claustrophobic when I'm there, not only because the country is so tiny, but also because the pressure of the race in and of itself makes you feel small.

Yes, Monaco may have all the funding, but I hate the track. It's a street circuit, meaning that it's almost impossible to overtake. Most of the streets are blocked off, which means that the grid is tighter when it comes to the width of the track. A lot of drivers have crashed in Monaco, which is why it's known for its extreme difficulty.

It's not that I don't like the fact that it's a challenge, it's more about the fact that drivers drive dirty when it comes to tight spaces. That's why it's so popular; people like the thrill. But it's not interesting to me in any way. I mean, no one can pass anyone, so what's the fun in that? It's just like every other Grand Prix, but seen as something more than it really is.

Grabbing my Bose noise-cancelling headphones, I put them on, trying to get some quiet. Taking out my Louis Vuitton blanket and pillow, I make myself comfortable in the chair, then pull out the recliner.

Before I fall asleep, Mr. Donatello walks into our part of the plane.

This never happens. He apparently likes to be alone in his grumpy land which resides at the back of the plane, far away from my personal space.

I think he's going to walk past me, but instead, he turns around and faces me directly. I just stare up at him, confused. He starts talking. All I see is his mouth moving.

Why can't I hear him?

Hungover me is stupid, he reaches over and takes my headphones off.

"I'm taking time out of my schedule to ask you how you feel."

"You don't have to take time out of your precious schedule for me. You have two eyes, I'm alive, that's all that should matter to you."

"I'm being nice for once, and you decide to berate me, yet again, with your stubbornness."

"If you would have phrased it in a friendly and caring way, I probably wouldn't have been stubborn," I mock him in a butchered Italian accent. "I was taking time out of my precious schedule to do the bare minimum."

"You look like shit, just so you know," he says casually.

"I don't see how you can see me while I have sunglasses and a hat on. So, how could you possibly know I look like shit?" I raise my eyebrow at him.

"Because your vibe is all wrong. You might be covering it up, but I see through people. It's my job, and you are the definition of transparent."

"If only you knew." I give him a glare that he can't see under my glasses for my own satisfaction. "I couldn't care less what other people think, much less you."

"Exactly. My point made," he responds.

"You didn't answer my first question," his tone is filled with annoyance and a hint of care.

"I'm fine, just feel like death is upon me."

He chuckles.

MORPHINE

"Well, if you need anything, ask the flight attendant. She will assist you. As long as you don't have the same conversation with her as you just had with me."

He walks back into his dungeon of doom, and I scowl. I bring the blanket close to my face and put my headphones back on, trying to fall asleep.

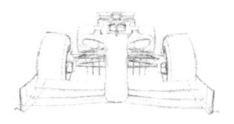

Feeling someone shove me a little, I slowly open my eyes to see the flight attendant waking me up. "We just landed." She smiles at me with the fake customer service toothy grin. I nod as I get up, realizing that right in front of me, Mr. Donatello is waiting with Xavier at his side. Packing all my things up, I take my glasses off and rub my eyes, then fix my baseball cap so my hair isn't everywhere.

Getting out of my seat, I grab my backpack and the small duffel bag where I keep my pillow and blanket. Walking out of the aisle, I'm met with both men looking at me. Seeing I'm ready, they walk down the steps. My stomach grumbles out loud.

I am hungry.

Both Xavier and Mr. Donatello turn back around and look at me after they hear the sound. I just stare at them innocently, like I didn't hear anything.

"I think we should get something to eat. I know a good

Mediterranean place close to where we are staying," Mr. Donatello suddenly suggests. Xavier agrees with a nod.

"I'm making a reservation now," Mr. Donatello confirms while tapping things on his phone.

"Done. We have a table in ten minutes, let's go."

They both start walking, and I just stand there dumbfounded, but I will never say no to food. I go after them, running in anticipation.

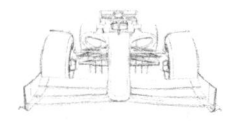

We finally make it to the restaurant that Mr. Donatello was talking about. It's overlooking the beach and the food smells incredible. I'm drooling in my seat.

I haven't eaten anything since I woke up with my hangover this morning, which is unusual because after a hangover I'm usually hungry. I love food in general, so when my head is crushing my skull, I eat more than normal.

Grabbing some of the pita bread, I spread hummus on it so fast I probably look like I've been starved. Taking a bite of the bread, I groan in satisfaction. When I finish, I look at Mr. Donatello right in front of me. He's staring at me.

"What?"

"You have something here." He points at the side of my lip. I try to wipe it off, nothing transfers onto my finger. I lift my head up at him confused.

"It's not that hard to wipe food off your lip. Of course you can't do a simple task," mid-sentence, he stands up and looks at the spot where I apparently had hummus. He takes his thumb and wipes it off, his thumb folding my lower lip. I stare him straight in the eye and gawk, breaking eye contact to look down at his lips before he says something.

"It's gone now." He sits back down, breaking the stare and looking at his napkin to wipe the residue off his finger.

"You know I'm sitting right here." Xavier gives us a mischievous look.

"Anyway, we have a gala tonight at ten. It's important that you guys walk around and charm the investors. Dress your best. It's an F1 event, so there will be a red carpet and other teams will be stalking investors trying to engage them before us. You both need to be on your A-game," Mr. Donatello says.

Xavier and I nod as we both keep eating our food.

"Who do we have to seduce tonight? Give us a pregame of sorts," Xavier mutters with his mouth still full. Enjoying my food, I pick and choose from what Mr. Donatello says, lifting my head up and nodding as he goes over on about potential investors.

"All done! I just have to set your hair so that you look as

good as possible on that red carpet tonight," my hairstylist Erica says from behind me. I nod when she starts applying hairspray to my now slick straight hair, flattening all the flyaways.

I wanted to go for a powerful look since this isn't an event to be fucking around at. A line of black is smoked out on my water line and leads up to my eyelid. I opted for a black smokey eye as well as a bit of white in the inner corners of my eyes. The fake eyelashes cover the majority of my lash line, and the look is complemented by a bare lip.

My makeup is accompanied by a custom gown sent to me by none other than Mr. Donatello's ex-wife's atelier.

Adèle fashion house.

They reached out to me to see if I wanted to wear a custom gown of theirs as PR. I had to think about it for a while, but I ended up saying yes after I saw the gown. Crystals encrust the bodice, and the low sleeves give it a bit of an edge. The leg slit has dangling crystals all the way down my leg.

It's stunning.

Having someone help me put it on, I look in the mirror, running my hands over the fabric. Grabbing my boob tape, I shove my babies up and apply the tape swiftly. Putting the straps on again, I give it another look.

Perfect.

I grab my shoes and put the stunning black 6-inch Adèle heels on slowly. I love how they make me look, but as some say, "beauty is pain." My feet throb against the hard platform that conforms to my feet. Despite being death traps, they make me look damn good. Picking up my clutch, I take a deep breath before walking out the door.

I make my way down to the lobby, and hop into the black car waiting for me. I open Instagram and see that Xavier is already at the party, looking dapper. While browsing, I notice that the event extends from the lobby of the Hôtel de Paris all the way to the restaurant, which is a little further inside. Monaco is known for its eccentric regency vibes. Despite being a small country, the government is loaded, or should I say, the Royal Family is.

The Hôtel De Paris is the gem of Monte-Carlo and has been seen in dozens of films. The lobby is beautiful on its own, but the restaurant is even prettier. The ceiling is adorned with gold leaf details. The whole place just screams money.

Making it to the entrance of the hotel, I see the carpet, the blazing red color adding to the whole ambiance of the moment. It's not a long carpet by any means, but the F1 logo is plastered all over the black background, and you can occasionally see investors' logos. Eventually, two white men, who I assume have hefty wallets, walk off, and the security guard opens the rope for me to walk past. Posing for a few pictures, I walk away, waving and thanking the photographers.

The gala is in full swing as I walk up the stairs. Team principals talk with investors at every corner, while drivers talk to other drivers. Laughter can be heard as the chatter spreads. Champagne glasses sit on small white tables and are also in most people's hands. The colossal chandelier in the middle of the room shines on the dozens of people. I stand over them and observe for a moment until Xavier catches my attention. He is currently talking to Mr. Donatello. Xavier is facing me while Mr. Donatello's back is turned. He looks up in my direction with his eyes raised. I'm guessing Mr. Donatello must have realized his attention shifted off the conversation because he looks in my direction in curiosity.

We lock eyes.

Fuck, why does his gaze seem different this time? It might be shocking, but I feel small under his stare. Xavier, standing behind Mr. Donatello, looks at me in approval. He catches my eye and holds his hand up in a perfection symbol, winking at me then nodding enthusiastically. I laugh at him.

Walking down the stairs, I meet them in the middle of the restaurant turned ballroom.

"Ale, you look stunning," Xavier says, coming to hug me.

"Thank you, you don't look too bad yourself." He adjusts his bowtie and winks again in my direction, giving me his wide smile.

"Okay, enough with the flirting. Miss Castillo, I am going to need you to talk to the investor over there." Mr. Donatello points at an old guy sipping champagne near the bar. He has a little scruff but is extremely well put together.

"He's a huge part of Elektra's funding, but he was a bit

wary of you coming onto the team. His name is Edward Schultz. He owns Schultz Energy Drinks."

"Why was he wary of me coming onto the team?" Mr. Donatello looks reluctant to tell me for a second.

"Because you were a rookie coming into a high placing seat." I nod, understanding his point of view. I mean, anyone would be worried, but for the most part, Elektra is at the top of Constructors', and I'm currently residing in fourth in the Drivers' Championship. He has nothing to worry about.

"Okay, I can be very convincing."

"I don't know if I agree with that, Miss Castillo," Mr. Donatello says. I give him a glare as I walk off, beelining toward Edward Schultz.

I make my way to the bar, and I try to keep it casual by asking the bartender for a drink.

"A whiskey on the rocks, please." He nods and starts making the drink. I hear Mr. Shultz to my right.

"Maria Alejandra Castillo," he says in a knowing tone. I turn around trying to seem startled. I acknowledge him.

"Ah, Mr. Schultz, it's a pleasure to finally meet you."

"You know who I am?"

"Of course, why wouldn't I know the name of one of our primary investors?"

Lies. I found out who you were about three minutes ago.

The best way to charm a man is by stroking his ego. It's basic old men in power 101.

He nods and takes a drink from his champagne glass.

The bartender in front of me drops the glass of whiskey on the bar. I put down my clutch and take a sip.

"I heard you're a feisty thing." I look up, startled by his statement.

"I mean, I guess in certain situations. I wouldn't call it feisty, though, more like stubborn."

"Hmm. I've heard things about you and Luca Donatello always butting heads." It's not a secret that we don't necessarily get along, but it's not a big subject when it comes to media coverage. My question is, did Mr. Donatello say something to him?

"Mr. Donatello and I disagree occasionally, but only for the team's sake."

"Of course. Although, it is a little worrying from my perspective, if I'm being transparent."

"How so?"

"Well, when it comes to your track record, on and off the grid, they are vastly different to how you have been behaving as of late, with Luca in particular."

"I don't quite understand what you mean? But I can understand your reluctance. When it comes to race car drivers, we can be unreliable at times. But I can assure you that Elektra is currently first in the Constructors' Championship and Xavier and I are in the top four when it comes to the Drivers' Championship. We are a good duo and are determined to give everyone, especially investors like you, an amazing result. Xavier might have more experience than me, but that doesn't mean I'm not just as capable."

"You think that I'm worried about you being a rookie? No, that's not the case. Even though it may be a concern for some, it didn't even cross my mind. Tons of new talent come falling into the sport, and if a team sees a future in a specific driver, so be it." He shrugs. I look over at Mr. Donatello, who is looking over at us like World War Three is about to begin.

You son of a bitch.

"So, what is your problem with me driving for Elektra, Mr. Shultz?"

Be careful with what you're about to say, old man.

"You know."

"I don't know," I counter.

"I mean it's obvious that you're different from most drivers."

"In what way?"

"Well, I mean you're a—" he gestures down my dress.

"A woman," I finish his sentence for him.

"Yes, exactly. You get what I mean." He nods at me while smiling. This man doesn't even notice his own misogyny. It's utterly disgusting.

"Actually, I don't get what you mean."

"It's nothing personal, Maria. It's business."

I hate when people call me Maria.

"Don't call me Maria, it's Miss Castillo to you. You act like me being a woman is a disease, and that's certainly not something that I respond well to."

"Face it. Scientifically and genetically, you're inferior. It's alarming that you're in a position of power."

"Scientifically and genetically are the same thing." I roll my eyes.

"You understand what I mean, Miss Castillo. I bet you're a nice girl, but this is something that needs to be said."

That's it. Something that needs to be said, my ass.

"First off, I'm not a girl, I'm a woman. Furthermore, I do for Formula One is far more than all that money you happen to possess. Elektra's sales have spiked in the last four months I've been driving for the team. My merch sells as much as Xavier's. Not to mention how much ratings have spiked for F1 channels across the globe. I have an exclusive brand deal with Nike and high fashion ateliers with lots of money, which I happen to be currently wearing.

"When it comes to genetics, I have beaten nineteen other men at their own game in more than one race this year. So, you sitting here, telling me that just because I'm a woman means that I'm bad for business or that I am genetically inferior, is bullshit," I counter.

"My whole career, I have had to deal with men like you who use the same argument repeatedly. For once in a man's goddamn life, can he be original, because you sure aren't. You have treated me like shit on the bottom of your shoe, yet you stand here in front of me saying *I'm* bad for business. Oh please. Honey, I'm the best investment you'll ever make." I down the rest of my whiskey, slamming the glass onto the bar.

"I hope you have a dreadful evening, Mr. Shultz, and if your wife ever needs someone to get her off, I know just the man for it. Or even a woman, because we do everything better." I smile at him like the conversation was pleasant.

Walking away and past Mr. Donatello, I make my way into an empty room just below the entrance stairs.

Perfect.

How do men have the audacity?

They get all defensive when we say men are shit, but do nothing to repair their image.

I attempt to calm myself down before I eventually just say fuck it and avoid all contact with men. Quite frankly, most of my interactions with them are utterly infuriating.

Breathe in.

Breathe out.

While I'm doing my breathing exercises, I hear the door open behind me. Of course, *he* followed me.

"Just go away. I'm attempting to not think that the whole male race should be extinct from this planet."

"You just pissed off an important investor. What the fuck did you just do?" Mr. Donatello says in an aggravated tone.

"I told off a misogynistic asshole. That's what I did, no more, no less."

"I don't care if you have opposing views. What you were supposed to do is try to convince him otherwise."

"Convince him otherwise, huh? You told me that he was worried about me being a rookie, not me being a woman, or, in his words, 'a genetically inferior girl.' You sent me to a guaranteed shit show and it's not opposing views, it's having human decency. You think that he could say those things to me, and I would stand there helpless? Think again, old man."

"*Cazzo!* We needed those funds for next year's prototype. You just fucked up ten-million-dollars in funding."

"ME?! You mean him. How could you want to be associated with that?"

"'That' has money," he says.

"You can find a new investor. Don't blame me for what that man said." I step closer.

"It's not that easy. You don't understand business, do you?" He steps away.

"What did you just say?" I question.

"I said you don't understand business!"

"Stop spewing bullshit."

He steps closer to me. "You're so infuriating," he says.

"No, *you're* infuriating!"

I hear his breath from beside me as we make eye contact. Next thing I know, we collide. I'm kissing him. He's kissing me, but not with adoration or any emotion a normal kiss would possess. It's raw, frustrating. His hands go into my hair, and I pull him closer as my hands grip his shirt. Following each other's every movement, our lips move as one. He bites my bottom lip and I moan. Grabbing my hair, he pulls my head back as he runs his nose down my neck. Holy fuck.

Alejandra, what are you doing?

I pull away and look at him breathlessly. I touch my lips

where Mr. Donatello's just were. I feel like I'm suffocating in this room. I need air. I walk past him and out the door, fixing my hair as I walk out. Finding the exit to the street, I breathe in fresh oxygen, since all of mine seems to have just left my body.

I'm pacing back and forth on the sidewalk.

Maria Alejandra Castillo, what the fuck did you do?

I don't even know at this point. Luca Donatello is one of the most egocentric, self-centered assholes I know, and I just kissed him. Not to mention, he's my boss. MY BOSS. It was kind of a two-person thing though. He did kiss me back. But that doesn't mean that it was okay. I just don't know what to feel. I scream into my hands, trying to release all my built-up rage.

Sitting down on the curb, I close my eyes, and try to do a breathing technique to calm down. All I can see, and feel, is his nose trailing down my neck and the way he pulled my hair. The way it felt to have my body against his and his lips on mine. In my thoughts, I realize something. I liked it.

Why the fuck did I like it?

CHAPTER TWENTY
MARIA ALEJANDRA

I haven't directly spoken to Mr. Donatello since Monaco. It's a weird situation. Most times when I'm uncomfortable, I take those situations and use them to my advantage. But this is different.

I kissed him. And now I've avoided him at all costs, but he hasn't made any effort to see me either. Which isn't something I can complain about. I only see him when necessary, like at briefings or occasionally at PR appearances.

This will be one of the first times that I'm going to have to speak to him in weeks. We've already gone to Azerbaijan as well as Canada. Now we're at Silverstone, about an hour and a half outside of London, and one of my favorite races of the season. England loves Elektra, and since the three of us are the face of the brand, they're making us go on a sightseeing tour around London for the YouTube channel.

Yes, that's right. All three of us.

Normally, the YouTube channel is just a compilation of me and Xavier tasting weird food and guessing words from each other's languages. Those videos weren't that hard because my and Xavier's first languages are similar in a way. Nonetheless, it's apparently entertaining for fans to watch. But now they want Mr. Donatello to be a part of this PR campaign since everyone loves him so much.

Mostly female fans. I don't blame them.

This day is about to be the bane of my existence. I'm currently on a train with Xavier at my side, and Mr. Donatello is on his way in his private car. We have about twenty minutes left of our train ride, and it hasn't been that eventful.

I've been listening to my melancholy music playlist, which consists mostly of Taylor Swift, James Arthur, and Tom Odell, while looking out the window. The English landscape is beautiful, and I've heard it's even prettier from England to Scotland. I've always wanted to go to Scotland, especially after seeing some pictures on Pinterest, but its just never happened.

"What are you thinking about, Rookie?" Xavier says out of the blue.

"Nothing, just thinking about what it would be like to take a train from England to Scotland. They say it's incredible, although the weather is shit apparently."

"I've never been, but I've heard the same thing. I know a few people from Scotland, and quite frankly, I don't understand a thing they say."

"Their accents are pretty thick," I agree.

"It's hard for me to even understand a British person with a formal accent, but if you ever go to Newcastle . . . good luck." I laugh at his comment.

"You're just a ray of sunshine, aren't you?" I tell him.

"Most of the time, I guess. Sometimes people think that just because I have a bright personality, that I'm not driven or I always go with the flow. But, it has its perks. I mean, I try to make the most out of any situation I'm in."

I smile at him. Xavier is one of the best people I know. I can see the public appeal.

"Just because you make people smile doesn't mean you have to always uphold that image. You know that right?"

"I do." He nods somberly. This man has problems, doesn't he? I just want to hug the shit out of him.

"At least I'm not always grumpy like Mr. Donatello. It's hard to make a man like that crack." He grins.

I groan. "Don't even get me started on him." He chuckles.

"I still don't get why you hate each other so much. I mean, he may not be the most approachable person, but you aren't either, Ale."

"I know that, but I have no choice. At least, I still have fun. He doesn't. I swear he's a robot whose life purpose is to be a buzzkill."

"He's just serious about his job, that's normal. I'm extremely serious about what I do for a living," Xavier says.

"The difference between you and him is that you always

smile, and that man doesn't ever crack. He doesn't even say 'thank you' half of the time."

"I've noticed that, but like I said before, he probably has a lot of demons."

"Yeah, I guess. Also, why do you always bring up Mr. Donatello every time I talk to you?" Xavier is a very nosy person. I love it because when there's gossip, he knows it all. But in this situation, I'm praying he doesn't know anything. This boy has spidey senses. He probably even has his Spider-Man suit in his backpack ready to go.

"Because I know you're both going to fall in love and live happily ever after. That much is obvious."

"He hates me. That much is obvious," I say. He shakes his head like I'm stupid.

"He may be distant, but have you realized what he does when you're around? When we were in Miami, he paid over a thousand dollars for a room just because you were sad when the receptionist said we couldn't go in. We both know he hates Versace for some reason, probably because it ruins the Italian reputation," he gasps for dramatic effect at the end of his sentence.

"That was one time."

"Or the time that you were falling on the floor in a club, and he carried you out, chasing after you when you ran away from him. He then put you into the car with a trash bag in hand. He was constantly asking you if you were feeling okay. And just to make my argument even more solid than it is already, he carried you to your room when you passed out in the car. He tucked you in and then left an Advil and a bottle of cold water at your side. It was from the mini fridge though, which I highly disapproved of. Who would want to participate in the scam that is a mini fridge?" He shivers in disgust.

"That's common human decency." I shake my head.

"Which you constantly say he lacks."

"That doesn't mean anything. The man is disgusted by my presence."

"Whatever you say," he sings out the last syllable, elongating it.

One thing about Xavier is that he has an overactive imagination. Most of the time, I love him for it, but in this particular case, not so much.

"Ladies and gentlemen, we have arrived at Waterloo train station. You may take your bags out of the compartment above you. Make sure to check for any lost items in the process. Thank you for your cooperation, and welcome to London."

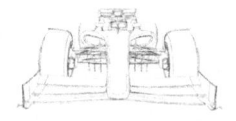

I'm on a huge red tourist bus in the middle of London, the ones with cameras on the ledge at the beginning of the seating area. I'm also holding a tripod, so that the social media team can get us from every angle. Xavier is looking over the side of the bus at the streets around him while Mr. Donatello sits comfortably in a seat looking down at his phone.

The bus stops right in front of Big Ben. I gaze up at the building in front of us.

"It's not as tall as I imagined."

"That's because most people from all around the world hear that it's one of the tallest buildings in the world. They're wrong," I hear Mr. Donatello say from behind me.

"I mean, it's a staple for most," I respond.

"Yeah, just like the castle in Disneyland; it's miniscule compared to Disney World's version," he says, trying to solidify his argument. But I turn around abruptly at the word Disneyland coming out of his mouth.

"I would have never imagined those words coming out of your mouth. The big question is, how can you even compare?"

"My ex-wife was obsessed with theme parks and we would go every so often." I still at the mention of his wife.

"I bet that was a pleasant experience for you." He looks at me with a stoic expression.

"It was one of the most unpleasant experiences I have ever had in my life, just like that marriage. Children running around everywhere, greasy food, long lines, and those stupid little ears that cost half of your life savings."

"It's all a part of the magic! Though I could live with the mental image of you in those ears for the rest of my life."

"That's where you're wrong. I would never put those ears on."

We hear someone walk up the steps and turn to see one of the social media team members appear.

"Okay, everyone, we have access to the Palace and the Tower of London if you will all come down and follow me." He gestures towards the exit of the bus.

Passing Mr. Donatello, I walk down the stairs, closing the distance between me and the door. Sitting down on the concrete, I nestle more into my wool coat. Fuck, it's cold. It's supposed to be summer! At least the sun's out. I guess since we're close to the river, it's bound to be breezy. I'm Mexican. I don't just hate the cold; I loathe it. We follow and make our way to the entrance of the castle.

"During the winter, the castle isn't open to visitors. Buckingham Palace is open during the summer as the Royal Family are on holiday at Balmoral."

He keeps talking about the history of the castle and how much London has industrialized over the years to become the metropolitan wonder it is today. We follow him as he continues speaking about the palace. It truly is beautiful. When it comes to historical wonders, I'm all here for it.

Finally, we exit the palace after three miles of walking and make our way through an opening that leads to the Tower of London. Walking into The Crown Jewels exhibition, I gasp in awe. Obviously, I can't touch anything, but it's breathtaking. The tour guide discusses how they use them during the coronation rituals and in what order. It's a super tedious ceremony. I stop in front of an emerald crown, which shines in comparison to the others. It is by far my favorite piece out of the whole collection.

Mr. Donatello creeps up like the leech he is.

"That's Queen Victoria's emerald tiara, it was her favorite. Most say it's because it was her month's birthstone," he says.

"Emeralds have always been my favorite gemstone, and this just solidifies my obsession. If I was a queen, this would be my favorite too." He nods as he walks away to look around again. Walking out of the collection, we make our way around the outdoor area leading to the tower.

"This was where Anne Boleyn was wrongfully accused by King Henry VIII of adultery and was ultimately executed." Poor girl, that's what happens when men are in power. This only confirms my thought process about how men are trash.

We make our way inside the tower. It's eerie and the light shines only in a few spots as very tiny windows go up the base of the tower. The stairs ascend in a spiral motion, and we make our way up until we reach the room at the top. It's a small space, meaning that Mr. Donatello is directly behind me. I can feel his breath on the base of my neck and the tension could break glass.

Thank God for the tour guide. He opens the door so we can walk in and see where countless prisoners were kept.

How fun.

"This tower is not only infamous for the executions held

by King Henry VIII, but this very room is where Queen Elizabeth I, also known as 'The Virgin Queen,' was imprisoned in 1554 for her involvement in Wyatt's Rebellion. Just twelve years later, the Queen would imprison Princess Margaret Douglas, Countess of Lennox, here. She was released after the murder of Henry Stuart, Lord Darnley, who was the second husband of Mary, Queen of Scots. Queen Elizabeth I reigned for forty-two years."

Power makes people do crazy things, just like love. Seeing powerful—and maybe a bit unhinged—women like Queen Elizabeth I in a position like she was, is just the start of female empowerment. Just like Queen Elizabeth II, who has been the longest reigning monarch in English history.

These things define women like me, and that's why women's history is so powerful. It gives us strength, it gives us a say, and it paves the path to who we are.

We, as women, are all queens, no matter what may be said. The past and the present show us nothing less than the possibility of an empowered future.

Looking around the room, I notice it's only me and Mr. Donatello now. When did the rest of them leave?

"Where are Xavier and the tour guide?" I ask him.

"Xavier is hung up on how the king killed his wives in that very square." He points down at the outdoor area of the tower. Mr. Donatello continues, "So, he dragged the tour guide down there with him to give him more information." I watch as Xavier looks at the man, horrified at what he's hearing. I can't help but laugh and Mr. Donatello chuckles behind me.

I spin around when I hear that foreign sound come out of his mouth.

"Did you just chuckle?" I stare at him dumbfounded.

"Yes, Alejandra, it's a normal response. I mean look at his face."

"I've never heard you laugh. Ever," I say.

"You are mistaken." He looks down at me with a serious face and then turns around, looking at the ceiling and observing his surroundings. Silence hangs in the air; a very tense silence.

"Are we just not going to talk about it?" I say rapidly so I don't have to hear the words coming out of my mouth, but I can't just sit here without at least addressing it.

"I believe you're talking about the kiss?" I look at him with a "duh" expression. "No, we aren't. It's not necessary to address," he responds.

"I don't know about you, Mr. Robot, but I address situations, so I don't have all these pent-up emotions like you do. It needs to be talked about." He crosses his arms and bends his head down close to my face.

"No, we don't need to talk about it, because it is never going to happen again." With that he walks out, gliding down the stairs.

Dickwad.

CHAPTER TWENTY-ONE
MARIA ALEJANDRA

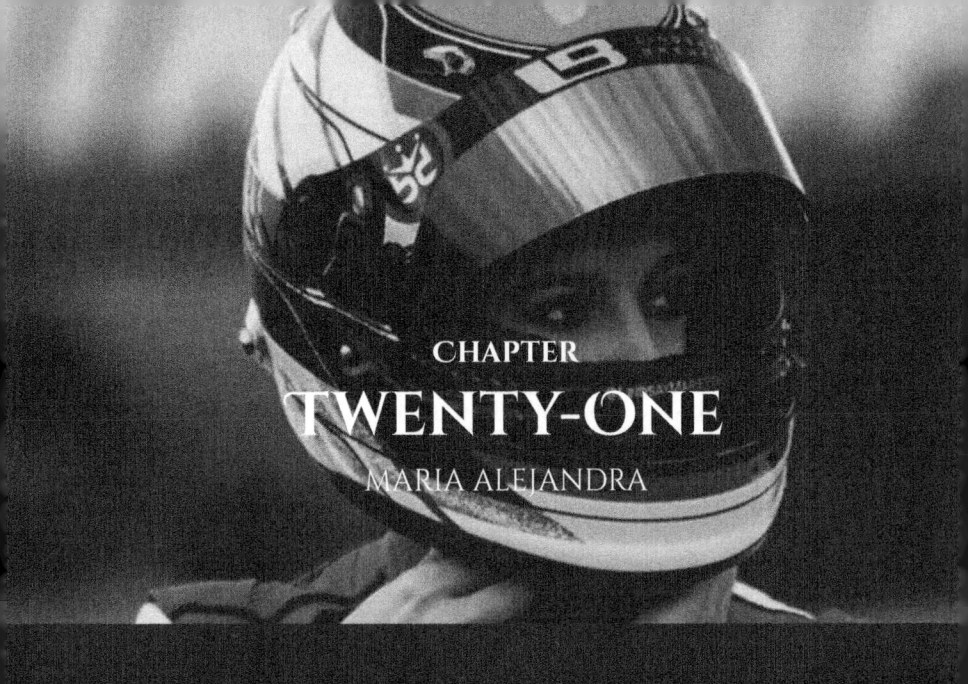

France, known for its beaches and cities. What I know it for is the mecca for rude people. There are French drivers who have always been nice to me, and I don't like to generalize, but I haven't met many people in France who have welcomed me with open arms. They act like they hate foreigners—mostly in Paris—but what they don't realize is that those foreigners are one of the major sources of their country's economy. It's not just me; they even hate the French Canadians!

A few days ago, the French Grand Prix took place. Xavier and I had a good race. Now I'm in Paris collaborating with Adèle Couture. After the red carpet in Monaco, they wanted me to be part of a campaign and be an ambassador of sorts. I was skeptical about it for obvious reasons, all involving Mr. Donatello.

They contacted me in regard to their all-black line. Which I'm perfect for since it *is* my signature color after all. I would like to believe that I was the inspiration for such a collection, but I highly doubt it.

I take a sip of my coffee, then set it down to take a bite out of my croissant. On my way to the atelier, I saw this cute little coffee shop, and since I was about twenty minutes early, I decided to stop for a bite. The French waitress is giving me a nasty side eye when I wave at her to come over. Little does she know that I'll be asking for the check so I won't have to see her face again.

You're welcome.

"Can you please bring the check?" She nods with a face that tells me she's disgusted by my existence. My question is, has she ever heard of customer service? Because this bitch wasn't even trained in the art of being decent.

A few minutes later, she brings me the check and I sign the little piece of paper. Before I go, I make sure everything is correct and then push the chair back under the table.

Even if the waitress thinks she's the best type of person on earth and I'm simply scum in her city, disrespecting her or not cleaning up after myself won't make the situation any better.

Striding out of the café, I only walk a few feet before I reach the atelier. I reach for the handle, swinging the door open and step into a marble covered room. Bright lights cast aglare onto my form. A muted pink tone shines on each part of the structure. Looking up ahead, I see spiral staircases leading up to what I assume is a showroom. Ahead of me on the right are two big white doors with glass windows side by side. I can't see through them because a mesh white curtain blocks any view.

To my left, I see a circular receptionist desk with a woman on the phone speaking French. Above her, the words, *"Adèle Maison de Mode"* radiate in a rose gold shimmer, almost blinding me in the process. Everything about this place screams upscale. I don't know whether to be scared or impressed. Mostly frightened, I would say. What if they ask me a question like, "What type of brands do you usually wear?" What am I supposed to say?

I usually wear one of your competitors: Dior, Yves Saint Laurent—which happens to be my favorite—Chanel, and occasionally Louis Vuitton's black accessories. Would you like me to go on?

God forbid I tell the truth. One of my many talents is lying when necessary. I know, I know I shouldn't be proud of that, but it helps in some situations. My overall nature is to be brutally honest, but once a situation is read, your responses should be chosen carefully.

"Miss Castillo." I turn my head like the fucking Flash. A man that seems to be in his early sixties walks up to me with his hand extended. I take it with a firm grip. He laughs.

Why is he laughing?

"What a handshake! Such a strong grip," he exclaims,

his French accent dripping off of every syllable. He's handsome for his age, gray hair shines in all different tones throughout his mane. He has scruff on his chin. But the thing I notice more than anything is how well-dressed he is. I mean, he works at a fashion brand, so it makes sense.

I may or may not have a thing for older men. I know, my daddy issues are coming out. Wait, I don't have daddy issues, or do I? If I do, that makes the situation even worse. I mean, my dad killed my mother, so I'm going to have to say that I'm the spokesperson for daddy issues. But I love my dad . . . oh my god, I have problems.

Snapping out of my thoughts, I hear him go on, "I'm André Manon, welcome to *Adèle Maison de Mode*. It's a pleasure to finally meet you." Along with working here, he's also the founder, CEO, and creator of Adèle, and the ex-father-in-law of my current team principal. Way to make a girl feel even more overwhelmed.

"The pleasure is all mine. I didn't know you would be the one showing me around."

He grins. "Why wouldn't I be the one showing you my creations? I may be old, but I am still very hands-on. I don't plan on retiring anytime soon." He laughs, and I do the same.

"Well, I'm very excited to be here. It's an honor to be posing for such an iconic line." I smile genuinely, and he nods.

Gesturing toward the staircase, he says, "Okay, so I think

I'll start by showing you our showroom and archive, which are upstairs. Please, after you." I walk up ahead of him. Keeping my hand on the rail, I slowly walk up the stairs. Stepping into a small doorway arch, I make my way through an empty space. My eyes are met with custom couture gowns. *I'm in heaven.*

"As a fashion house, we think that you are the perfect fit for the black line. Adèle is known for its color and liveliness. Our preferred color, as you can probably tell, is a light pink tone. This isn't news to anyone. I know you did your research before coming here. Adèle is a brand based on my daughter, as the brand is named after her. But it is also her lifestyle, which is why our signature is her favorite color. Every time I sketch out a design, I think of it on her first.

"This collection is very different. The muse is 'powerful women'. The color black is seen as a universal color for potential and the unknown itself. That's why I knew you would be the best one to launch it. And the fact that you only wear black doesn't hurt."

"I know I've said this before, but I am incredibly honored that you thought of me as the ambassador for such a powerful new creative outlet for your brand. My only question is why didn't you pick your daughter for this collection? Isn't she a strong woman as well?"

"Because *mon père* knows I wouldn't be caught dead in black." I turn my head to see a long-legged, beautiful toothgapped woman. Adèle.

ABORT, ABORT.

"*Mon amour,* I didn't know you were here," he exclaims in joy, looking at his daughter.

"And miss out on such a special occasion? Never." She gives him a small smug smile, and he beams at her. This man is obsessed. *She* doesn't have daddy issues. That much is evident.

I wonder if she has mommy issues though.

At this point, Google is my best friend, and I may have stalked her once or twice.

I was interested. It's not my fault that my brain wanted to see Mr. Donatello's ex-wife's extensive history. That was before the kiss though . . . okay, I'm lying. I may have stalked her Instagram after the kiss. BUT THAT DOES NOT MATTER.

Her father was married to her mother for eleven years. In that time span, they had two children, Antoine Manon and Adèle Manon (they have a thing for A names, apparently). They got divorced when she was nine and her brother was eleven. Antoine came out as bisexual during their divorce, declaring that he was indeed in love with one of his investors at the time. He and his husband have been happily together for twenty-four years.

I swear to God, I need to stop stalking people I meet. Don't even get me started on the Google searches I did on Xavier.

"I was just telling Miss Castillo here the history of our brand."

"It's a pleasure to meet you, Adèle. I have heard so many things."

"I'm guessing from my father, not Luca." They both laugh, and I chuckle awkwardly. Way to kill a compliment. But I mean, she's not wrong. Mr. Donatello is the definition of Fort fucking Knox when it comes to any topic on his personal life.

Mr. Manon continues to walk me around the archive, and I stop in front of a bright gold dress. It's stunning, possibly my favorite out of the collection. The fabric is something like the chainmail would see on a knight's armor below his helmet. The train is long and metallic; the gold shimmers.

"I can see that's your favorite. I like to call it 'the dress of shining armor'."

I love it.

"I made this dress when Adèle was a little girl. She saw Queen Victoria in a museum the first time she was in London and asked me why the women in that time didn't wear dresses made out of metal since it would protect them. She isn't very fond of English history, but I wanted to take her to a museum, and it just happened to pop up in her little brilliant brain. The next day, I was glued to my sketch pad trying to get it right. The bodice and form are meant to keep little from the eye but also to cover up enough for a man to want more. The chainmail as her armor as the modern woman fights her way through a sexist world. It's not just a garment, it's a story."

"Your inspiration is so fascinating," I tell him.

"You're looking right at her. It isn't hard when your

daughter is the inspiration for many." He looks at her caringly, and she returns the look.

Best dad-daughter duo ever.

"Enough of the showroom, I think it's time to show you the new collection," Adèle says suddenly, and her dad agrees with a small nod. They take me through doors that lead to a big office space.

The building looks small from the front, but it's a maze in here.

We come upon another staircase at the end of the office space, which I assume leads to the same place the doors in the lobby lead to.

Reaching the top, we walk into a large room where women in white coats work with Singer machines while others scurry around with fabrics and measuring tapes.

"This is where the magic happens, or as most people call it, an atelier."

"It's amazing," I tell him in awe.

"*Adrienne, sortez-moi les dessins pour la collection noire,*" he tells a woman, and she runs for what I assume are the designs. Shortly after, she brings out several white bags with the word *Adèle* on them.

Hanging them up on racks, she spreads them out. Mr. Manon walks up to one of the garments and pulls the zipper down. I gasp.

I'm obsessed.

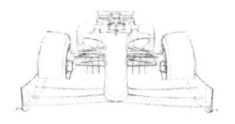

"Tilt your head back so that it touches your neck; basically just look at the ceiling. Also, can you put your hands in your pockets for me?" Doing as the photographer, Crue, tells me, I pose.

After seeing the garments and absolutely loving every single one of them, the makeup and hair girls descended on me as if they were about to give me Botox and an eyebrow lift. They quickly escorted me to the chair and worked their magic. My hair is straightened, and I have a natural makeup look on my face. Layers of foundation cover up every pimple and discoloration known to man. Lip gloss and a shimmer shadow were applied shortly afterward. My makeup has a matte finish, and let me tell you . . . my skin has never looked better.

I was also quickly introduced to the world-renowned high fashion photographer, Crue Thomas. Coming from first-generation immigrant parents, he moved to France when he was just a child.

He's hot as fuck.

"Ugh, you are fucking brilliant," he says as he keeps taking photos. This man does wonders for a woman's ego.

I think I'm in love.

I'm posing in the "signature" pantsuit, as Mr. Manon likes to call it. He's very passionate about his clothing. He told me the full story behind each piece. This look in particular embodies gender-neutral clothing and gives a sort of masculine look to the female body. Since Adèle is known for its hyper-feminine pieces, he wanted to do something vastly different.

I don't have a shirt underneath the straight suit jacket. It curves at the waist, giving it a flattering finish. The pants are completely straight-legged while hugging the ass. The accessories are composed of a belt with silver embellishments as well as metallic rings scattered on my fingers.

"Okay, shall we get you into look two?" I almost burst from joy; it's my favorite look out of them all.

"Yes, please." I grin like the fucking Cheshire Cat.

Walking back into the changing area, which is pretty much just a dressing barrier, I begin changing. When I came in, they told me it was okay to change in front of them, but I am not letting it all out for my potential boss to see. It may be the French way, but these people are not going to see my vagina on our first photoshoot. We can work up to that.

Taking off the suit carefully, I grab fishnet tights that are going to match the shorts and the corset bodice that has a sort of Matrix-style black leather coat paired with it. Slipping on the black ten-inch heel boots that are made of velvet, I feel like I'm in heaven.

I could be a model at this rate because I am damn good at it.

When Mr. Manon said that this line is made for strong women, he was not lying.

All these looks are so good. It's chic, modern, and still has that Adèle appeal all bundled up into one collection.

The assistants help me get everything sorted. I take a few steps out from behind the divider thing or whatever you call it.

"*Qu'est-ce que tu as encore fait, Adèle?*" I hear someone burst through the doors. Everyone looks up, including me.

Of course, he's here and why in the ever-loving fuck does he speak French so well?

What, is this man a parseltongue too?

"*Qu'est-ce que tu fais ici, Luc?*" Adèle sighs into her hands in frustration at his outburst.

"*Tu sais ce que je fais ici, tu penses que tu peux me poursuivre pour quatre millions de dollars alors qu'on a divorcé il y a des années. Ça va dans ta tête?*" Mr. Donatello holds up a piece of paper waving it in Adèle's face.

Am I witnessing a lover's quarrel? Someone get the popcorn.

Adèle finally ends the dialogue in French, so I can understand some of the words coming out of their mouths. "Let's talk about this in my office. Everyone keep the shoot going!" she yells out, waving her perfectly manicured fingers in a circle, before walking past Mr. Donatello, who is currently holding the door open.

Luca looks at Crue, giving him a nod before leaving.

Why am I kind of sad that they left? I would love to see the rest of that play out, even though I probably wouldn't have understood a word of it. I would be witnessing the real ex-housewives of high fashion and sports. Netflix, hire me.

"Let's go, everyone. Get Miss Castillo ready for the next shot," Crue yells out in his thick French accent.

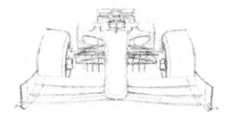

"Thank you so much, Mr. Manon, this experience will forever stay with me."

"You don't have to thank me, doll. What you did in there really captured everything I wanted. You were brilliant." I smile at him before waving as I make my way out. Hearing the door open behind me, I look over and see a pacing Mr. Donatello. Our eyes meet.

So much for not wanting to run into him.

"Tell Adèle to get it together, I don't appreciate her filing another lawsuit for no apparent reason. If either she or you try to step into my life again, I will ruin you," he says directly in André's face. He quickly walks out the door as I give Mr. Manon a sympathetic look before mouthing an apology in his direction. What does the old man have to do with all this? He just let his daughter marry the man she loved at the time. It's not his fault that Luca's parents happen to be assholes just like him. Rushing down the stairs, I find Mr. Donatello staring at me.

"What in the ever-loving fuck are you doing here, Miss Castillo?"

I laugh at him, give him a sneer, and then walk past his

standing form. He doesn't take long to catch up to my strides.

"You didn't answer my question, *ragazza*."

"Why do you care?"

"Because you were just in my ex-father-in-law's fashion house. Are you obsessed with me, Miss Castillo? Is that it?"

I stop in my tracks and slowly turn to face him menacingly.

"Obsessed? The only thing that I think I'm obsessed with is the fact that I just modeled for a high fashion campaign. Wearing a collection that they specifically chose me for," I say without wavering.

Bringing his thumb and middle finger to his temples he glares down to the floor. "You have got to be kidding me."

"What? Does it hurt your ego? I seem to look good in all the clothes that they gave me, and I even had the honor of wearing one of their dresses at the gala. Remember? I bet you didn't even notice I was wearing one of their gowns that day."

He looks up at me.

Well, that's until he literally grabs me by the throat and pulls me into him.

"You think you're so smart, little girl? I bet you loved wearing my ex-father-in-law's designer gown while I pulled your hair and kissed the ever-living fuck out of you. Did that arouse you, *ragazza?* Your neck fully exposed to me in that dark room or the way the soft gasps came tumbling from your mouth? Tell me . . . does it make you wet knowing that your stubbornness gets on my very last nerve?" I move a step closer, almost touching his lips with mine.

"The sad part is that you were too much of a pussy to rip it off." I smile, looking him straight in the eyes before walking in my hotel's direction.

CHAPTER
TWENTY-TWO
MARIA ALEJANDRA

Here we fucking go again. Being back in Italy comes with a migraine the size of Mr. Donatello's ego. The pretentious douchebag has another home race, and yet again, he's hounding us on placements from the last time we were in the country. I mean, come on, dude, give yourself a break.

Your team isn't even from Italy, your drivers aren't either. I get the "I must honor my country" bullshit, but what happens out there is me and Xavier's decision as well as the conditions and car's performance. Without being behind the wheel, he can only do so much.

It's not like today is race day or anything. It's quali, so he can calm his inner Karen down while we try to do everything we can.

"Luca, relax. We're going to do our best out there, so please, I ask you to have a little trust in us for once," I say soothingly as I put my hand on his shoulder. He shakes it off before grunting and walking away, stressed. He's like a ten-year-old boy, I swear to God.

"And the boss stomps off in a tantrum, just like someone else I know." Xavier side eyes me.

"I love you, but shut up."

He smiles. "You love me." His eye's glint with mischief as he fucking grins. I glare but he doesn't back down.

"I was nice to him, like you told me to be, and guess what? He still stomped off."

"He is a little fussy today, someone should feed him." Xavier jokes.

I laugh. "Agreed."

"One thing that I didn't fail to notice was your hand on Mr. Donatello's shoulder. Finally thinking about what I've been saying, huh?"

"Take that small amount of hope out of your eyes and throw it in the nearest trash can," I tell him.

"It will stay in my eyes until the end of time. As Yoda says, 'if he chooses to not believe and lack hope, he will fail every time.'"

"Did you just pull a Star Wars quote out of your ass?" I ask.

"Yes, ma'am!" he confirms.

"You're such a nerd," I joke.

"Proudly. If you want to offend me, you'll have to do more than that to phase me and my pretty face."

"Your ego just gets bigger the more time you spend with the devil's spawn."

"Just wait until you hear my Lord of The Rings quotes." His eyebrows raise at me while smirking as if he's making a sexual comment.

"Do you ever back down?" I ask.

"Never."

"Goodbye," I tell him before I start walking away and hear his laugh behind me.

"There's trouble in paradise today. Someone change these big babies' diapers. It appears they're both having extensive tantrums," Xavier yells from behind me. I smile a little before walking away.

Pinche Xavier, lo amo.

"We're finished here, I will see you all tomorrow," the lead diagnostics specialist says to the whole team, who, by the way, just got a second and third placement at qualifying. Mr. Donatello must be off his rocker because he still seems angry. The prick.

Walking away from everyone, I make my way to an empty garage. Everything is set in its place, and the black cover sits atop my car. I trace my finger from the top to the bottom. One thing that gives me more ecstasy than anything in the world is this car. Taking off the cover, I look around to make sure I'm alone.

I look at it with rigorous attention. The white lines and my number on the side. I still can't believe this is my life.

I hear a tool clank in the garage. I jolt up like I've just seen a ghost. Well, I mean, I'm not wrong. More like a demon, but same thing.

"Everyone left, Ale. Why are you still here?"

"I could ask you the same thing, Luca." He points at his desk, and I see his phone vibrate and flash.

"That's surprising. You never leave your phone anywhere."

"Not like it's any of your business, but my family has been hounding me about the result."

"It was a good result."

"It was fine, but my mom thinks otherwise." He sighs.

"Interesting."

"What are you implying, *ragazza*?"

"I just wouldn't have taken you as someone who has to please his family constantly."

"Don't talk about my family in that way."

"It seems I've hit a nerve," I taunt him.

"You know nothing." He walks to my side of the car so we're standing face to face.

"I know more than you think. You of all people should know that."

"But you are nowhere near smart, Miss Castillo."

Now that was a low blow. I mean, most of my statements about him haven't be very nice either. But at this point, I realize that we're tired. Tired of this. Tired of each other. Just physically and emotionally exhausted.

But neither of us will back down without a fight.

"I may not be Albert fucking Einstein, but I am perceptive. I know that you come from a prestigious family, a family that has put you under constant pressure since you were a child. You take all that frustration and anger and convert it into your personality, the way you treat people. You're picky. From the way you dress to the way you walk. You know what you want when you want it. In most situations at least. All the pressure you put on us stems from your own mistakes. Being born into an Italian family with a heritage that is so thick hasn't helped you. Everything they taught you is ingrained in your blood. But that doesn't mean that you have to put up with them treating you like shit.

"I can relate to most of the things that you've been through, even though you don't want to admit it. The constant pressure that you aren't supporting the people you're supposed to support. Your mother or father telling you that you're not enough. Those are the things that have made you who you are today. The way 'thank you' isn't present in your vocabulary or the way you hated me from the first moment you saw me. You're not a pushover, but when it comes to your family . . . you are easily swayed. The real question here, Mr. Donatello, is whether you want to confront it or not." I pause before continuing my "speech".

"I can't stand here and say I have faced my own situation. I visit my family as often as possible, but am I really addressing the issues? No. I know that, but do you?" I look up at him with a "so I'm a dumb bitch apparently" face. He grabs my wrist and pulls me in.

"You may be perceptive, Miss Castillo, but one of the biggest lies that I just heard come out of your mouth is the notion that I hate you. I don't hate you, Ale. I despise you." Our noses are touching now.

"Is that so, Luca? Well, I think that's the only thing we can agree on." I slam my lips onto his. He isn't shocked or even hesitant about the kiss. Our lips move together in a frenzied state. Pushing me onto the car, Luca takes my t-shirt off. He tugs it over my head and chucks it to the other side of the garage. I do the same, unbuttoning his shirt while his hands roam all over my body.

"I still loathe you, but you're hot as fuck. That I won't deny."

"Ditto, *ragazza*," he rasps.

Finally, I slip the last button from its hole, ripping his shirt off after what seems like hours. I run my hands over his chest. His chest goes up and down as he breathes heavily. I run my finger down the middle of his abs, making sure it touches every single crevice. Who made this man, fucking Hades?

I've seen him like this before, but now sweat droplets roll down his chest. He seems even more buff than he did before.

He pulls my head back, kissing all the way down to my

collarbone, grazing his teeth against my skin, making me hypersensitive. I can feel the cool steel of the car against my back. Licking and kissing all the way down to my bra, he looks up at me with a smirk before reaching to the back and unfastening it. He practically rips my bra off, setting my breasts free as he uses his hands to massage them. He brings his fingers down to play with my nipples, and I moan out, reacting to his touch.

"Fuck. You didn't tell me they were pierced."

"I don't remember having a conversation about my boobs."

The metal slides between both nipples as he begins to play with them as if they're toys. I can't handle this. I've never been this wet before. Bringing his mouth down, he starts licking and sucking, leaving multiple marks in his wake.

"These tits could start wars, *ragazza*." He presses up between my legs, both of us still fully clothed on the bottom half of our bodies. Even with the clothing separating us, I can feel his length and can already tell that it's going to hurt when it goes in. Fuck.

"You see what those pieces of metal do to me?" He presses his lips to my ear. "I'm going to fuck you like a dirty whore. After this, no man will ever touch this pretty little cunt and leave you satisfied. You'll be ruined."

He brings his fingers down my stomach slowly and I whine.

"You're already a needy little girl."

"I would never need anything of yours."

"Tsk, tsk. Bad move on your part. That means I'll just have to fuck you longer then."

Bringing his hands to the hem of my leggings, he slowly brings them down my thighs. He takes them off completely before spreading my legs open. He kneels in front of me, reaching up to move my panties aside.

"You say you don't need anything from me, *ragazza*, but your pussy says otherwise. You're already this wet. I can't imagine how much you could squirt."

"You think too highly of yourself. The only person to make me come is myself. Never in my life have I been able to squirt, and you most definitely won't be the one to do it."

"Let's prove that theory wrong." He starts circling around my opening and I shiver. His fingers keep circling and circling.

I let the shock of the amazing feeling run through me.

"Oh my god."

He slowly makes his way down to my center where he slides one finger in. The sound of gushing makes me quiver. It's too much. I can't. His finger enters and exits in a torturously slow rhythm.

"You love the sound, don't you? My finger inside your cunt letting your wetness spread all over my hand. It's music to my ears."

This man and his dirty mouth. He adds a second finger, and I clench around them. His pace is still slow as he adds his thumb, which resides on my clit. His other hand reaches up to my stomach. He stands up and leans over me, adjusting his finger position inside me, making them go in a downward angle, hitting the spot that's going to make me come undone. Both my arms fly out to grab something, but I find nothing to support me, I'm bent over the car. An F1 car is built with a slim front, which my back is bent over, with my legs and arms on either side.

His rhythm picks up, it's becoming too much. It's building and building. I come undone. I open my mouth to scream, but the sound is silenced by my ecstasy. Standing up, he looks me in the eye and shoves his finger that was just in my opening into his mouth, licking off every inch of my juices. I just can't anymore. I will say this only in my brain and not for anyone else.

"Just you wait, *ragazza*, that was just the first one. You haven't even had my cock inside of that sleek, tight opening." He smirks at me, but not his signature cocky, masochistic one. This version is primal. Animalistic.

Yes, please.

"Let's just see if you can deliver on everything you say, pretty boy." He chuckles while taking off his belt slowly, dropping it onto the floor. The thud echos around the garage. He slowly pulls down his zipper, taunting me in the process.

"I am no boy, *ragazza*. I'm a man." He pulls the top of his boxers down. Looking me in the eye a little while doing so. He does it again.

This man is daunting, not only in a sexual way, but in an absolute prick way.

"If you don't pull down those boxers in the next second, I will pull them off for you."

"Do it then." His arms dangle at the side of his body as he waits for me with a challenging look. One thing he knows is that challenges are something that I excel in.

Pushing off the car, I walk up to him slowly. I reach up to touch his top lip, sliding it down to his plump bottom one. I bring my thumb down across the center of his chest, maintaining eye contact the whole time. Finally reaching the top of his boxer briefs, I pull them down forcefully. I keep my gaze locked with his until he grabs me and kisses me again. Setting me down onto the car forcefully, he pins me down with his weight.

"You never got to see it, *ragazza*. Well, feel it then if you're so eager."

He takes his tip and rubs it against me. Everything in me spasms. I moan uncontrollably at the sensation.

"You think you're ready, little girl? Are you ready to take the cock of a man eighteen years older than you? You talk a big game until you actually feel it rip you open, giving you such intense pleasure that you see stars. Forget about the stars you saw in the observatory; I'm about to make you see the whole fucking galaxy."

He enters me abruptly. Luckily, I'm already extremely wet. I hate to say this, but the man is big. Well-endowed would be an extreme understatement. The feeling isn't painful, but it's uncomfortable at first. I almost yelped when he entered me, but I kept it in while my eyes crossed.

Before he starts moving, he lets me adjust while adorning kisses all over my body. When I know I'm ready, I start grinding against him, searching for friction. He moves slowly and it feels good, and then it feels otherworldly.

"Fuck, *raggaza*. You're such a good girl for me, aren't you?"

"Filthy words coming from such a poised man."

"Admit it, you like it. Just a second ago, you told me you don't need me for anything, and now look at you, begging like the whore you are."

Why was that hot, oh my god do I have a degradation kink? NO, absolutely not. I will not stand for it.

My body is rebelling against my head. His words set my skin on fire.

"Faster."

He listens for once in his goddamn life. He enters me and exits like his life depends on it.

"Fuck," he groans, making me squeeze around him like a vice. A man who exhibits his pleasure makes him ten times hotter, it's scientifically proven.

My nails knead into his skin. He pounds into me while his head nuzzles into the crook of my neck, biting and nibbling. I think I found the sex messiah because I sure feel like I'm in heaven.

He continues to thrust in and out of me, hitting places I never even knew existed before him. Using my hand and toys occasionally fills the void for a while, but nothing compares to the feeling of a dick entering you. Everything about it is raw. Maybe it's just his dick. I've never had this type of experience with any other man. Before him, I only had one boyfriend, and he never made me come. He would get off extremely fast and just leave me there. I thought it was supposed to be like that until I gave myself my first orgasm with my own hand.

That's the sad and empowering part of it all. The sad part being the fact that most men don't even know how to make a woman moan. The empowering part is that I can do without wanting sex constantly. Getting myself off takes me ten minutes. It really isn't that hard, but for most men, you have to be a rocket scientist. I know my body better than any other person. No man knows how to play it better than I can.

Well, maybe Luca does, who is currently railing me into oblivion. The orgasm builds. I'm about to feel one of the best inner and outer body experiences of my life. It enrages me almost as much as it excites me. I fucking explode and scream audibly this time. Yet again, I'm ashamed to say this, but Luca is right. I don't see stars, but rather the whole universe exploding in front of me.

My body falls limp as he pulls out of me, jerking off onto my stomach. Looking up at him, I drag my index finger through his mess and take up a little bit of it. Sucking it off the pad of my digit, that's his reward for a job well done. Because cum isn't an appealing thing to swallow.

"Fuck," Luca responds.

I lay down right beside my 21.2-million-dollar car that I just had sex on, and Luca lies beside me. We both stare up at the ceiling in a moment of silence for the sacred act that just occurred.

"You're a minx, you know that? A twenty-year-old soul-sucking she-devil, that happened to be one the best fucks of my life."

I laugh. "You're leaving out the part where you also happen to be my boss and we're both public figures in the biggest racing sport on the planet."

"Fuck me," he groans.

"I just did."

"I see you're on a high."

I snap out of my haze of bliss for a moment. "I am not on a high, especially not from you of all people."

"Why lie at this point? It's not like we're going to get married. This was a one-time thing, that's all. Do you understand me?"

"This happened on a whim. We were both pissed and sexually frustrated, that's all." I reassure him and myself.

"I believe this is the second time we have ever agreed on something."

"See, it isn't so hard," I mutter. He stands up and begins putting his clothes on in front of me.

"Don't get used to it," he says before taking in everything around us.

Getting up, I do the same. Fixing my appearance, I opt

for grabbing a cloth nearby to clean myself up. His cum trails down from the center of my breasts all the way down to my stomach. Wiping it swiftly, I make sure it didn't get anywhere else.

At least we know he has good aim.

Putting the black cover on top of the car just like before, I make sure everything is the way it was prior to having mind-blowing sex at the workplace.

Great Ale, you're such a saint. Your mom would be so proud of you.

Looking at my phone, I see that it's only eleven, so the gates should still be open.

"Fuck," I say as I realize something that will result in the most awkward drive of my life.

"What?" Luca questions.

"I drove here with Xavier. I don't have a way to get back."

He sighs, running his hands through his thick, coarse black hair that I just so happened to see in a different place only minutes ago.

Snap out of it, Ale.

"I think the obvious assessment is that you ride with me." I look at him with a "duh" face, but he continues. "My car is outside, come."

"I already did, just regretting that it was with you." I push past him as he grabs his phone and keys.

The track is under security ninety-nine percent of the time, but just for safety precautions, they make sure everything is incredibly secure. Walking behind him, we make it to the car he drove for this race. Most drivers just take the same car everywhere, but Luca likes to keep things different occasionally. This weekend's car is a Ferrari in honor of his ancestors. If they ever became an F1 team, I bet he wouldn't just walk, he would run with all his Italian pride to work for them.

Jumping into the passenger's seat, I make myself as comfortable as possible on the black leather seats. Fastening my seatbelt, I look straight ahead as Luca turns the ignition on.

No, not Luca. Mr. Donatello. He's your boss, Ale.

Turning my head to the side that *Mr. Donatello* is not at, and I look out at the old building surrounding me. I've always loved Italy. When I was younger, Rome was my favorite place in Europe until I went to Croatia. Italy used to remind me of the Vatican; of its rich history and the people who lived inside.

Now the only thing it reminds me of is him.

Luca Donatello, the Italian bastard from hell who happens to have a magical dick.

CHAPTER TWENTY-THREE

MARIA ALEJANDRA

I got a podium at Monza. You can suck on that, Mr. Donatello.

Just like he sucked on your tits last night.

Oh, fuck off.

He better be giddy right now, considering Xavier got first and I got second. The results he wanted for his home race. So, he better not be annoyed or I will kick his teeth in.

"Rookie."

"Xavier." We smile at each other like idiots, then hug in delight.

"He better be happy with the result, or I will cut his dick off." I smile sweetly at him so that if any cameras take photos, they think we're having a nice conversation.

"I think that's a little extreme, but I agree to a certain extent."

"Welcome to the dark side, Mr. Smiley."

"Cutting off a man's manhood is the worst offense, especially when they're good at using it," Luca says with a shudder. I look at him horrified.

"How do you know how Mr. Donatello uses it?"

"I've heard that he's greatly endowed and knows how to please a woman."

"I doubt it, it's probably teeny-weeny."

"Wouldn't you like to know?" Xavier nudges me in the arm, and I playfully hit him on the back. "I'm going to go and get weighed before the podium starts. I'll see you there, silver champion."

I snarl at him. This man.

I walk toward my car to grab something before I go and follow Xavier. Finally getting the pieces I needed out of the car, I turn around and bump into something hard. More like *someone* hard.

Oh my god. Of course, you had to say that in your head about someone you fucked. Get it together, Ale.

"Hello, Mr. Donatello."

"You just called my cock, and I quote "teeny-weeny,' in front of your teammate, but your screams last night said otherwise."

"How did you even hear that?"

"You didn't notice me lingering behind you and Xavier?"

"Don't flatter yourself, old man. When you're around, I barely notice."

He scoffs."I could care less if you called my dick small,

Miss Castillo. What I care about is why the fuck you were even on the subject."

"For your information, Mr. Donatello, I was informing Xavier before you came in that if you weren't happy with this result, I would chop your dick off."

"Interesting. Why wouldn't I be happy with the result? I mean it's the best result he and you could have possibly gotten."

"Because you seem to find everything that we do inadequate to your standards. You're lucky that you have two drivers that are so self-assured that they don't let what you say affect them as much as others."

"Ale, I don't find everything you do inadequate. Annoying, yes. But you wouldn't be here if you weren't as high as my standards are."

"You just complimented me. Did Jesus come back?" I look around waiting for the reckoning to come upon us.

"No, but me fucking you on that car last night was the blessing you never knew you needed. I definitely helped you win; I'm your new messiah."

"In your dreams." I turn and storm off towards my podium.

"So, what are you doing for the minor break we have this

week?" I ask Xavier, figuring he may go home or make his way to LA.

"I'm going to Portugal for the week to spend time with my family. You?"

"Nothing. I was going to go home, but I was thinking of going around Italy and taking in the sights. Be a tourist for once." He smiles.

"Why don't you go around with Luc—"

"What about me?" Mr. Donatello questions as he walks in.

"I was just asking the rookie here if she thinks that you're going to stay in Italy for our week off."

What are you doing, Xavier? You better not be asking what I think you're asking.

"I am. But no plan is set. I'm going to my family's estate for two days. I leave today. Then afterwards, I might go somewhere else to have a break."

"What a coincidence. Ale is going to be staying in Italy too. She was just telling me she doesn't know where to go or what to do. Maybe you can show her around?"

Of course, he said that. Mr. Matchmaker over here.

"Mr. Donatello, I was just going to go to Rome for a few days, that's all. I can make it around by myself."

"Nonsense. There's no better way to experience Rome than with an Italian present."

"I could ask my friend Giovanni. He can show me around. You don't have to."

"No, I will accompany you, but you will have to go to my family's estate first before we do anything else."

"But—"

"Don't make excuses, *ragazza*. You will not be going around with your Italian boy toy, Georgio."

"His name is Giovanni, and there's really no need."

"Nope, I offered. I'm your boss, and you will be coming with me. Consider it a business trip of sorts. Get your shit together, we'll be leaving in forty minutes max." With that he walks away, leaving no room for further dispute. I turn around and look at Xavier in disbelief.

"Xavier, are you fucking serious?"

"Yes, ma'am. The tension is getting too intense at this point. Just fuck already." I still, my eyes opening a little wider than usual. He looks at me in realization.

"Rookie, no." I look at him tight lipped, his jaw drops. Then he jumps up and smiles at me.

"I'm a physic medium at this point. I'm so proud of the love story that's about to ensue." I slap him on his arm.

"There is no love story about to ensue. I don't even know what you're alluding to. Nothing has happened."

"No need to hide it, Ale. I'm not going to ask you if it was good. I may be bright and happy, but I'm not dumb. You fucked him, period. Now it's time for you to say your 'I love you's' and get married."

"Nothing happened."

"I'm so ready to see you in a wedding dress, I better be

one of the groomsmen. I expect nothing less. I wonder what Luca would pick out for your engagement ring."

"You think you're so funny."

"I am. But that's beside the point. I'm predicting your whole future in this moment, let me just think about my vision." He puts his finger on his temples and closes his eyes. He continues to speak. "I can see it now. You'll get married in a vineyard in *Italia*, your dress will be a lacy Grace Kelly sort of look."

"*Cállate, pendejo.*" He just grins at me, and I return it with a disgusted look on my face.

"I'm going to go pack now because you just sent me on the most dreadful trip of my life."

"You said that wrong. You mean your future is in front of your eyes."

I walk away, turning my back to him. He can shove that love story up his ass. I will never have sex with or even kiss Mr. Donatello again.

"I wonder how many kids you'll have. Let me think. Five, probably to keep the Donatello legacy alive. I can just imagine you in a mama van."

I raise my middle finger up in the air and just before I walk out, I hear Xavier laughing in the background.

I hear a knock on my door just as I'm in the middle of an episode of The Karlssons. Who knew they would tell E! to fuck off and move to Hulu?

"I'm about to see how Kam reacted to her ex-husband obliterating her boyfriend, Peter Davis, on social media. So, whoever is at the door, would you kindly fuck off?"

"*Ragazza*, we're leaving now." I almost break my neck as it snaps in the direction of the sound. Is he serious? I stare at the door for a few minutes, hoping he'll get bored and leave.

"Get the fuck up now before I knock this door down." I groan out loud and get up, twisting the door open. I see him look behind me. My clothes are practically everywhere around my room.

What? I'm indecisive.

"I told you to be ready in forty minutes," he says in annoyance.

"I thought you were just saying that to appease Xavier. I was under the impression that you were joking."

"I never joke."

"Well, that's the only truth I've ever heard come out of your mouth."

"Yes, and the fact that I told you I had a big dick."

"You may be well endowed, but just by saying that you've shrunk your dick down five inches." I hold up my index finger and thumb, leaving a miniscule space in between them. Bringing my hand to eye level, I squint to make the whole gesture hurt his ego more. He slaps my hand away.

"Pack. Now."

"So you've apparently turned into my father?" He pushes past me, grabbing all my clothes and throwing them onto the bed. He starts folding them. "You were serious?" I groan, slapping my palm against my head.

"Isn't that obvious, Ale?"

"Don't call me that, it's too casual."

"What we did yesterday was far from casual. Or professional," he mutters.

"You told me that was a one-time thing."

"It was," he reaffirms.

"So, why are you speaking to me so casually?"

"Because I've seen you naked." His hand gestures up and down my body. He gives me a look, one that makes up for undressing me all over again with his eyes.

"So what? I've seen you naked and I still call you Mr. Donatello."

"That's a choice you've made. Now come help me pack your things so I can show you around Italy the right way." We have a stare down for a few seconds before I back down and throw my hands up.

"You're going to at least let me finish the episode while we pack." I pick up the remote and Kam's crying starts sounding through the speakers again.

"Dear god, she sounds like a dying walrus." His Italian accent messes with the word "walrus". I want to laugh, but I would *never*.

"Hey! She's going through a tough time."

He rolls his eyes before stacking all my tops in one place.

"How do you pack? By color or type of clothing?"

"Oh my god, does Mr. Donatello have a packing fetish?"

"Answer the goddamn question, *ragazza*."

"I usually just shove it all in."

He looks at me disapprovingly.

"That will not do. All your clothes will wrinkle, and you won't know where anything is. We will do it by type of clothing."

"Yes, daddy," I say sarcastically. Realizing what I said, I stiffen. Ale, you did not just say that.

Unfortunately, you just did.

He looks up at me and stops everything. His eyes widen and a clear awkward silence spreads throughout the room.

"Umm moving on." I run past him to the bathroom muttering a quick, "I'm going to just put away my toiletries."

The TV is still playing in the background, and I can hear Kyson on the phone. Grabbing all my makeup and skin care, I stuff them in a bag. I replay everything that just happened in my head. I swear to god, I can't deal with my mouth anymore.

Snatching my suitcase from the floor, I bring it over to the bed. I see Mr. Donatello staring at the screen in front of him.

"I would have never thought of you as a Karlsson viewer," I mutter under my breath.

"I'm not."

"What you're currently doing tells me otherwise."

"What I'm doing is analyzing why the fuck her rapper ex-husband would be posting all of this on social media."

"Because they've been going through a lot of things when it comes to his mental health. Also, because he still thinks their marriage can be saved."

He chuckles, continuing to watch.

"There is no plausible answer as to why Peter sent a message to Kyson saying, 'I'm in bed with your wife.'" His face is full of shock, and I can't help but laugh.

Did I just laugh? This is bad, Mr. Donatello can be funny. I refuse to believe it.

"Welcome to the world of The Karlssons."

"It's fucking stupid, but I can get the appeal."

"It's not stupid, its entertaining."

"I never said it wasn't entertaining, Ale. I was simply saying that these women make almost as much money as us for getting butt implants and causing drama."

"Um, excuse me? They're human beings."

"I never said they weren't. I couldn't care less if their body composition is solely silicone. I've always thought that if you feel better about yourself, then do anything to accomplish that. I'm simply stating that the people watch this because they don't have enough drama going on in their own lives. So, they watch sisters make money off of nothing but their talentless lives."

"Thanks for the compliment," I mutter.

"You're the exception. You have too much going on in

your life, most of which includes me, so you already have enough on your plate." He smirks up at me.

This motherfucke—

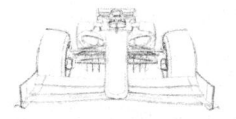

Spending an hour and forty-nine minutes in a car with Mr. Donatello has been far from interesting. Our conversations have consisted of work and his family.

He grew up on an estate in Florence. He told me about how his house has an amazing view overlooking the city. There's a massive garden he says he never liked and a gazebo that sits in the middle of all the flowers.

I'm expecting something big and extremely Italian. I also found out a lot of things that he and I have in common when it comes to our childhoods. We're both from privileged families and grew up on an estate. The only difference is our environments, which were extremely different, and the morals that structured the dynamics vastly opposed.

His family also hates what my whole life was based on: *organized crime*. He's happened to mention it almost a gazillion times. I can feel his hatred from here and it still sends a chill down my spine. It's not like I didn't know about his whole vendetta on the subject. But hearing him talk about it is different from Xavier explaining it to me.

His mom is the standard setter of the family because he

never had a father. His mother married rich, and his dad died at the hands of the mafia.

Yay me! I'm at the center of his family's pain. Cue dramatic cry.

He told me that she's basically the head of the household and was both the female and male example in his life. He was supposed to take over his family's business, which is a part of many endeavors, the main one being the primary source of wine all over Italy. But he always knew he wanted to be an F1 driver—*another thing we have in common.*

His younger brother, Bernard, took over the family business at the age of eighteen. Now he's thirty years old with a horrid wife—*words of Mr. Donatello*—and three children that Luca adores. It was cool to see him talk about children so fondly. I would never have seen him as the type. I have little cousins, but no nieces or nephews, thank god. It's not that I hate children, but most of the time they ruin everything. They're cool and stuff, but I don't have the time or energy for them.

Especially after the childhood that I went through. I don't want my children to experience anything like it. I've never been fond of the possibility, but it's not something that I'll completely write off.

Brain, why are you thinking about children? No.

That part of my life isn't completely closed off because León wants to breed an entire population. I asked him once how many children he wanted, and he said ten. May god bless him and his offspring, as well as his sanity.

My father has many children from many different women. I was his only legitimate child. He asked me if I wanted to take over once. I gave him a scathing look, and he got the message loud and clear. He chose León as his successor because he was the result of his favorite mistress. Having hundreds of siblings that you don't know about is quite thrilling in a way. On the rare occasions we left the estate, I would stare at other children we saw along the way and see if they looked like my dad in any way. Most of the time, my brain would say "yes". I love my father, but he's a man whore.

"Here it is," Mr. Donatello announces as we reach a grand gate that has the initial D in a circle in the middle of the gate. Looking ahead, a dirt road with trees lining it lead up to what I assume is the main entrance. I can't see it from here because the entry road is long.

"That gate says a lot. In Sinaloa, we have a gate but would never put an initial or family emblem on it. A little egotistical, don't you think?"

He scoffs at me.

"It shows how much pride we have in our family. If you think that's egotistical, just wait till you meet them."

He didn't have to tell me that; I'd already assumed it. I mean, Mr. Donatello couldn't have become the way he is on his own.

Driving up the road, we make a left that leads to a massive doorway. The doorway has the same circle that was on the center of the gate. But there is no "D" on it this time; instead it's a vine with grapes. I assume it symbolizes their wine empire. Jumping out of the car, I go to grab my stuff from the back so we can make our way inside. Before I can even reach for my luggage, he stops me with his hand.

"There is no need for that. Umberto will grab them and take them up to our rooms."

"Umberto?" I question him.

"The butler, he's family."

"I'm rich, but not that rich."

"Europeans do it differently." He winks. Disgusting.

Stop lying to yourself. You got butterflies, pendeja.

Walking over to the door, he opens it swiftly, holding it out so I can walk through. Inside, I'm met with a grand entrance. It's not huge, but the room is shaped into a circle with a white table in the middle. On top is a statue of a woman with her head tilted to the side as she wraps her arms over her chest. It's not a full-body one, only from the middle of her stomach up, but you can tell it's good quality. The inside of the house is white marble, which contrasts with the classic Italian brick on the outside.

"Luca!" I hear a feminine voice shout in excitement from the doorway.

"Mamma," he responds.

An ultra-feminine, refined brunette woman walks through the door. Her hair is a mix of chocolatey brown and gray strands. She's on the older side, but not old enough to be his mom.

She looks clean. She could be a part of an anti-aging Neutrogena commercial.

"*Ragazzo mio come sei stato,*" she says, her whole body dripping in adoration.

"*Bene, solo lavoro,*" he responds with his usual stoic facade. This man can't even show his mother a little bit of affection.

Red flag.

Realizing there's someone else in the room, she looks over at me.

"Mamma, this is Alejandra," he introduces me. "She's a driver for the team."

"Hi. It's nice to meet you, your house is beautiful." I reach my hand out to shake, and she takes it.

"I have heard a lot about you, it's nice to put the name with a face." I smile at her accent which is thicker than Luca's. "I hear an accent, where are you from?" she asks softly.

"Mexico."

"Ah, the land of the cartel."

I stand there awkwardly.

Of course, she brings that up . . .

"Mama, she isn't in any way affiliated with the cartel."

GREAT. Kill me now.

I laugh, trying to soothe the tension. What a way to generalize a whole country, even though I am one of the few people you'll meet who is affiliated. But that doesn't mean Mexicans everywhere have anything to do with it.

"Most Mexicans aren't a part of the cartel, just like most Italians aren't a part of the mafia. Mexico is known for many things, even though most people think of drugs and organized crime first. That doesn't mean there aren't other things my country offers," I say calmly, so I don't sound rude or snappy.

"I like her," she says to her son before walking towards the rest of the house. He looks at me before following his mother. I trail after him.

Everything is nude all around me. They must like neutrals because that's all I see.

"I am sure Luca will give you a tour around. After all, he is the most informed about the history of the estate. I will see you both later for dinner." She gives us a short smile and walks away.

"Do you want the tour, or would you rather go up to your room and rest before a very long and dreadful dinner?"

"I think I'll have the tour. After all, you are the most informed."

"Be nice or I won't tell you about the most interesting parts."

I gasp, putting my hand over my heart. "That would be a crime."

"This house was built as the symbol of my family. It has been with us for generations. My great-grandparents didn't like the extravagant ambiance that was prevalent in Italian houses at the time. They wanted a modern approach for theirs." He walks through the living room and into the gardens.

"Even though things have been renovated, the estate has never lost what they truly saw in it. The view is what sold it for them."

We make our way past all the trees and make it to a gazebo featuring the same marble from the interior of the house. I stand there in awe. I can see the entirety of Florence from up here. The appeal is very apparent. His family has taste, I won't deny that.

"That Basilica you see up ahead is the trademark of Florence. Catedral de Santa María del Fiore was built by the Medici Family. We can go see it if you would like."

"I'd love to."

He nods at me.

"The gardens are simple, my *bisnonna* loved botany. Her husband would do anything for her, so, he made her the perfect garden"

The greenery is different from the garden we have in Sinaloa. Ours stretches over acres of land. This one has trees on both sides and a large flower shrine in the middle. Every flower and plant you could think of sits in buckets of soil.

"My family makes wine because of her. My great-grandfather started it all because she loved the outdoors so much that he wanted to dedicate his profession to something she loved. We have many wineries across Italy, each with a huge amount of property on top that doubles all the money we make. The family imports and exports all over the country as well as internationally."

I stop in front of the same statue that I saw in the entrance, but this time it's the full body version. I can feel him closing in behind me.

"I see you have taken a liking to the statue that defined my bisnonnis life. This is a custom statue of Aphrodite, the ancient Greek goddess of beauty. My great-grandfather would always call his wife 'goddess' because that's how he saw her. I've never heard of a love story where two people were so enamored with each other." He takes a strand of my hair and places it over my shoulder softly. This man really wants me to have a heart attack.

"That type of love is what I aspire to have some day," I say abruptly.

"That type of love is rare."

"But not impossible," I correct him.

We just stand there for a while, taking in the statue with a clear sense of tension between us. The hand that he touched my hair with is now lightly caressing my back and shoulders. I feel chills all throughout my body. He walks up close to my ear. I can feel his breath on my skin. I shiver.

"We should go inside," he mutters and walks away, too fast for my liking. I follow behind him leisurely as I take in the gardens.

He stands at the top of the steps that lead to the garden, waiting for me to catch up. Finally meeting him there, he looks up and I follow his gaze.

"There are seven bedrooms upstairs and one downstairs. That is my mother's room. You will be staying in the suite right next to me. Shall we go up?"

I nod as he leads me upstairs.

"Were your parents in love?" I ask. The question probably too personal. I immediately regret asking as soon as it comes out of my mouth. His head whips around, his eyes meeting mine. At first the gaze is hard, but then softens once he realizes that it's a genuine question. I mean, why wouldn't it be? I just heard a whole story about his grandpa dedicating his whole life to a woman. I want to know more.

"My father was very much in love with my mother. But my mother, not so much. It became apparent throughout their relationship that my mom was here for the benefits. But I don't exactly blame her; she came from a tough life."

We finally make it to the top of the steps, and he leads me to a small room. "This will be your room. I'm right next door if you need anything."

"Thank you."

DID I JUST SAY THANK YOU?

"You're welcome."

DID HE JUST SAY YOU'RE WELCOME?

What the fuck have we become?

CHAPTER
TWENTY-FOUR

MARIA ALEJANDRA

His brother's wife is indeed horrid.

Yesterday, I met his whole family for dinner around a spacious table made of birch. I had life-changing pasta as well as some soul-shattering wine. The only thing I heard the whole time from his brother's wife was how much she hated Bernardo. If you hate him so much, why are you with him?

Her excuse was that she has children with him, but what I concluded is that she wants his money. I don't like coming to bad conclusions about women. I've advocated my whole life that women should support women, but Emma is the epitome of all that is annoying in the world. She just wouldn't quit yapping.

She was also hitting on Luca the whole time. I was bothered by that, not because I'm jealous, but because she's married to his brother!

To be honest, I really enjoyed everyone else yesterday. Luca's family life is juicy, and it's cool to see him in a different dynamic apart from work. He's still an asshole, even to his family, but he does seem different. He's different around me too, which is weird.

Starting with the fact that he says "thank you". We also don't bicker as often. Don't get me wrong, we aren't in *The Matrix*. He and I still make snarky comments to each other, but it isn't the entirety of our conversations anymore.

Improvement, if I say so myself.

I'm back sitting in a car on my way to another part of Italy that I'm ecstatic to see. I ended up going around Florence alone because Mr. Donatello had some work to deal with. Something about improvements for the car, so I left him to go around and see the sights. Much to his distaste, as he said I would do it all wrong, so he made me an extensive list of the places to go and see.

It was great.

He would make a fantastic Italian travel agent. There were so many beautiful sights, and I even managed to take some photos while I was there.

I posted it on Instagram and Mr. Donatello was the first to hit like. He proceeded to text me constantly to ensure I was okay and yelled at me via text to follow his list. I rebelled a few times, but he doesn't need to know that.

Who would have guessed this would be happening? Absolutely no one. I kind of like it too. I'm betraying myself.

We are in Rome.

A city with history at every turn and the best gelato ever made.

As we pull into the main avenue which overlooks the Vatican, I look over at Mr. Donatello, who's still staring at his phone like he has been for basically the whole trip.

"You're missing it."

"Missing what, Ale?"

"The power of entering your capital city."

"I've seen it entirely too many times."

I rip his phone out of his hand and he immediately grabs my wrist while I'm attempting to throw it out the window beside me. I don't succeed as he tugs my wrist in his direction.

"For the rest of this trip, you're leaving your phone in the hotel," I tell him.

"That's impossible, and you know that." Luca says.

"It's not impossible, and you will listen to me." I yell at him.

"You think this is funny, little girl? You will give me my phone back now!"

"Nope." I tell him.

"Don't play with me, *ragazza*." He growls out.

"I thought you were smarter than that, Mr. Donatello. Our whole relationship is a game. We just don't know who's going to win it yet." I tell him.

"We both know it's me." He teases.

"Eh. Wrong."

"You're exhausting." He replies.

"You're the one who dragged me here. I could be spending an awesome time with Giovanni, who wouldn't be looking down at his phone the whole ti—"

Cutting me off, he slams his lips on mine. Shoving me into the door while pinning me down. The kiss is cutting off my oxygen supply. I can't breathe.

Pulling back, Mr. Donatello has his phone in hand.

That son of a bitch.

"You play dirty," I snarl.

"Like you said, this is a game."

"Not a game where you break the rules deliberately," I point out.

"I will kiss you whenever I want."

"Yeah, you just so happened to kiss me to get your phone back." I hold my middle finger up to provoke him.

"No, I just wanted to shut you up."

"You're such a gentleman," I say sarcastically, before he goes back to typing.

Leaving the hotel, I walk out before Mr. Donatello can tell that I'm gone. He wants to play dirty? Fine, then bring it on, bitch. Taking out my phone, I set up my maps app so that I can get something to eat before I sightsee.

I'm starving.

Thinking about what I'm in the mood for, I let my phone direct me to a pizza place that's five blocks away from where I'm at.

Pressing start, I walk and walk until my legs can barely move anymore. Reaching the pizza place, I stride in and kindly ask for a seat. They lead me to a table for two, but I won't be needing the other seat. I laugh demonically inside.

The waitress swiftly hands me the menu. Looking down at the array of options, I order a simple pizza. The difference between Italy and different countries is that their crust isn't thick like many others. It's thin and baked to crispy perfection.

The way it should be.

What a shame that Mr. Donatello isn't here to lecture me on the history of how the pizza was created.

The waitress sets down my food as my phone buzzes on the table, moving slightly.

1 Message from The Devil's Spawn

Groaning, I decide to open it.

The Devil's Spawn: Where the fuck are you?

I decide to leave him on read and take a bite out of my pizza, moaning in delight.

There's nothing like pizza in Rome, everywhere else in the world is doing it wrong.

My phone dings again.

The Devil's Spawn: Ragazza. If you don't tell me where you are, I will find you and throw you over my shoulder in front of all of Rome.

I leave him on read again. Suck it, asshole. I hear another ding five seconds later.

Clingy much?

The Devil's Spawn: So be it. Have it your way.

Yeah right. There's no way he's going to find me. He should just accept his fate.

Going back to eating my pizza, I enjoy every bite of it and I people watch while eating. I like to take in my surroundings as much as possible. I hear a ring come from the door, and see a fuming Mr. Donatello walk in. I jolt in shock. Not even looking around, he beelines straight for my table.

Leaning back against my chair, I press my whole body into it hoping that it consumes me. Yanking my wrists, he pulls me towards him, and his chest collides with mine.

"What did I say?" he growls.

"I don't know, what did you say again?" I try to seem clueless.

"Have you checked your phone?"

"Oh, you mean the texts. I don't think that's considered words coming out of—" I squeal as Mr. Donatello throws me over his shoulders. "What the fuck are you doing?"

"Staying true to my word." Keeping one arm wrapped around my body, he reaches his other arm into his pocket. He yanks it out with one arm while his other is still wrapped around my thighs. He pulls out about twenty-five euros and throws them on the table. Shoving the wallet back into his pocket, he walks out while I'm hanging over his shoulder. I start hitting his back with my arms.

I'm not six, but I want off.

"Why are you such an asshole?"

"That's a good question." He sighs as we walk down a few blocks before he stops abruptly. I snap my head up, wondering why he stopped and then see the Vatican within eyesight.

"Are you going to let me down now?" I growl.

"Nope."

"I swear to God, Luca, if you don't put me down, I will figure out how to put a curse on you."

"In your dreams, *ragazza*."

"That's what you say now, but once you see a dead crow on your doorstep, you'll think differently." He pulls me off his shoulder and drops me down onto my feet. I wipe down my clothes and look up at him with a scowl.

"I stay true to my word. You'd do well to learn that now."

I look at him for a second. Just because he goes by his word does not mean that he has to throw me over his shoulder like I'm a child. I could obviously jump off, but today was not the day to break my skull open. I stare at the Vatican's exterior in fascination. It's definitely a wonder, but I'm curious about what it's like on the inside. When I came to Rome last time, I didn't get to see the interior. I've always wanted to go in but haven't gotten the chance.

"Are you ready to go in, *ragazza*?"

"Oh, so we *are* going in?"

He walks way too fast for my liking, and I run to catch up. Making our way to the entrance on the other side of the cathedral, where we wait in line to enter.

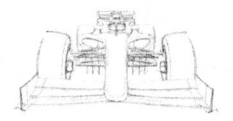

We had to go through fucking immigration. I am well versed in history, but why is the Vatican its own country?

Someone, please explain.

I get it, it's holy land. But if it really was such a sacred place, then why let tourists in?

The Catholic Church is already loaded as it is. They have thousands of paintings that all cost millions, and here I am paying twenty euros just to go through the museum.

Make it make sense.

While my family is Catholic, I happen to be one of the odd people out, as is my brother. I still prefer to believe in a higher power, but am unsure whether that is god or karma. My brother has said that he still believes in Aztec mythology. Sometimes I question if he really does believe. I mean, they're known for giving sacrifices to their Gods, so each God is at peace with their people. My brother does make sacrifices, *that I am certain of.* That's his job anyway. Whatever keeps him going I'm fine with, but it is mythology for a reason.

Making our way through the Basilica, Mr. Donatello is at

my side. The whole ambiance is mesmerizing. One thing I'll say about the Vatican is that it's breathtakingly creepy. I don't know what it is, but there's an ominous feeling in the building. The architecture for its period is impressive, and the vast art collection gives it an appealing gleam, but I don't vibe with the aura.

We keep walking through the huge space, finally meeting the altar. I admire the work. It's truly beautiful here. Chilling in a way, but that is the essence of its beauty. Sometimes, the ugliest things are the most appealing.

"It's stunning. That I won't argue with."

He's standing right next to me, our shoulders almost touching. I can feel his hand brushing against mine. I breathe in and out as our knuckles brush each other's.

Alejandra breathe, it's not like he's going to hold your hand.

"It is," he agrees.

We stand there in comfortable silence, our hands barely touching. I reach my fingers out slightly as I turn my hand around, so my palm is facing the top of his. He reaches out slowly, the pads of our fingers colliding.

Breathe.

He lingers there for a second, both of us still facing the altar. Then grabs my hand, intertwining our fingers. I can hear his breathing falter as our hands stay molded together.

Looking up, I admire the sun beam that shines on the wood engravings. I turn my head to the right of the altar, *NC VNA FIDES* engraved in the marble.

"It means 'to be rather than to seem in faith'."

I nod and hum, and he goes on, "Living in faithfulness is stronger than to pretend to do so."

He unlatches his hand slowly from mine. That alone snaps me out of my haze, and my brain recovers from that experience. Don't tell me he speaks Latin. That's so not safe for anyone.

Personal Reminder: never call him a grosseria in Spanish.

"Ready for your next exceptional Italian experience?"

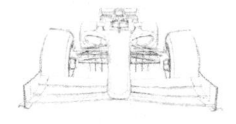

It's not an exceptional Italian experience. Dying of heat stroke is a more apt description. I can still hear Luca's voice in the back of my head saying, "Here's something that you must know a lot about" as he gestured to the Spanish steps.

Este cabrón.

Who knew that walking up a few steps would become a marathon? I swear I have been pooped on by a pigeon, shoved like the world was ending, and have been in the background of every tourist's photo. I'm almost at the top and I let him know that I'll strangle him when I get to the last step.

He's skipping steps like he's climbing Mount Everest at this point, while I trail behind him, dying of heat and dehydration.

Two more steps. One more step.

I swear, there better be an utterly breath-taking view at the top of this death trap, or else. We finally reach the top, and I turn around.

Nope.

I face him with a deadly look that radiates my urge to murder him.

"What, *ragazza*? You don't like it?"

"Are you fucking serious? You just made me climb stairs designed for giant-footed people, just for this to be the result?!" I wave at the view manically.

"It's a staple here."

I snort at that.

"Well, it shouldn't be."

"It represents the close relationship between the eternal city and the sacred part of Rome. It's the widest staircase in Europe. Impressive, isn't it?"

"Nope."

"I quite like them." He smirks at me like he's planning my demise in the process.

He almost succeeded.

"I swear to all things holy that when you go to Mexico, I will drag you up Teotihuacan and you will climb up every small-footed person's step there is."

"Is that a promise?" His eyebrow quirks. I hate his look of success. So, I examine my surroundings, trying to find a bottle of water in my vicinity. Of course, there is none.

I sigh in defeat.

This will never happen again.

I start walking down the steps not even acknowledging his presence. I feel like I'm running to find some water.

"Admitting defeat, are you, Ale?"

I turn around slowly and spit out, "Never."

CHAPTER TWENTY-FIVE
LUCA DONATELLO.

One thing that I've realized while in this woman's presence is that I can tolerate her existence. It was just days ago when the mere thought of her made me want to clench my hands into fists and force her into listening to me for once.

But I quite like her fight, it's thrilling to finally find someone who can match me. It's an interesting turn of events.

"Can you bring me a glass of *Cannonau di Sardegna, por favore?*" she says in Italian with a slight accent.

The waiter nods and looks at me, "What about you, sir?"

"*Niente per me.*" I give him a slight shoo-off wave before he nods and then walks away in *una fretta*.

"Why do you never drink?" I hear. Randomly said by none other than the woman herself.

"Because it was my vice once."

"You know, that's a very vague answer. You don't have to open up if you don't want to. I'm just curious." She shrugs, and I sigh.

"When I was very young, wine was influential in my family's dynamic. It is the family business, so to speak. Since then, I've seen it as an important part of my life. When I started driving, a lot of new things were introduced to me. But one of those things was one that I was familiar with. Alcohol. It started off as a crutch to stay away from all the drugs. I always thought of them as something that you could never run away from, but little did I know that I was holding something just as potent. I started drinking when I was worried, mad, sad, happy, and every emotion you could fathom. It was a while before I realized I had a problem. My first sip was when I was twelve and my last when I was thirty." She nods.

"If it helps, alcohol and I have never mixed well."

I chuckle. "Trust me, I know," I respond.

"Oh god, please don't tell me you know about the Monaco incident."

"I'm your boss. I know everything. Plus the person's yacht you were on happens to be a close friend."

She throws her hands up in the air, and covers her face in embarrassment. "That makes it even worse," she utters from beneath her palms.

"Don't worry, he thought it was funny."

"Thank god that didn't go completely public. I can thank my publicists for that."

Little does she know that all of F1 knows about it, but that's a conversation for another day.

The waiter brings the wine over and she takes a sip, moaning in the process. My dick twitches a little, I won't lie. This whole trip has made me question my relationship with Ale. I don't do relationships anymore, but she makes me think a little differently.

I've noticed that I don't like her talking about other men, let alone touching them. When she mentioned Giovanni at Monza, I kept my anger in. I don't know this guy, but him showing her around my country was a no for me on all accounts.

When I was with Adèle, I didn't feel a smidge of jealousy, but that definitely backfired in the long run. With Ale, it seems to be running through my veins. The only guy I don't care about her spending time with is Xavier. He is way too friendly to make her think of him as anything other than a friend. She's too hot-headed for him. But now, even her smile makes my dick react, and her defiance gives me blue balls. She's becoming an integral part of my life, and I don't hate it.

"Why is the wine so much better here? It's a crime."

"It's not, we basically invented wine," I respond.

"I doubt that."

"The Armenians actually did. But the Greeks claim they did. Apparently, they believe it was created by Dionysus, the god of wine, which we both know isn't true," I elaborate.

"I like to think that the Greek gods existed, but everything says otherwise." She takes another sip of her wine. Her top lip is completely drenched in the liquid. It makes me want to go up and lick it off. I couldn't care less about my sobriety at the moment. She's my new booze. I hold myself back, staying away from the forbidden fruit, figuratively and literally. She goes on.

"Imagine that the gods were so scandalous, it would make everything better. It would be like a telenovela in the sky." The only thing I admire the Greeks for is that they made their gods so much like them. Scandalous, sex-driven, and vengeful.

"If you could be any Greek god, who would you be?" she asks.

"Zeus."

"Basic answer," she deadpans.

"How so?"

"He's the god of thunder and the ruler of everyone. It shows that you like being in control of everything and everyone."

"You're right. But I could never control you, even if I was Zeus."

"Finally, something worth hearing comes out of your mouth." She laughs.

"What about you?" I question.

"This is obvious. Athena. I know it's my middle name, but I think it fits, being the goddess of war and all."

"I see you more as an Aphrodite. I didn't know your middle name was Athena," I say.

"And here I thought you knew everything about me. My dad liked to give his children middle names that have to do with mythology. He gave my brother, Mictlantecuhtli and me, Athena. I think he did well as they represent who we are in a way." I've heard of parents naming all their children with the same letter, but never a specific middle name.

"I think it's an interesting take on someone's name."

She nods in agreement. "All I know is if I ever have children, I would never give my child a name they would have to live through high school with. I was homeschooled, but if my child was going to live a normal life, which I would hope for, I have seen high school TV shows and I will not stand for any bullying."

"I've never understood the thought of naming a kid a repulsive name. I've heard some pretty stupid ones before." She laughs as the streetlight shines above her.

"I'll see you tomorrow, then."

"Today was bearable," I responded abruptly.

"What a random compliment." She snorts, and I look at her as she gazes down at her shoes, snapping out of her thoughts. She takes out her key card from her pocket, and slips it into the reader. The light flashes green and lets out a sound, confirming the card's authenticity. Twisting the doorknob, she opens the door and walks in. It's like the whole thing goes in slow motion as I see the door almost close. I know what I'm about to do and I won't regret it a single bit.

I push the door open, and it swings, banging against the wall. The sound makes Ale flinch, turning around in shock. Giving me a stare that is surprised and dumbfounded at the same time. She's standing at the foot of the bed.

"What are you doin—" I push her onto the mattress.

"Che Dio mi aiuti, quando sono con te."

"English, please," she says. I chuckle.

"I can assure you, *raggazza*. There will be no words coming out of your mouth, only screams. Those can be in whatever language you like. Preferably using your tongue."

She tries to stand up only to be pushed back up against the mattress, this time with my hands around her wrists.

"Are you trying to run your mouth again, little girl? Why don't we see how it works up and down my cock?" I press my nose into her neck. She gasps, her back arching.

"I don't think my words will be as filthy as the words that come out of that mouth." Her face is close to mine, she runs her finger on my lips.

"Hm. My mouth can do even dirtier things to that cunt of yours." I shove my hand into her pants, and my fingertips meet lace. *Fuck.*

"Did you wear these for me, *ragazza*? Do you like the thought of your much older boss grabbing this tight wet pussy?" I move my finger inside of her underwear, slipping a finger in. Making it to her opening, I can feel the outline of her cunt. She's dripping.

"Don't flatter yourself."

"Too late for that. Your juices are spreading all over my fingers. Your body is so responsive, yet that mouth is the exact opposite."

"I believe that's called hating someone."

"You don't hate me. Just like I don't hate you," I whisper

"So now you know what I'm thinking?" She bites her lip as my finger continues to slowly caress the inseam of her opening.

"I know why you do things. I also know why you don't want to be so responsive to me."

She moans out. "My body betrays my mind."

"That I'm grateful for, but that mouth still needs work." Removing my hand from her cunt I hear her whine.

"What's wrong, baby? Are you whining like the little brat you are?"

"You're such a tease." Grabbing my hand, she attempts to shove my hand back down to her panties again.

"Such a needy little girl, yet so spoiled. You should learn how to earn the satisfaction of a man's dick." I push off the bed and look down at her. "Take them off," I say, gesturing to my pants.

She looks at me like the nymph she is. She stands up and reaches for my belt. Circling the metal, she finally undoes the clasp, pulling the leather out of the belt loops. She goes to my zipper, getting hold of the slider. Looking up at me while she pulls it down, slowly licking her plump, red lips. That plump little opening will soon be corrupted by the presence of my dick. Reaching to the waist of my slacks, she shoves them down and is met with my briefs.

I grab her chin, forcing her eyes to meet mine.

"Are you going to be a good girl?" I raise an eyebrow.

"Yes."

"I don't buy it."

"I could just bite your dick off." She smiles. How very funny of her.

"I never took you for the blood play type, *ragazza*." A horrified look spreads across her face. *That's what I thought.* I take off my boxers and push her down so she's kneeling in front of me.

"Look at you, worshiping and praying up to me. Who knew that I'd have the power of making you my needy little whore."

"What an egotistical statement." She squirms. She can say anything she wants, but I know it turns her on.

"What did I say about that mouth?" I ask her.

"I could say the same about yours."

"Spit." I point at my erection standing up right in front of her. She does as I ask with a look of defiance on her face.

"Now suck." Grabbing my shaft, she starts with an up and down motion. I breathe in, it feels almost as good as her tight little pussy. Bringing her mouth towards my erection, she licks the tip slowly.

"Defiant as always." Shoving my cock in her mouth, I take a deep breath as it hits the back of her throat. Her eyes start watering while she looks up at me. I grab her hair, keeping her mouth milking my cock.

Seeing a single tear trail down her face, I smirk. Letting go of her hair, I brush the tear off her cheek and take the salty drop into my mouth. "Look at you, sacrificing tears to your new God. How does that make your defiance feel, baby?" She doesn't stop or even flinch. She continues licking and sucking my dick like it's a damn popsicle. I know I'm close. This woman is a pro at giving head. I feel her saliva and tongue collide while creating a beautiful mess around her lips that I can't wait to mark with my cum. In that instant, I release into her mouth. I pull my cock back and rub the rest of what's left on my tip all over her lips.

She swallows every last drop, licking her lips of the rest. Standing up in front of me, she stares at me with a look of distaste.

"Now, what am I supposed to do with that look of yours? Haven't you learned your lesson, *ragazza*?"

She just smiles at me mockingly. "No, you are *The* Luca Donatello. You have millions of women lined up and ripe for the taking. I'm not going to be just one of the ones you throw off to the side." I just look at her and tilt my head in interest.

"Is that jealousy, *raggazza*?"

"In your dreams, Donatello." She looks away and out the

window where the Colosseum can be seen. I take a hold of her chin and force our glares to meet again.

"You, of all people, know I'm selective. I haven't slept with another woman for months, only you."

Her eyes soften as she slams her lips on mine. I shove her pants down. I'm met with the lace panties I felt against my fingertips just earlier. Helping her slip out of her shirt, I see her bra. Her tits are almost completely bare, and the fabric does nothing to cover them. Her nipples peek out, and I feel myself getting hard again. She gapes at me while I admire her.

"*Fottutamente squisito,*" I sigh and grab her by her hips, bringing her towards me.

Ripping the bra and undergarments off, I'm met with her naked body. She's fucking molded for me at this point. I've never found anyone as attractive as this woman. Laying her down on the bed, I kiss her softly before I enter her abruptly. Her head leans back in bliss.

"You like that don't you, *raggazza*?"

She moans as I enter her opening. "*Verga,*" she shouts, and I keep going slowly, making sure to reach every part inside her. Everything is so slick and messy. I'm bare inside of her. I know she's on birth control because of her medical records that I read when she first came to the team. I wasn't looking for it per say, but I happened to stumble upon it. I mean, I can't let a drug addict on the team. If she would have told me to use a condom, I would do it without a thought.

The rhythm becomes deeper and deeper as time passes. Her moaning fills the room as the bed moves back and forth slowly. I love being buried in her. The first time this happened, it wasn't planned; that's what made it hotter. As time went on, I couldn't help but find her attractive all the same. My fantasies would run wild with thoughts of fucking her in a bed or even on top of an F1 car. To be fair, it was always one of my goals, but she's an F1 driver, and that made me even hornier. It happened to come to fruition, and now I can say that I fucked this girl on top of my life's work.

But the months of wanting to have sex with her is in the past as my cock slides in and out of her. This is way better than my dreams.

She clenches and I groan out. Fuck. This is way too good.

"Do you love clenching around my cock, little girl?"

"Yes," she whispers. Her face tells me she's close, so I pick up the speed. The echo of our skin slapping together sounds like Beethoven playing Piano Sonata No.14.

We work swiftly in harmony as our bodies collide in song, and she comes all around me. She grabs a pillow from behind her, muffling her screams.

I rip the pillow out of her hand and keep going until I come undone. I groan one last time forcefully, letting my cum drip inside and outside her cunt. As always, it looks fucking delectable, almost as much as her.

I drop down beside her, and our heavy breaths start to die down.

"You will never do that again," I say menacingly. She looks over at me, disappointed.

"What do you mean?" she mutters out, still breathing heavily.

"I don't ever want to see you muffle your screams; I love hearing your ecstasy."

She smiles. "You like screamers, do you?"

"Not really, but I like to hear them when they come out of your mouth." I drag my finger across her lips.

"Well, you're going to be hearing more of them. You still owe me one more orgasm after what you made me do earlier."

I laugh out loud, she turns to look at me horrified and jumps up, leaving an array of pillows falling behind her.

"Did you just laugh?" She looks at me in bewilderment.

"It's a normal human reaction to something humorous."

"You're also smiling. To the person who put me in this simulation, you can take me out now, I know your plans," she screams at the ceiling, and I smile up at her.

"How is this shocking to you?"

"I swear to god if you smile at me again, I will literally think I'm in *The Truman Show*."

"Sorry, baby, but I'm all real."

"Way to ruin the mood with your arrogance." She throws a pillow at my face. "You were doing so well," she grunts.

"I would think me being real is something that you would appreciate." I push her down and place my arms at her sides so that I'm hovering over her. I start kissing down her body as she submits to my touch.

"What is this?" I see her looking down at me with a serious face, wanting me to clarify the situation we're in. Well, we just did some filthy things to each other in a hotel room in Rome. The bed is a mess, and there are pillows on the ground at our side.

"Whatever we want it to be." Then I kiss her, making sure that this feeling never ends.

CHAPTER
TWENTY-SIX
MARIA ALEJANDRA

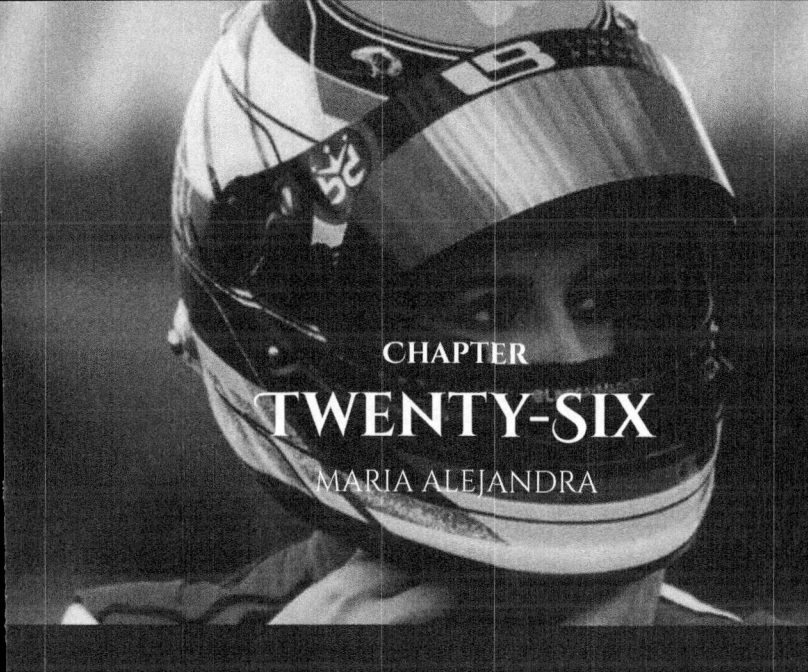

"Well, that's a wrap for today's race! The next time you'll see us is at the Mexican Grand Prix." I hear in my headphones as I set my phone down on the table in front of me. I'm in my apartment in Mexico City. Everyone has two weeks off from racing again. But this time, I was able to come home to my sweet little Mexican apartment. Sometimes, I forget how much I love it here, in my own space. Because I travel, almost always due to my job, I forget about every little detail I put into my home.

Home.

That's such a warm word, and sometimes I don't feel like I have one until I come back. For most of my life, I was stuck in a house that I thought I loved, when in reality, it's the place where all my trauma stems from. I haven't been back in years. I only see my family in another atmosphere because I don't want the resentment I hold towards my father to come up out of nowhere.

The mere thought of going back makes me hyperventilate.

After what happened in Rome, Luca and I are on good terms. We've pretty much fucked in every space possible, inside the paddock and our hotel rooms. It's pointless now to be in separate hotel rooms; I either stay in his or he stays in mine.

We talk a ton, which is weird because just a few weeks ago, I hated his delectable ass. He laughs more and smiles occasionally, but he's still the same asshole I used to hate. The only difference now is that I get to fuck him on the side while he tells me his likes and dislikes, which he has a lot of. When we're in public, there are occasional glances, but he keeps a straight face. We still argue almost all the time, but that's okay. I know we both like it just as much as we like to have casual sex.

It's not like we're together or anything. I don't have feelings for him, and he doesn't have any for me, and that's okay.

But I'm starting to like him a little bit.

What monster have I become?

He is very sophisticated. Apart from his bad boy—more like edgy— man exterior, all his interests are so fancy. He only listens to classical music—mostly Beethoven—and it's been established that he has a thing for art history.

He's knowledgeable in most things, which can be incredibly frustrating. I talk about something, and he'll always correct me. Can he let me be dumb for once? I personally think it's the Italian in him, but I would never say that to his smug face. He's lucky to be well-endowed and somewhat fascinating.

After our race in Texas, we went our separate ways. Because of a delay, the Mexican Grand Prix was held back a week. It turned our break of a few days became two whole weeks. The weird part is that all the other locations had already set back their schedules for a week or two before it was announced. I don't really think much of it. After all, it means rest and more sleep. I still wake up every morning to get my workout in with my trainer, mostly resistance exercises to keep me lean. I love boxing. It helps release all the tension and shit on my mind. When I used to hate Luca, I happened to work out more than twice a day with a punching bag. I imagined it was him and it was thrilling.

Now, he has to be all bearable and everything and also have a magical dick and tongue. *Which helps.*

Looking at my outline in the full-body mirror ahead, I decide that I love the outfit I'm wearing. I put on a breezy tulle dress with some silver jewelry and combat boots. I like it. It's girlier than usual.

Today, I have plans to meet my best friend, Violetta, in El Zocalo. It's the huge cathedral that sits in the middle of everything. It's basically the center of Mexico City. The square is buzzing with noise and life.

I've always loved it there, and so does Violetta. I met her when I went to Acapulco for a tennis tournament she was playing in. She and I got along really well, and now we're basically inseparable. Being a star-studded player, it helps that she travels for work almost as much as I do.

She is probably one of the best professional tennis players right now. Wimbledon is on her list of things to do this year, as it should be. She really is an incredible player. It's cool having a best friend with a drive like mine, even though she is a little different. Being the observant person she is, her soft-spoken personality can come off as shy, but really, she just likes to observe a person before she converses with them, and that's where we're opposites. I happen to say what's on my mind, but it's the perfect balance.Mexican professional female athlete besties.

Walking out of my room, I pace down a couple of stairs, and reach for my keys. I press the elevator and wait for it to arrive.

VIOLETTA: *Estoy arriba. Nos conseguí una mesa antes de que otro turista pudiera hacerlo.*

ME: *Ok. Estoy Subiendo.*

Turning my phone off, I put it in my purse and look up at El Palacio de Bellas Artes. It's still one of my favorite things to look at in el centro de la ciudad. The orange, yellow, and black ombre basilica at the top makes it such a wonder. It feels so grand, like something you would see in France, which would make sense since it obviously has some European inspiration due to the Spanish colonization in the fifteenth century.

I turn away, walking to the Sears in the front of the palace. Walking in, I make it to the elevator that takes me to the terrace above. The café overlooks Bellas Artes. Violetta and I found it on YouTube when we were sixteen. Taking on our dreams, training every day, and coming here afterwards for coffee.

I make it to the designated floor and see her blonde locks swing over her shoulder when she turns around to look at me. Her distinct style contrasts with mine. She loves color. Pastels and muted colorful tones. She has an eclectic style, which I can assume takes some criticism from her two fashionable twin sisters, Cleo and Chanel.

I squeal as we hug.

"¡Siento que no te he visto en mucho tiempo!"

"Bueno, es porque no nos hemos visto," she responds, our conversation continues in Spanish.

"True, but we do text every day." I point at her and she smiles.

"That we do." She reaches for a sugar packet in the middle of the table, pouring it into her coffee mug and swirls it around with one of those little wooden sticks. The waiter comes over to greet me, asking for my order.

"A black coffee please." He nods, going over to the barista area.

"You and your tasteless concoction." Her face turns into one of disgust.

"What? At least I don't do drugs."

"That I'm grateful for because you would be abusing the shit out of it."

I give her a judgmental look.

"So how have you been?" she questions while taking a sip of her coffee. I pause for a moment, not wanting to tell her about how I'm casually sleeping with my boss, who is also one of the world's most renowned veteran F1 drivers.

"Good, how about you?" I touch her hand, hoping it will make her take this conversation swiftly away from its focus on me.

"Good. I still have to deal with my younger sisters coming to my apartment every day. Even though I moved out just to get away from both of them."

I laugh. "I remember the days when you thought that they were going to burn your closet down." I point out as she groans.

"Now that they can drive and know where my spare key is, I still have to worry about it to this day."

The waiter comes over with my coffee, setting it down in front of me. I nod and say a quick thank you.

"I can't imagine those two driving."

"You don't even want to know. When they're both in one car, they're lethal. One has severe road rage and the other blasts the music at full volume."

I laugh, trying to imagine the twins in a car. "I can't

believe how big they're getting. I remember the days when we were eighteen and they were freshly fourteen. I saw Cleo's Instagram a few days ago, and she's getting really good."

She nods. "Her and the MUA influencer dream, her looks and style keep getting shinier by the day. I swear she's like a shedding cat but instead of hair it's glitter."

I chuckle. "I bet Chanel hates that." I take another sip of my coffee.

"Oh, she does. I hear her tell Cleo constantly that she's tacky, you know her, and the *haute le mode*. She actually saw your collaboration with Adèle and freaked out. You know that her dream is to work as a designer there."

I nod. "I thought of her when I was in the atelier. It totally fits her vibe and everything. Hyper feminine and such."

"Yep. Chanel may not have said nice things about the collection, but she did say you looked great. You know her and the color black don't match. I swear, the only thing those two have in common is their taste in men. Unattainable and much older."

I still.

"How so?" I question, interested.

"You know girls and their crushes. Cleo is obsessed with this painter, Exodus Wolf. He's a judge on her favorite British makeup reality TV show. And naturally, Chanel is obsessed with Antoine Manon, the prestigious heir to the Adèle fashion house. Both are twelve years older. Sometimes

I don't understand how we are blood related. I mean, I got sports, and they got glamor. I still love the two heathens though." She shrugs.

"At least we have one thing in common," I mutter under my breath, hoping Vio won't catch it.

"What do you mean by having one thing in common?" She looks at me with interest.

"Nothing." I try to guide the situation somewhere else.

"Ale. I'm your best friend. You know you can tell me anything and I'll take it to my grave." She reassures me but also seems offended that I haven't told her something. But this shit is a bomb the size of Jupiter, and I don't know how to say it without an over-the-top reaction. But knowing Violetta, she won't have any reaction and she might stay quiet for a second.

"I may be seeing someone way older than me."

"Who?" she asks in interest.

"Remember the person I used to text you about saying that I wanted to push him off of a building?"

She processes my words, eyes wide once the realization hits.

"No," she whispers.

"Maybe." I look at her observantly, waiting for her next reaction.

"But he's your boss, Ale."

"Yeah, I know, that makes it sound even worse than it is." I rub my forehead in discomfort.

"The man is eighteen years older, but at the same time, good for you I guess."

I look up at her in shock.

"I was not expecting you to be so open to it, Vio." I look at her with my mouth agape.

"It is kind of shocking, but when I think about it more, you've always liked people who challenge you. I've known since we were fourteen that you were going to end up with someone with balls as big as yours, figuratively and literally speaking."

"You're exaggerating." I roll my eyes.

"Your taste has always been very selective," she responds.

"Right, just like my first boyfriend who turned out to be a psychopath. Yeah, my taste is just great," I say sarcastically.

"You're right. I understand the swearing-off-of-all-blondes thing. He was horrible, but you've always liked a challenge. Believe it or not, your ex was more than a challenge, and you liked the thrill."

"Like you haven't been obsessed with my brother all your *pinche* life." I look at her with a smirk on my face, and she slaps me on the shoulder playfully.

"I don't like him anymore, especially with the whole I'm-the-devil-himself thing."

I knew Violetta was obsessed with my brother since we were young, always following him around. At the time, he wasn't who he is today, which happens to be a cold-blooded killer. As I've said before, I love him to death, but he has a lot of blood on his hands.

Before my father molded him into his heir, he was nice and funny. Exactly Violetta's type. Until he knew she was obsessed with him, and he told her right to her face that he was the devil incarnate. She says she's sworn him off since then, but I don't believe her. My brother is many things, and one of them is a charmer with the ladies.

She's known about my family since she was young. Her family is based in Mexico City, and they also have a house in Acapulco that my father took a liking to. He asked Violetta's father if he could use it a few times. He welcomed him with open arms, thinking he was the CEO everyone thinks him to be. Until he caught him smuggling drugs into a car. Weirdly enough, both of our dads are fucked up, so he didn't even flinch. Both families are old friends. At least her dad didn't kill his wife, that would be too perfect for the both of them.

"I prefer more of the golden retriever type now," she says, trying to convince me she's over my brother.

"I guess we just have very different opinions when it comes to men."

She laughs. "Have you told him about your family yet?"

I sigh. One more thing I have to think about. "About that. His whole family has a vendetta against organized crime, so nope, not going to do that ever."

"You're going to have to tell him eventually. He's your boyfriend."

I hear that word and cringe. "He's not my boyfriend."

"Okay," she says slowly.

"What?"

"You're talking about him like he's a big deal. He may have a magical dick, but if you keep having sex with him, you're going to have to address the word you hate so much."

"I don't hate it."

"You have commitment issues, Ale."

"I do not," I refute.

"Do too. Don't deny it, you're a Gemini, it's in your chart."

"Don't spew that zodiac crap to me."

"What's his sign?"

I look at her. "What the fuck is that supposed to do? Absolutely nothing."

"It's everything. Now tell me, what's his zodiac sign?"

"Leo," I whisper.

"You do like him!" she exclaims.

"Stop with that, Vio, I don't. I hated him a few weeks ago. He's just bearable now."

"You wouldn't have known his zodiac sign if you didn't like him," she points out and I cringe.

"I know what you're about to say, and I don't think I'm going to like it."

"The fact that you're a Gemini and he's a Leo says a lot, Ale. He's most likely feeling the same way you are. The only difference is, if you want to pull the man, you have to compliment him. It's the only way to his heart."

"He is an egotistical bastard, that's for sure." I inhale and exhale slowly, trying to understand all the words coming out of my best friend's mouth.

"You always tell me zodiacs are fake, but you just admitted defeat. I win!"

"You do not."

She just laughs as we keep sipping our coffee and carry on with our conversation. Far away from my problems.

Luca is in my apartment.

I repeat, Luca Donatello is standing in front of me. I just walked in to be met with a cool breeze and his heated stare. His posture is as straight as ever, clad in black sweatpants and a hoodie.

It's decided. I am going fucking crazy.

"What are you doing here?" I ask him in alarm.

"I got bored in Italy, so I came here," he says nonchalantly.

"How did you even know I was in Mexico?"

"You and your friend are all over Instagram." He hands me his phone; I scroll through the pictures of me and Violetta enjoying our coffees.

"Didn't realize I was famous now."

"Are you serious? You're the first female F1 driver. You don't think people will be taking photos of you everywhere? Get used to it, that's what comes with being on the grid."

"I guess it doesn't help that my best friend also happens to be a professional tennis player," I say indecisively. I've never had my picture taken while I was out. This is a weird feeling, and I don't know how to process it.

"Don't you find it a little intrusive to walk into a person's home without their prior knowledge?" I say to him.

"Whatever you say, baby," he sighs.

Did this man just call me baby outside of the bedroom? He really wants to get laid, doesn't he?

He grabs the remote to the TV beside me and turns it on. I look at him weirdly.

"Stop looking at me like that, *ragazza*. Now, what do you want to watch?" He scoots closer. Is this man being somewhat casual and romantic with me right now?

Where has the real Mr. Donatello gone? Because at this moment he's gone to outer space.

"What about *The House of Gucci*? I know you love that movie with your whole soul." I look at him knowingly, ready for his snarky remark. It never comes. He turns back to the TV and begins putting the title in the search bar.

"I was kidding. You don't have to go through two hours of pain for me." He just looks at me while pressing play, smirking once the white glow of the TV hits his features.

"I've never seen the movie. I only know the story. You've captured my interest with your remark." Of course, he's doing this as a reverse annoyance tactic.

Reaching the thirty-minute mark when Patrizia and Maurizio are happy, his family is brought into the picture again.

"She reminds me of my ex-wife." I jump. Is he really going to mention his past with me? I'm now thoroughly freaked out.

"What did you just say?" I need to clarify that I heard him right because at this point, my brain cells are less than zero.

"Patrizia reminds me of Adèle."

"Are you okay? I think you have the plague." I press my hand against his forehead, looking for any sign of a fever. He grabs my wrist and pulls it down.

"I'm being open about something for once, and this is how you react." He scoffs.

"Excuse me if you being the opposite of closed off for once is peculiar."

"You've never asked, so how am I supposed to tell you things you want to know about?"

This is really weird.

"Okay, so if you're so open, please go on about how your ex-wife has any relation to a psychopath?"

"Adèle isn't a psychopath. She's just overly spoiled."

"You call me spoiled all the time. What a great way to start."

"You're not spoiled in the way she is. The one time her father didn't give her what she wanted, she hurt people in the process, including me." He sighs and goes on. I listen carefully, interested.

"When I first met her, I was on a yacht having dinner with one of my investors. I remember seeing her for the first time. She was so proper and poised. I knew I needed to get to know her. We talked for hours, and I was immediately entranced by her. She didn't give much away, and yet, I felt like I knew her. Afterwards, I walked her back to her hotel in Monaco. I wanted to kiss her that night, but I knew she would refuse, so I didn't.

"I went on to race, never once forgetting our conversation. I won that year, and she came running up to me. At that moment, I knew that she was mine. But she was never mine to keep. Maybe in my heart, but not in hers. I was never in hers. I fell for her. Hard. One thing led to another, and I found myself asking her father for her hand. I was a stupid, love-sick boy back then, and all I wanted was her. Her father accepted, but one thing stood out to me when I was leaving. He said something very ominous. *I'm glad she moved on.* I stopped but didn't turn to ask him anything. I just stood there thinking, who had she moved on from? Why did he tell me this now?

"I walked out and didn't touch the subject. That is, until I walked in on her fucking another man who she claimed to be the love of her life."

I just sat there and looked at him with wide eyes. She cheated on him. Now that, I wasn't expecting.

"I was shocked," he continued. "The funny thing is, I

didn't cry. I just felt broken, I guess. I don't do well with emotion, and holy fuck did she take everything out of me. I told my mom I wanted to break off the engagement. She said no because they had ties to families that she wanted to know more about. You know, the ironic thing is my life has always been surrounded by organized crime. I've never hated anything more."

He could have left that detail out, it's almost like he knows . . .

"So, I married her until my mom had drained out every last drop of information she could get. The whole time we were married, I was miserable. Drinking like it was my lifeline. She always had him around, and by that point, I was friends with him. I know the whole situation is fucked." He sighs and looks at me, his hard exterior returning.

"Why didn't she just marry the guy she was in love with? It doesn't make sense," I ask him.

"Because of her dad. One thing about Adèle is that she needs her father's approval for everything. He coddled her as a child and still does, if you couldn't tell. But this is the one thing he refused to give her."

"Why did her father say no?"

"Because her and Crue fell in love when they were young."

I smack my hand over my mouth, interrupting his sentence. Holy. Fuck.

"The fucking photographer?"

He nods. "It's not his fault he fell for a rich socialite and his family were normal people. They met when he was taking photos around Paris on his little disposable camera. He saw her and was gobsmacked. She tends to have that effect on people."

"I still don't get it."

"Her father is a classist, Alejandra."

"Of course, he would be one of the only people I collaborate with," I whine, and he laughs.

"Yep."

"I need to pull out of that ambassador role immediately." I get up to grab my phone before he pulls me into him.

"You will not be doing that. Nobody knows this, but Antoine is taking over soon. Why do you think I was at the office when you were there? Adèle filed a lawsuit again so she could take some money out of me before her precious little daddy doesn't have the funds to support her lifestyle."

"Her dad is the founder. There's no way she isn't getting as much money as before." I look at him like he's dumb.

"Antoine hates his family."

"Wow. What a ball of fucked up family dynamics."

He laughs at my comment. "No wonder he was my favorite," he tells me.

"What about her being pregnant and everything?" I ask him.

"I see you've done your research. I knew she wasn't pregnant with my child, but I didn't say anything. I just made her take a paternity test."

"You could have exposed her. Why didn't you?"

"Because I knew what she was feeling wasn't completely

her fault. She loved someone she couldn't have and took it all out on our relationship. I was fine with that for a while, but there came a point where I was tired and ready to get out. I wanted her to be happy, even if it wasn't with me. But the only way that could happen is if I stayed and didn't say anything."

I feel a pang in my chest. What the fuck is this? I swear to God, if this is emotional jealousy I'm feeling right now, I can't bear the thought.

"Why are you telling me all this?"

"Because I don't do love, *ragazza,* and I don't want you to get hurt."

"Don't worry. You don't have to be concerned about that," I reassure him.

He smiles sadly.

Wrong idea acquired.

CHAPTER
TWENTY-SEVEN
MARIA ALEJANDRA

I wake up to a tongue in my lower region, and I moan.

Santo Dios, did I just wake up in heaven?

I grab onto a head of hair and look down at Mr. Donatello, looking up at me while underneath the covers. I feel his tongue brush my clit and suck it softly. That alone almost makes me come. He licks, sucks, and then spits. This is too much. My haze is being lifted and lifted until I reach a point at which I can't keep going any longer. I come. Hard. But I don't just come, I have an out of body experience. I also feel like I'm peeing. I stiffen and realize that I just squirted. I look down at him in horror, and he looks up at me in amusement.

"Did you just squirt?"

"You saw it for yourself, you tell me."

"You're really snarky for someone who just reached the stars and back." He quirks an eyebrow.

"I'm not going to say I didn't like it." I look up at the ceiling, wallowing in my embarrassment, until I feel him grab a hold of my chin, shoving it down to look at him.

"Never be embarrassed for how I make you feel." He crawls up just a little and kisses my lips harshly, pulling back. "How do you taste, *ragazza*?"

"I'd say it tastes like rebellion." I smirk at him and lift my eyebrows up and down at him. He smiles at me.

That will never get old.

"Now, that's cheesy."

Yeah, I kind of agree. Not my best line.

He plops beside me and sprawls out against the sheets. I nuzzle into my pillow, relaxing. It took me a while to go to sleep yesterday. All I could think about was what he said to me last night. Not the whole Adèle thing, even though I may be a little jealous that she is the only woman he's ever going to love.

Stop betraying yourself, Ale. There's a reason why you don't do relationships.

The thing that bothered me was that the only reason he opened up to me was to tell me he could never do this. I can understand why he is the way he is; I'm exactly the same. But it did hurt a little bit.

"What are you thinking about?" I see a disheveled Luca beside me, and it's beautiful. There's just something about a man with his guard down. Before I can respond, I hear a phone ring on Luca's side of the bed.

So, he has a side now...

I'm fucked. He holds it against his ear as he spits fluent Italian into the phone. I squirm. Something about this man speaking Italian gets me horny.

"*Suona bene, sarò lì il più presto possibile.*" He ends the call and looks at me.

"I have to go. That was my friend. He told me there are investors going to a gala tonight in Paris. I have to drain every ounce of funding out of them so that the designs for next year can be attainable."

I nod, understanding his need to leave.

Grabbing his bag, he starts packing everything. He grabs clothes from his suitcase, and walks into the bathroom, coming out a few seconds later looking fresh as ever.

Why is this man so attractive? It should be illegal.

He grabs my face and kisses me before he says goodbye. Before I hear the door close, I shout, "Text me when you land!" No response is to be heard, but I hear the sound of the door closing, signifying his absence.

This all feels so domestic.

Disgusting.

Laying back down on my pillow, I fall asleep with the tranquility of my inevitable fate. I like him, maybe too much for my liking, as well as his.

I wake up to the sound of my buzzing phone. Clutching my phone, I press accept, and hear Luca in my ear.

"I'm in Paris," he states bluntly.

"So, you did hear me before you left?" I bite my lip and smile.

"How could I not?"

"When did you land?"

"Two hours ago." I check the time and it's already 8 pm. I fell back asleep at 8 this morning. Fuck, he took everything out of me last night, didn't he? I want to say something, but I just stay silent. There are lines that are hard to cross with him. I'm tiptoeing around them because I don't want to become too much or too little. He sighs and responds with the same gesture. We sit on the phone in a comfortable silence.

"I miss you," I whisper, scared of what I'm saying to him.

"I miss you too." He exhales once the words come out of his mouth.

What have we become?

"I guess I'll see you later..." I respond.

"I'll be back in a few days, *ragazza*." The line cuts, and I immediately miss the days when we bickered for hours. It didn't make me overthink as much as I am right now. Of course, the day after he tells me he can't in any way love me, I catch feelings.

ME: *Estoy jodida.*

VIOLETTA: *No soy lectora de mentes, Ale.*

Groaning, I keep on typing my feelings out because I

would never tell Luca how I feel. This relationship is a product of predisposed failure. Everything is against us. From ourselves all the way to the fact that he would never approve of where I come from. He hates everything I was created in.

ME: *Al día siguiente que dice que no puede amar, me empieza a gustar.*

VIOLETTA: He's spewing bullshit. Everyone can love. It's a matter of whether they want to address their own feelings or not.

I leave her on read and look up at the ceiling, trying to process her words. I could try my best to change him, but I don't want to. I've achieved many things, and Mr. Donatello may be one of them. But I can only do so much.

I hear my phone ding beside me, I grab it and the notification reads that my favorite WAG F1 Instagram handle posted recently.

Before I started racing, I was always interested in the concept of driver's wives and girlfriends. Being a professional female athlete, I've always wanted someone to make a HAB account for female drivers. But I don't know if that'll ever happen.

Tapping on the notification, the face ID on my phone unlocks. I can't lie. I like to see new photos of my fellow drivers being carefree and in love. It makes up for my most evidently shitty love life.

The Instagram logo pops up, then redirects me to a picture of Luca and Adèle kissing. I think it's an old photo for a second, but then I see the exact same outfit he was wearing when he left.

Trying to keep my morale up, I look at the caption. The thing I like about this page in particular is that they give exact dates to when every picture was taken.

F1WAGS4LIFE: *10/26/22 Luca Donatello and his ex-wife, the infamous Adèle Manon, seen kissing outside of her father's atelier today in the city of love. The big question here: is the divorced couple back together?*

I don't react, don't even break a sweat. I may be infuriated on the inside, but I don't like to react to a man's faults. I've experienced many of those in my life. This wouldn't make him special in any way.

I grab my laptop from my side table and rip it open. Furious typing can be heard echoing around me as I book a flight to Paris. After buying a hotel room for two nights, I get up and grab my suitcase. Making a few calls, I zip my suitcase closed and walk out of my apartment, making my way to the airport.

I'm about to make a bitch remember what he lost.

CHAPTER
TWENTY-EIGHT
MARIA ALEJANDRA.

"It looks amazing, Ale!" Madeline, my hair stylist, says while shrieking at the same time. I look at my new, just-above-the-shoulder length hair. It's as straight as uncooked spaghetti and I like this new look. After calling my hair, makeup artist, and styling team, they all flew in with me for the gala.

His gala that he so needed to attend, where he just happened to trip into kissing his ex. I'm going for something completely different than usual. You can call it a mental breakdown. I call it making a man drop to his knees in front of me. My vibe won't change after this, but I need to feel fresh to shed him off my skin.

"I like it. It's giving *kneel before me* vibes." My stylist says. I stare at myself in the mirror knowingly. While I love it, I kind of miss my curls. But I know they'll come back with time. Hair grows back, but embarrassment never washes away.

I'm not mad about the fact that he kissed her, it gave me a reality check of sorts. I'm pissed that he was playing me the whole time.

This makeup look is so weird on me, but it will match the dress that I picked specifically for this. It was inspired by the women he kissed on the streets of Paris, hand-picked from her daddy's couture collection.

I'm going from my usual matte makeup to a glowy look. The base is wet in a way and my eyeshadow is a gold shimmer surrounding my eyelids. I kept my lashes natural with a little bit of lift by adding single extensions. My nude lip remains with a shimmer gloss over the top.

"The dress just got here," Giselle says behind me. Being my stylist and all, she blew this last minute "project" out of her ass.

I see the gold dress in front of me in all its glory. What a perfect name for such a special occasion.

Dropping my robe to the ground, I slide in, and it's a perfect fit. Zipping it up, I see the metallic gold material draped over the naked parts of my skin. I look at myself and see someone different. I recognize a fighter in my reflection. Ready to lure him in and kill him silently. I should have protected my heart from all of this. This dress pays homage to who I am and who I was before him. A fucking queen.

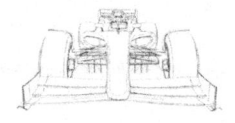

"You, of all people, know that this has to be perfectly timed out," I say a little too aggressively to my publicist, Lauren.

"Ale, I know. But we've been sitting here for thirty minutes and the event coordinators are calling for you to get out of the car." I sigh in defeat and jump out of the seat from the side where no one can see me walk onto the concrete sidewalk. Just as my feet hit the floor, I hear shouting.

"Luca, look over here!"

I turn my head to Lauren, and she gives me a knowing look in return. When I told her I needed to get an invite for this gala, she was all for it.

I don't make a lot of public appearances, only because I get busy or occupied by the hecticness that is the Elektra calendar. Now that I have a little bit of time off, my vendetta is welcomed with open arms.

The idea to fly to Paris and attend the gala without Luca knowing about it was a hard task to take on. Usually, when you attend a gala of this magnitude, they like to announce who will be attending on a list. This helps people like Luca find investors they might think are interested. But somehow, with the magic that is Lauren, we got it done. She can be very persuasive when she wants something.

One of the instrumental parts of this scheme is to make

sure that Luca goes in first so that I can walk up behind him, smacking him in the face with my presence. It's working so far, aside from roadblocks happening at every turn, but it's nothing I can't handle.

Crossing the street, all the photographers turn their attention from Mr. Donatello to me. They start yelling my name instead of his as they scramble for their cameras.

That's more like it. Not such the golden boy anymore, huh?

I walk up the stairs, looking down at each step I pass. I give them some poses once I reach the top of the stairs. I don't want to give too much, just enough for them to wonder why I'm here.

"ALE, I LOVE YOU!"

I smile at them, waving in their direction.

"I love you too," I mouth to a fan. Words that the man of the hour couldn't say in his wildest dreams. I keep going down, giving all the photographers shots of my every movement before reaching the end.

"He was staring at you the whole time," I hear Lauren say beside me.

I smirk. "Good."

Walking into the event is a lavish expensive experience. To me, every gala looks the same, either old Hollywood vibes or modern architecture.

"I'll see you later."

Lauren nods, walking back to the car just around the corner. Taking a deep breath, I straighten my posture and stroll in with everything I have inside of me.

I quite literally bolt to the bar and order a glass of champagne once I walk in. This reminds me of Monaco, where he and I kissed for the first time. It's no different. I hear French being spoken all around me with the same hatred I felt for him at the time. The only difference is that he won't get a single peep or kiss out of me. He kissed that all goodbye when he left me in my apartment to go meet up with his ex.

I walk around observing my surroundings, and then I see his eyes.

Staring at me.

I keep eye contact. He makes his way through the crowd. There are two things I can do in this moment:

1. Walk away without a word.
2. Give him the bare minimum.

He reaches me and I opt for number two. Let's see if he'll explain himself.

"I didn't think I'd see you here."

"Okay." I sip my champagne while looking up at him.

He gets closer, looking around while his breath fans across my ear. "You look ravishing."

I roll my eyes, stepping back. Swirling the fancy alcoholic beverage with my middle finger, I let the silence sit for a second. Taking the tip of my digit into my mouth, I suck off the liquid.

"I know." Turning my back to him, I walk away.

I'm bored, meaning I want to leave. I think this whole thing has proven its point. I walk towards the exit after getting a text from the driver who brought me here. That is, until I feel a hand grab my wrist, pulling me into another room. I already know who pulled me in and I don't think I like it.

"Why are you so pissed off at me? Because as I recall, the last time we talked, you said you missed me."

I snort. "The mere thought that you don't know what you did wrong infuriates me in every possible way you can think of," I say, my back still turned to him.

"I'm sorry for not knowing about the intense grudges you hold just because I exist."

"You know what, I was really starting to like you. But don't worry. All that disappeared when I saw you kissing your ex-wife yesterday after leaving me in my apartment." I turn around and smile. He freezes.

"How the fuck do you know about that?"

"Aw. Are you scared that your side piece knows about what you do when she isn't around?" I raise my eyebrows at him and dare him to say anything.

"Stop saying you're a side piece. You are far from that."

"Well, the picture told me differently."

"Where did you see this picture?" he asks.

"On a WAGS Instagram page. Don't ask me how or why I saw it, that's irrelevant."

"I paid off the pap right away, like I always do when we do something neither of us expect. How did this get out? I paid him five thousand dollars, Ale!"

"Wait, they have pictures of us?!" I screech.

"They don't. I always make sure they're deleted off their camera right away. If this gets out," he points at me and then himself rapidly, "we would both be fucked, and you know that."

I just look at him, knowing he's trying to run away from the main issue.

"You saying that you thought that they were deleted makes this even worse. You were just going to lie to my face and tell me that you weren't fucking anyone else, then go straight to your cheating ex-wife."

"We didn't fuck. She kissed me and I pushed her back right after she jumped on me."

"Why were you even with her in the first place?" I raise an eyebrow at him.

"Because I was getting my divorce papers finalized," he whispers, and I get even angrier.

"They weren't even finalized when you decided to start using me?!?"

"That's not the way it is, and you know it. Our divorce process was long after the whole pregnancy and money scandal, it took a few years to finally have it all in place. I went to go get them yesterday because I had asked her for them-" He stops and then keeps going, not finishing his previous sentence. "She's engaged to Crue. Her father finally approved, and right before she kissed me, she told me that this was our parting gift. She thinks I'm still hung up on her."

"Are you?"

"Hell no. You should know that by now, Ale."

"I actually don't know. Remember when you told me you can't love anyone, especially me." I look at him with a knowing face.

"Every single second that I have known you, I have been infuriated by your presence. But there came a time when I liked that comfort. I realized when I saw Adèle yesterday that every single thing I felt for her was fake. It wasn't love. It was infatuation. With you, it's different, it's raw, and I'm not going to let you walk away just because of a misunderstanding."

"It looked like you were kissing her back. One thing I don't do is cheaters, so if you are one, Mr. Donatello, say it right now. Put your ego and self-absorbed dick away." I'm heaving at this point. I don't know how to react or what to believe. I've been around liars my whole life and I don't want another one becoming my boyfriend.

Did I just say boyfriend?

"Do not call me Mr. Donatello. This will not go back to what it used to be."

I take one step towards him. "Isn't it? I mean, you did kiss your ex-wife and didn't tell me. If there was such an easy explanation, why didn't you just communicate? Because I would have found out sooner or later. Our every move is watched, and you know that."

"You're finally accepting that, I never thought I'd see the day."

"Answer the question, Donatello."

"The reason I didn't tell you was because I didn't feel anything. And I also didn't want to lose you."

I suck in a breath. This isn't happening. My commitment and daddy issues are really showing right now.

"What do you want me to say, that I automatically forgive you? Because I don't."

"No, I just want you to understand that the kiss was not something I wanted, and it made me realize that the only person I have ever been in 'love' with never actually existed."

I turn around, putting my hands on my hips, looking up at the ceiling. I hear him step towards me and he wraps his arms around my waist. He nuzzles his head in my neck and sighs in defeat.

"Did you get the sponsor you wanted?" I ask and it's followed by his laughter.

"After the conversation we just had, you bring that up?"

"Would you like me to continue to yell at you? Because I could do that."

"Yes. We have the prototype we wanted for next year."

"You mean Xavier and you."

"No. I mean us, Ale."

I close my eyes and relax. I don't want to freak out after what just happened before the segue into this conversation. I just keep silent as he kisses down my neck softly. I melt against him. Damn him for bringing my walls down. They're up for a reason, sir.

"I like this." He brushes through my newly cut hair with his fingers.

"Do you?"

"Oh, very much so." He looks at me with hunger.

"Hm. Let's see about that." I drag him out of the room. "I'm leaving, but if you find out where I'm staying, you can meet me in the room." I walk away thinking about all the things I want to do to him. Because this time I will be in control.

The night is still young, after all.

CHAPTER TWENTY-NINE

LUCA DONATELLO.

I find myself at her door, which is not shocking in the slightest. I was surprised when she brought up the situation with Adéle. After the whole explanation, I knew that I would have to work on the pieces she's still wary about. When she told me to come to her hotel room, I was shocked. But finding her hotel room was easy. I might have found out where she was staying as soon as she walked onto the carpet. Just in case she wasn't going to talk to me and I'd have to track her down.

My hand lingers over the doorknob, which with one little twist will lead to her room. Putting all of my egotistical energy away, as Ale calls it, I knock. I hear shuffling happen before she swings the door open, still wearing her dress. I'm met with my bare-faced and no heels *ragazza*. She's pulled her newly short hair back and it barely fits into her hair tie because of the length.

When I saw that it wasn't a wig, my dick immediately went stiff. There's just something about the way short hair compliments her bone structure. It makes her look even more tempting than she already is.

Pulling me in by my collar, I'm caught off guard as she drags me in, pushing me onto the bed. Taking my wrist, she runs the palm of my hand and fingers down her dress. "You see this beautiful dress that your woman is wearing?"

I look at her instantly when she says *my* woman.

"Yes."

"Well, it also happens to be made by your ex-father-in-law, and I'm going to ride you while reminding you who you belong to."

I quirk my eyebrow at her. "Who said I was yours? I remember a time when you said you weren't an object and now you say I am. Wouldn't you call that contradicting, *ragazza*?"

"The difference in this situation is that you fucked up, I didn't."

"I didn't, Adèle did."

She gives me a look, speculation written all over it. "Hmm. Well, that's precisely why I will be riding your cock in this dress."

I'm amused that she thinks she's in control. But for tonight, I'll set it aside.

Shoving my pants down, she takes her panties off slowly in front of me, teasing me. My erection is standing up in the cold air, out and naked. Just by looking at her face, I know she's excited. She's most definitely a cock tease, especially in that dress. She crawls onto the bed, bringing her legs to the sides of mine. She's hovering over me. Grabbing my shaft, she starts rubbing it against her opening.

She tries to gather a little more wetness between us before she starts fucking me. Her dress is completely covering my view of her pussy. I hate it, so I lift up the hem before she slaps my hand.

"You don't get the satisfaction of seeing me grind against you, at least not tonight. That's something we'll have to talk about in the future." She's gasping at the feeling of my hardness contrasting her softness. It's a match, and I can feel her getting wetter by the minute. My precum slides over her clit, helping with the natural lubricant spreading all over our sexes.

"There's something else I need you to know. You do not grab, pull, or shove this dress. It stays on all night. I will not have a custom couture dress lent to me be ripped just because you are a needy oaf." She moans in response to the friction.

"Yes, little girl." I feel her clench when she rubs my tip against the hollow part of her pussy. When she feels like she's slippery enough, she shoves my cock inside her and I groan as she muffles a scream.

"What did I say about screaming?"

"What did I say about you speaking?"

I bite back a response, knowing that she will just give me a rebuttal. I don't think she realizes that if I wanted to, I could overpower her. I'm letting her do this. But I would never do that, especially not now when she needs this and the way I feel about her makes me want to give it to her even more.

She starts going up and down. Her hands are on my chest as her motions go slowly, her eyes close, trying to feel every movement as she rides me. I've always loved this position, but more so with her. As always, she knows what she's doing.

The flexible little thing she is, moves off my shaft before she falls back down. Each motion makes her moan. Her rhythm gets faster, and I can feel her tighten around me even more than before. She's close. I want to touch her and overstimulate her. But I don't due to her orders. I just watch her hair, that was previously up, become a wild mess around her perfect face.

I see the dress bunch up a little with every motion. Fuck me. The sight of her in that dress makes me go stiff. I can't believe she's fucking me in my ex-wife's dress. It's the sexiest thing I have ever seen.

I throw my head back when the buildup starts to happen. Her pussy is squeezing me so tight that I almost lose it. She cums and she keeps going, knowing I need this release too. She's almost limp around me but keeps pumping until I shoot deep inside her. Her whole body convulses at the pleasure.

This is quite possibly the best thing that's happened in my existence. I groan in ecstasy. Fuck is she good. That makes it all the more venomous.

"You're lucky that I even let you come."

"Thank you for that."

"You're welcome. I'm quite good at it." She smirks, looking down at me.

"You are and if you mention another man when you're in bed with me, I will find him and strangle him with my own two hands."

"There you go ruining the moment."

"How so?"

"With your controlling ways."

"You're the jealous type too, *ragazza*. And don't deny it."

"I may be, but I don't want to kill every woman you've been with. That would be a life's mission, and I don't plan on making everything in my life about you."

"I don't believe that for a second. Once I'm done with you, all you're going to do is think about me."

She gets up and crosses her arms. "So, you are going to get rid of me once you're done."

"It's a figure of speech."

"Yeah, well, it's not very convincing."

I gape at her. "What's going to convince you otherwise?" She thinks for a good minute before she looks at me and says the one thing I was not expecting.

"Kneel." She points at the ground in front of her. I stand up and do just that. I get on my knees. She looks down at me with all the confidence only a woman can possess.

"You're going to make me come with your tongue."

I start kissing up her thighs, making my way to her entrance. Opening her seam, I take two of my fingers and start massaging her pussy gently in a scissor motion. She leans back against the TV stand with both her hands supporting her weight. Her mouth agape at the sensation. She's spread out for me to feast on. I latch my mouth onto her clit and suck gently. Doing that for what seems like hours, I take my tongue and do a very large lick, from her entrance to her clit. I can taste the mix of our juices, and I've never tasted anything like it.

My tongue penetrates her opening as my thumb finds her clit. I suck gently on her clit and shove two fingers inside of her, curling them at the exact angle that makes her scream. I lick her from front to back before shoving my tongue deep inside of her, relishing in her reaction. Pinching her clit, she screams out into the open air. I love it when she doesn't take away the pleasure of hearing her ecstasy.

"How'd you get so good at that?" Her breath is unsteady as she speaks.

"I could say the same to you."

She shuts up in that moment, realizing what I'm saying to her. I don't want her talking about other men when I'm around, I think she would want the same thing in return. I've always loved giving women head, but not as much as making them come on my dick.

Before Ale, sex was simply an unfulfilling transaction that I always made for my own pleasure. I wasn't a dickhead; I let the woman have her high. I'm perceptive and try to understand a woman's movements even in my haze. But there is something about Ale that makes that haze lift, and all I see is her.

She's a drug, one I can't stop taking.

Her mouth opens and her eyes roll to the back of her head. She's done for. As I make her come with my mouth, her breath starts slowing down and I watch her look at the ceiling with a smile. I like it when she approves of me making her come undone. Her smile makes my ego crash through the roof because I'm the one responsible for it.

"It's unfair to humankind how good you are at that."

I smirk. "Well, at least it's not unfair for you because I don't plan on giving anyone else what you get from me."

"I like the sound of that."

I stand up, getting off my knees. "Oh, baby, I do too." I crash our lips together, locking. They move as one. Her hands roam around my whole body.

"Am I forgiven?" I pull us apart and she looks at me with her plump red bruised lips, ripe for the taking.

"You may be forgiven, but this will not be forgotten. One thing you should know about me is I hold grudges. If this ever happens again, I will cut your dick off when you least expect it." She smiles giving me a look opposite of her words.

"I'll take that."

I mean what I say, I'll grab onto anything she gives me. The scary part is that there isn't anything that this woman could do to make me leave.

Nothing.

CHAPTER THIRTY
MARIA ALEJANDRA.

Paris was great, amazing in fact. We spent a few extra days together shut in our hotel room.

Yes, our *hotel room. Weird. Extremely concerning.*

It felt like literal sunshine and rainbows, as we fucked each other every night and ended it by talking about ourselves. The one thing that I have yet to mention is the fact that my family is literally the epitome of organized crime. You might be asking why I'm so scared about this. I should just spit it out, right?

No. I should not. Even though these days have been some of the best of my life, my brain keeps telling me that it'll never work out, which I fear is spot on.

I don't know how to break the news. It's not like we're officially together; at least we haven't said those words. But I feel the inevitability of it. The future isn't something we talk about. Mostly, we like to talk about the past and the present, but never the future. So how am I supposed to tell someone that I continually have sex with, maybe even my boyfriend, that I grew up in a world that he despises?

I know him well enough now to know he will not take this well. At all. Not well is probably an understatement. Because in my head, it's way worse than that. It's fury mixed with hatred. Those are the two things that I don't want a man that I might have feelings for to feel towards me.

I'm the queen of relationship advice, but I'm not living it. Quite the opposite, actually. I remember a time where I always said: if a man doesn't accept you for who you are, then that doesn't make them a good partner.

In my defense, I was never talking about my dark side or the demons of the person I was giving advice to. It's not like I'm proud of it, but it's my family. They're all I know, and that life was part of me for so many years. I don't live in it, nor will I ever. But I do love my brother and even my father, despite their business dealings.

I just can't get my head out of my ass.

It's all a mindfuck, the incentive being one that I can't understand.

I know I'm complicated, and sometimes I contradict myself. But being a bad bitch is a mentality, and I plan to harness that when I do eventually tell him.

Meaning, maybe in four years. Preferably never.

He's going to want to meet my family one day, and he's going to stumble around a corner and see a room full of drugs, weapons, or maybe even someone being tortured. It wouldn't be the best environment for our kids, but at least then I would have something to keep us together.

Ale, you're so fucked up.

Relationships aren't built on lies, and I know that. I would never want him to lie to me, but it would make me a hypocrite if I didn't tell him.

Polanco is the place I call home. I'm walking around the streets days before my home Grand Prix, hand in hand with Luca. It's summer and the sun is blazing, meaning that we're both wearing sunglasses and baseball caps. Hoping that we're going around incognito. I don't know if it's working. If anyone were to hear the conversation I'm planning on having with him, not only would the government be after me, but my own blood would probably kill me.

It's depressing if you think about it. It's not like my dad has any feelings in his poor little black heart. He did kill my mother. I'm a part of her, and in his mind, that will justify murdering my ass.

You need to stop thinking too much and enjoy the next moments in which you and Luca are happy. Because they're about to come to an end in a few hours.

"Where are we going?" Luca questions.

"The castle here in Mexico, it's called El Castillo de Chapultepec. It's on a mountain so that you can see all the way from Polanco to La Condesa. When Mexico was invaded by the Spanish, a lot of European settlers came and conquered. When the Spanish were weakened here in

Mexico, an Austrian archduke was placed as emperor. He took control of the castle and made it extremely European."

He nods when we enter the forest-like park. The uphill climb is a few miles away. I can see it in the distance.

"Remember when I told you I would get you back for making me walk up the Spanish steps?"

He looks at me, nodding, and I smile.

"This is payback." Motioning at the slant, he gives me a look.

"And?" He doesn't know what he's in for.

"You'll just have to experience its greatness. The view is beautiful." I'm trying to make him not realize that there's going to be a full walking experience that most people can't get through. It's about a forty-minute uphill climb.

"I can promise you, *ragazza*, this is going to be nothing like you going up minor steps and losing your breath as if you were going to have a heart attack."

"It's so much worse." I walk past him and start walking. He follows behind.

"You know I would have never taken Mexico for having a castle."

"The first time we met, I defended my country. I thought you would have taken the impression that we have everything."

"I doubt it."

"Don't offend your girl's country, embrace it."

He goes quiet. Did I go too far with the "your girl" thing? Maybe I'm taking this way too seriously and nothing is really happening. Way to give me a panic attack on top of the one I'm already having.

We continue walking with our arms swinging and legs bending due to the incline. I see people running past me. They're obviously doing some type of workout; their attire alludes to it.

"Why would people give themselves the pain of running up this?"

"We are professional athletes, and you say that." I quirk my eyebrow.

"Ex-professional athlete, *ragazza*. And I have the image of you dying while walking up a few steps in Italy ingrained in my head."

I look at him, offended. "A few steps? Are you serious? I walked up a marathon's worth of stairs. Don't question my stamina." He laughs when I point a finger at him.

"I'm not questioning your stamina, baby. There have been many occasions where your stamina was stronger than mine." He winks and gives me a knowing expression.

Pervert.

I keep walking, not feeling like responding to his comment about our sex life. He should be happy about it. I can keep up with his man-whore personality. What a great line, I should have said that to him. It would have been the perfect comeback.

"How does this keep going?" He's breathing hard now.

"I stay true to my word, that's something you should

have learned by now." I love throwing his words back at him.

"I just don't understand why people do this leisurely."

I turn my head so he can see the view. "Because of this." I gesture towards the untouched grass and trees spreading all the way to the industrial side of the city. He looks and relaxes at the sight.

"I would never have taken Mexico City as such a nice-looking *città*."

I look at him, dumbfounded. "Are you admitting defeat, Luca?"

"No. As I recall, my argument was that Florence is better, and that's a fact."

I sneer. "Just wait until you get to the top." I shoot him back a wink that he threw at me earlier.

Walking up for about another twenty minutes, we make it to the top. At this point, we're both heaving. I need water. I was prepared this time. Grabbing my bag, I unzip it and take out my black Hydro Flask.

I take a swig of it, the coolness hits the back of my throat and all my senses relax. There's nothing like cold water when you're dying of dehydration. I hand the water bottle to him, and he drinks out of it.

"This is sad," I point out.

"What do you mean?"

"I mean the fact that both of us were, slash are, F1 drivers and get dehydrated by walking up a slanted road.

We've been withdrawn from water and dried out like apricots in our cars, and yet this is more difficult."

"Don't make this more disappointing than it is, *ragazza*."

"Nothing is more disappointing than this."

He chuckles. "That I agree on."

I grab his wrist, dragging him with me. "Come on, let's go. You can see this view later. The one that's important is the one from the inside."

After going all around this eclectic piece of Renaissance history, it happened to impress Luca one or two times. I mentally pat myself on the back.

"It's sad that you can't see it from the outside as much anymore."

"All the vegetation is a result of purpose. When the Aztecans built their pyramids, it was all torn down by the Spanish due to their religious denomination. Vegetation was their favorite thing. For example, in Puebla, the biggest pyramid in the world is covered in plants and trees, and at the top sits a church."

"I've always found colonization a disrespect to every cultural aspect known to man."

"Yep. Mexico City was previously known as the Aztec City of

the Gods. It was filled with a completely different type of architecture. If it hadn't burned to the ground, it would have been one of the seven wonders of the world. If you see the mockups of what it looked like, it would have been marvelous to see."

"I love when you talk history to me." He smiles, but not with his teeth. It's a different look for him. It's genuine. Everything about this man is. I've noticed that he doesn't smile often because it wouldn't be genuine.

I like that most of all because he smiles more when I'm around, which I take as a personal compliment to my sense of humor and aura.

"It's always been a passion. If I wasn't an F1 driver, I would probably be a historian specializing in Mexican history. If the Spanish never came, we would be speaking Nahuatl." Reaching the terrace, the black and white tiles span over the whole deck. Then, boom, there's the view. You can see all of Polanco from up here and have an unobstructed view of the top of almost every high rise.

"It really is nice up here."

"Just think, just before the trees came in, you could see *La Reforma,* previously known as the *El Paseo de la Emperatriz.*"

He focuses all his attention on me. "Why did they change it? I think it's a perfect name for such a long street."

"Because once Mexican independence came, the whole meaning of the street was built so that you could connect the imperial residence to the city center. Mexicans don't like the idea of a monarchy, so they named it after the liberal reform. Why do you think *El Ángel de Independencia* was built? To show that they were no longer in power, and it was the people in control. It's basically the structure of democracy."

"I guess that's fair," he says to me, seeming to like the history lesson.

"It's more than fair. Mexico was under a hierarchy for most of its history after having its people slaughtered. Thankfully, the rich history still runs through our veins."

"I like you and your strong opinions." He looks at me, then kisses me softly. What a way to get to a woman with a history kink's heart.

He pulls back and I see it then. He likes me. I get chills.

Scary.

I have to tell him. All I can hope for is an understanding reaction, but I know it will be far from that.

"I don't want whatever this is to start off on the wrong foot." I say softly and he looks over at me again.

"I agree."

"Secrets and lies don't start off a relationship well. I've been telling you that in my own way for a while now, and one thing I'm not is a hypocrite."

He quirks an eyebrow. "Who said we were in a relationship?" Just by the look on his face, I can tell he's being sarcastic. I slap him on the shoulder, and he laughs.

"You're not gonna like what I'm about to say to you. All I ask is that you don't lash out." I sigh in dread. He takes his finger and moves my chin towards him.

"I can promise you, Ale, that whatever you say right now will never affect this."

I don't believe him.

"Don't say something you're not going to believe after this conversation."

"You're making me think the worst, *ragazza*."

"Well, because it is." I stay quiet for a second trying to form my words in the best way.

"Spit it out, Ale."

"When I first found out you hated organized crime, I knew in that moment I was fucked. Xavier happened to tell me, and I was worried in that instant. Not because I had feelings for you at the time, but because my career comes first. I plead in front of you right now that when you get infuriated and disgusted by my presence, set it aside and don't tell anyone, because if this gets out, I won't be able to fulfill my life's purpose and I'll be in danger." He stays silent and I can already tell he might know what's coming, so I just spit it out.

"I grew up in a life that wasn't my choice. My dad runs the biggest cartel in Mexico and my brother runs the underworld of the city." I keep my breath in after I exhaled all those words, waiting for the bomb to drop.

Instead, he bursts out laughing. I look at him, making sure he understands it isn't a joke. The look pains me when I direct it at him.

He stops laughing as the news settles in. When he realizes the inevitable truth that the girl he has feelings for is everything he hates. I want to cry, and bad bitches don't shed a tear.

I see his jaw clench as he looks away, pacing back and forth between me and a tree a few feet away. Then he stops in front of the big plant, turning around to look at me again. I've never seen this man speechless, but in this moment, it's the definition of his whole facade.

"I—" He shuts his mouth and just stares at me in shock. I'm not going to push anything out of him; that's the last thing I want right now. But when he walks away, all I can do is chase after him. Pushing past all the tourists, he makes his way down all the stairs swiftly. I try to keep up, but his long legs do not help.

He finally reaches the exit, and I hear the person who says goodbye to people say, "I hope you have a good day, sir."

In a thick accent, he replies, "Fuck you." He literally runs past him. The greeter stands in shock.

"Sorry. He's like this because of me. You know, couples and their problems."

He smiles weakly, and I run past him.

Luca already at the top of the slant. Standing a few feet away from him, I stop in defeat as he keeps walking, raking my hands through my hair in desperation. I see him stop and look the other way before he begins walking again.

This is so much worse than I could have ever imagined.

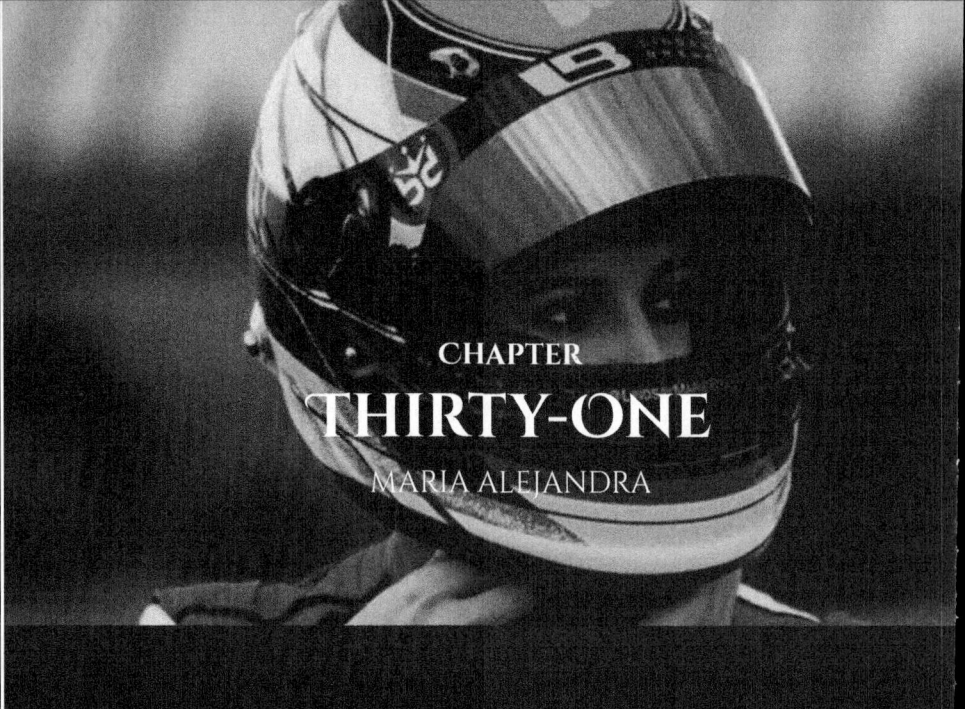

CHAPTER THIRTY-ONE

MARIA ALEJANDRA

My eyes hurt, my head is pounding, and I feel like I've been drained. Let's just say that crying is something that I've been doing for hours. I didn't even cry this much when I realized how abusive my ex was. I don't understand why this is so much worse. I hated this man and now I'm crying over him.

Fuck my life.

The thing we definitely have in common is the fact that organized crime has changed our lives. I knew that this was going to affect me someday, and it was like a slap in the face. I have to see him tomorrow morning for practice, and I don't know how I'm gonna take it.

I've been locked in a dark room for approximately two days. My phone is off, and I don't feel like entertaining anyone. That's until I hear my front door open. Who the hell is here? I gave Nieves the day off, and only one person has my key.

Footsteps echo off the walls. I'm just waiting for this person to come in and see me wallowing in the dark. The door flies open, and I'm met with a male figure. One I don't want to deal with right now. I groan audibly at his presence.

"Maria Alejandra Atena Castillo, levántate ahorita antes de que te saque de tus penas."

I stay under the covers, hoping he'll let it go and leave. He doesn't and instead grabs my blanket, shoving it off me.

"Déjame en paz, imbécil."

"That's no way to talk to your older brother, Ale. I swear to God if you don't get up, I will drag you by your feet."

"Remind me to take my key away from you."

"Too late. I've already made copies."

I turn to look at him with a scowl. "How did you even know I was here?"

"Because I haven't heard from you in two days. I texted Vio, and she said that the last she heard from you was at the same time as me. But the day you disappeared, she got an ominous text from you. It was then I knew you weren't fine, but thankfully alive."

"I don't feel alive," I groan.

"You sent a text to your best friend saying, 'Kill me now.' *Porqué crees que vine aquí?*"

"I wasn't lying, I feel like I'm dying."

He grabs me, shoving me onto my feet. Startled at the sudden movement, my head starts spinning.

"Well, you're not, so whatever happened to you, deal with it. I'm taking you to the opera."

"That would be a no." The thought of getting up and dressing myself makes me want to scream.

"Don't test me, *princessa*."

I look at him and snarl. "I'm not in the mood to watch a woman screaming for hours to old ass music," I say.

"You've always loved the opera, don't lie to me. I know you better than you know yourself. So, we're going because I have something to deal with tonight."

"If I go, I will not be left alone for a minute, because you know how the other cartel Dons herd towards me like mosquitos." I give him a look and just stand there.

"You won't be. Vio is coming with us."

I run my hands through my hair and accept the fact that he's going to drag me out, like the good brother he is. He knows that when this happens, I need to dress up and do something. But I do not want to do that right now.

"You need to stop getting her hopes up, you know."

He rolls his eyes. "I'm not doing that. She knows that we would never work in the slightest. Her little crush isn't even a thought anymore; it's in the past."

"Hmm." I look at him in judgment. No matter what he does, she will always like him, and sadly, I have no idea how to get it into his head that she's every man's wet dream.

"I'll see you there in three hours, and Vio will be there as well. I swear to god, Ale, if I don't see you there by the time it starts, Lucero and Sebastian will come and drag you out."

"Okay, I'll go."

I hate this more than the situation I'm in with Luca. He walks out, the door shuts, and I get off my ass. My feet hit the floor for the first time in days, and I make my way to the bathroom, dreading having to put a fancy dress on then slather myself with makeup.

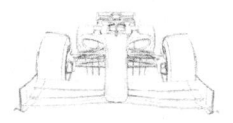

"Apparently, it's really good," Violetta says next to me as we walk up the stairs in *El Palacio de Bellas Artes*. Following León up the big, old, extremely expensive steps, he is greeted by everyone and their mom.

I however have all of León's admirers glancing towards me. I keep the conversation going with Vio to show I don't want to talk to anyone I don't know without saying go away.

"If he stops one more time, I will strangle him with the exact same tactics he taught me on how to block someone's air duct." I shoot a sweet smile in Vio's direction, and she bursts out laughing.

"He is the CEO of one of the most important companies in all of Mexico. Everyone wants to talk to him," she tells me like I don't already know that.

"You mean the drug trade empire? The one that includes killing people without a flinch."

She gives me a harsh look.

I throw my hands up. "What? You know it's true."

Sighing, she looks the other way. "I know. That's just the worst part of it all. He was such a sweet boy, and something corrupted him. I just want to know what."

I observe León shaking hands and smiling at people. "Not a what, but a who. *Mi Padre*."

"I have a feeling it's more than that," she says.

"Listen. My brother is a killer. He was trained by the best, my father. He grew up as his bastard child. His mother was constantly being beaten by the sperm donor who created us, because he didn't like the emotions he was feeling towards her. Don't get me wrong, León would never lay a hand on a woman; it's too personal for him. My father was great to me, but he would do anything for that little boy to become exactly like him." I point at my brother. "My father didn't succeed; he's so much worse," I say before I walk past her towards our viewing box. The one designated to our family name is all the way at the top with a perfect view.

I'm exactly what Luca said I was. I come from a long line of murderers. That doesn't mean I don't love them with my whole heart. It's selfish of me, but if that's a crime, so be it. I'll be the woman with her murdering family at her side.

I sit down in my black Valentino dress that has jewels encrusted at the top of the cleavage. There's a huge slit at the bottom. I slicked my hair back and put on stilettos. This is all anyone is getting from me tonight, nothing more, nothing less.

The opera house is beautiful as always, but it's much different than a European one. Instead of the gloomy look, there's a stained-glass religious Catholic piece on the ceiling. The stage is a wood color, and the seats are covered in red velvet to match the curtain that is currently covering the main stage. I was introduced to the opera by my brother. He has a taste for the finer things.

Just like Luca.

He sits next to me. I take my seat in the middle of him and Violetta. The crowd goes silent when the lights dim and the curtain goes up. The opera is *Lucia di Lammermoor*, one of León's favorites, and with reason. It's a creepy take on Romeo and Juliet, but not exactly. Basically, there's this girl who comes from a rich family in Scotland, who's feuding with another family. She falls in love with a member of that family. Her parents and brother disapprove. She gets married to another man, and on their wedding night, she kills her new husband after going crazy because she can't marry the man she truly loves. The mad scene is spectacular, and I've never seen it live before.

I turn to Violetta. "Who's playing Lucia?"

"This new breakout American opera singer, her name's Amelie Fox." I nod and turn my attention to the first act. A bunch of men come in and start speaking Italian.

Of course, it's in fucking Italian. I forgot most operas are. It's like he's following me everywhere I go.

The whole vibe of listening to and watching the opera is that you, as the viewer, don't understand jack shit. But through the way they act and use their voices, the storyline is clear. Even though the language isn't universal, the story is. That's the beauty of opera.

Suddenly, a red-haired woman comes out and I immediately know it's Lucia, or should I say, Amelie. Her mouth opens and I freeze. This woman is exceptional. I could listen to her voice for days. Luckily, I have three hours and fifteen minutes left.

Act one finishes.

It's time for the first intermission to start. I stay in my seat, stretching my limbs carefully. León walks out without a word. I turn my head to Violetta, who's looking out into the crowd.

"I wonder what's up with him?"

She turns her head towards me and nods. "I've never seen him so entranced in a performance before."

"Violetta, please don't tell me you were staring at him the whole time." I groan.

"It's not like that, when she started singing, I heard him stiffen in his chair. You were too entranced in her performance to take note."

"Why would he stiffen?" I ask her.

"I was wondering the same thing. You think he knows her?"

"Vio, he knows everyone, obviously."

She looks at me in realization and then gives me a shrug.

I think she really is over him, and I'm grateful. Any mention of León with a girl used to make her frustrated, but she doesn't even seem to care anymore.

Twenty minutes later, León comes back with his suit jacket in his hands and his sleeves rolled up. That means either one of two things. One, he just had sex—*something I would not like to know about*. Two, he told his men to *talk* to someone—*more like beat the life out of them*.

I don't see any blood or sign of force; it could be neither of the two. The lights dim again as the curtain rises for a second time. An angry Amelie walks out. This woman is an amazing performer.

Act two finishes.

León walks out again. Twenty minutes later, he comes back even more irritated than earlier. I give him a look; he returns it with malice. I ignore him just as I always do when he's like this. León usually treats me with warmth, but he can be cold at times.

Amelie walks out in a wedding dress covered in blood. On the edge of my seat, she starts using the actor who is playing dead. Imagining him as her lover who no longer loves her. She's mad, completely lost in her grief.

Chills.

A tear runs down my face, I'm in awe. She brings out the abuse of the character, all of her anger transforming into something more. I've never seen a mad scene like this ever. She's glorious as the light shines down on her.

The lights die down and I jump up. Clapping in amazement, having seen over forty operas in my lifetime this is truly the best. Everyone joins me below as we see the whole cast of the national Mexican opera bow. The curtains close and it's all over. I sigh, rubbing my hand around my mouth.

"I have never seen anything like her," I blurt out.

"She was phenomenal," Violetta agrees.

"She's a liability," León says before he walks out, and I look over at Violetta in bewilderment.

There is definitely something going on there.

CHAPTER THIRTY-TWO

MARIA ALEJANDRA.

The crowd is insane. Mexican pride is practically dripping off the stands. It feels so good to be at my first home race in my career. I have signed probably hundreds of caps and I may have cried once or twice at the same sign.

My whole family is with me today, which obviously includes Violetta. After my night out at the opera, I went to practice to find a non-present Luca. The day after qualifying, he was there but avoided my presence entirely, and today I watched an interviewer mention me in one of her questions.

He didn't even answer, he just stood there and said, "It really is cool to be in Mexico, I think the fans are very excited." Why doesn't someone just erase me from his memory while they're at it.

It's cool to be in Mexico, my ass.

I get it, he's pissed, but he knows how important this

race is to me. At least communicate somewhat. I know he must hate me, but that should not affect the team because, quite frankly, his behavior is childish.

Meanwhile, in the back of my head one phrase keeps replaying.

What if he's already said something?

Both my father and his heir are in the same room, not even breaking a sweat, thinking they're fine. What if they're not and the Federales are going to handcuff them and take them into custody? This isn't something my family has ever had to worry about, and I don't want to be the reason they spend the rest of their lives in jail.

"This is the paddock." I walk them around, letting them take everything in.

"I can't believe this is what you do every day," Violetta exclaims.

I turn around and smile genuinely at her. "Me either." I exhale and everyone looks at me.

"I am so happy for you, *princessa*. This has always been your path," my dad whispers and kisses the top of my forehead.

"*Gracias, Pa.*"

"So, this is the rookie's family." The familiar voice comes creeping up behind me, pushing me aside. He's now in full view of my guests.

"Xavier, this is my family." I introduce them as he reaches out to shake hands with my father and brother.

"Now I see where the attractive genes come from."

My head literally snaps towards him. "Did you just call me attractive?" I throw my hand over my heart.

"Of course, I did. Ale, it's common knowledge." I laugh. He looks over at Violetta and stops to stare.

Way to be obvious.

"This is my best friend, Violetta."

She smiles timidly. "Nice to meet you."

He gives her his charming smirk. "The pleasure is all mine."

She reaches out to shake his hand, but instead of holding it in a firm grip, he brings the top of her perfectly manicured fingers to his lips, kissing them gently.

Am I watching gentleman porn, what the fuck is this?

She blushes.

Violetta, please fall in love with this teddy bear of a man. He is perfect for you. I will go out of my way to be a matchmaker, if you're willing.

He lets go of her hand, refocusing his attention on all of us. "It was nice to meet all of you. I hope you enjoy the race today." Before he walks away, his gaze meets Violetta's, giving her a wink before striding off.

I almost squeal when she looks over at me with a knowing look. Did Xavier just hit on my best friend? I'm gonna have to talk to his cheeky ass after this race is over.

When my father gets a look at the car, he almost runs to see it. One moment he's in front of me, the next he's petting it. I burst out laughing.

"Papá, the team needs to keep working." He gives me a

look saying, *I'm staying.* León is smiling beside me as we watch him.

"Sir, I'm gonna have to politely tell you to step away from the vehicle." I tense when his accent runs through my ear drums. My dad's head snaps up.

He walks over to Luca shaking his hand. "It's very nice to meet my daughters' boss." Nodding, the Italian bastard walks away. I guess that's a normal reaction. *But it hurts nonetheless.*

"He's very friendly," my father says, and I chuckle.

"Like you're any nicer," I blurt out sarcastically, rolling my eyes. I lead them all out of the paddock and walk them to the club above the pits.

"This is where you'll be watching from. I got you all exclusive seats just for the race."

León walks over to me, hugging me into his side, then kisses my forehead. "Don't let that imbecile take away your shine today. You're gonna do great." He looks into my eyes while saying every word, making sure I know he means it. I melt.

"Te amo, hermano."

"I love you more." He turns, sitting down and crossing his legs while putting his glasses on.

"I'll see you both later." I wave at Violetta and my father.

Striding away, I take a deep breath and replay my brother's words. He's right. Luca can have all the time he needs, but that doesn't mean it should affect my career.

CHAPTER THIRTY-THREE
LUCA DONATELLO

How could she bring them here?

The audacity this woman possesses will always astound me. After what happened, she brought them here. In my presence!

I've been thinking, my mind on constant replay of what happened on the checkered terrace within the castle walls. I couldn't say anything, but I have so many questions. Ones that frighten me as much as my feelings for her do. Ones I must scrub from my mind until they no longer exist.

Her words, her face, and her pain make me go crazy. To say I was angry would be an understatement. I'm still furious.

She knew! She knew that organized crime was a trigger from my past. A part of my life that I would never get over. Did she use that to hurt me?

Every time I find something good, it always brings me

back to my father. The man who died on the steps of his own home in front of his wife and children. The shooter was a friend, one whom our family trusted. Until he shot my father in the head with a revolver. That is what these types of people do; *they kill.*

Her father and her brother kill. Hell, maybe even she does too.

Why can't I just tell someone? Why can't I just make her pay for playing me all this time when I was deep inside her? Showing my most vulnerable parts. The parts I don't show anyone, except for her.

All through my fake marriage, I never confided in Adèle, nor would I ever. The only people who know are the people my mother chooses to tell. The people who she thinks deserve to hear the story of our family tragedy. The legacy which we thrive on, eradicating people like Ale and her father.

Her father even came to introduce himself to me as well as her brother. The two people in her life that she said with her own words, would kill her if I said anything.

That's why I haven't, I will not be like them. Having a person's blood on my hands is not something my conscience needs or wants.

"Boss, the formation lap is done. We need you looking over intercoms." I nod, opening the diagnostics page on the screen in front of me.

First red light all the way to the fifth, and then it's lights out. The engines are heard all around *Autódromo Hermanos Rodríguez*.

Xavier qualified first with Ale in third. No overtaking was done at the beginning of this race. Xavier is about six seconds ahead of Amir and Ale is close behind by a few tenths. Fighting for the place, she gets past Amir. Cheers erupt and I stay still.

After keeping her placement for a good thirty laps, Amir overtakes her. *"Puta Madre,"* I can hear in the headset.

"You could've kept that placement," I tell her over the radio.

"Why don't you come over here and drive the car yourself? Oh yeah, I forgot. You're not a driver anymore." I don't respond, because if I do. It won't be anything nice.

Fifty laps in, Ale is falling behind. She's about to be taken off a podium with Ren close behind her. She knows that if she gives up this placement it'll be nearly impossible to get past him. She did that one time by some kind of miracle, but his strength is defense.

He passes her and she gets mad once again.

"I feel something wrong with the car. My brakes are wearing away."

I roll my eyes. "Stop making excuses for your horrible defensive strategies." Her strength is definitely speed. Everyone knows that, including her.

"I'm serious, Donatello. Check the diagnostics now." I sigh, turning to all the recent updates that the car is transmitting.

Fuck.

"Ale, you have to retire the car now!" I yell into my headset.

"What do you mean?" she yells.

"Your brakes aren't going to be working in one more lap."

She sighs. "Okay, going to the pits now."

She's at the final sector turning towards the straight. A few seconds later, all I hear is squealing before a loud crash. I turn to see a demolished car right at the entrance of the pit. She hit a barrier.

I see black and throw my headphones off.

I run.

I can see her from here. It's been long enough and she hasn't gotten out. Her head is dangling on the exterior of the car. I sprint even harder, turning the corner. Suddenly, I see her pushing herself out. I exhale in relief. Then, she falls. Her body appears lifeless as she drops right next to the car onto the ground. I run faster and am met with her body. Dropping to my knees next to her as I try to shake her awake.

"Ale, baby, you need to wake up or I will die knowing that I . . . that I never got to tell you that . . . I . . . I love you. *Ti amerò sempre.*" All I can feel, see, or hear next is a paramedic pulling me away from her as they put her on a gurney and carry her into an ambulance.

CHAPTER
THIRTY-FOUR
MARIA ALEJANDRA.

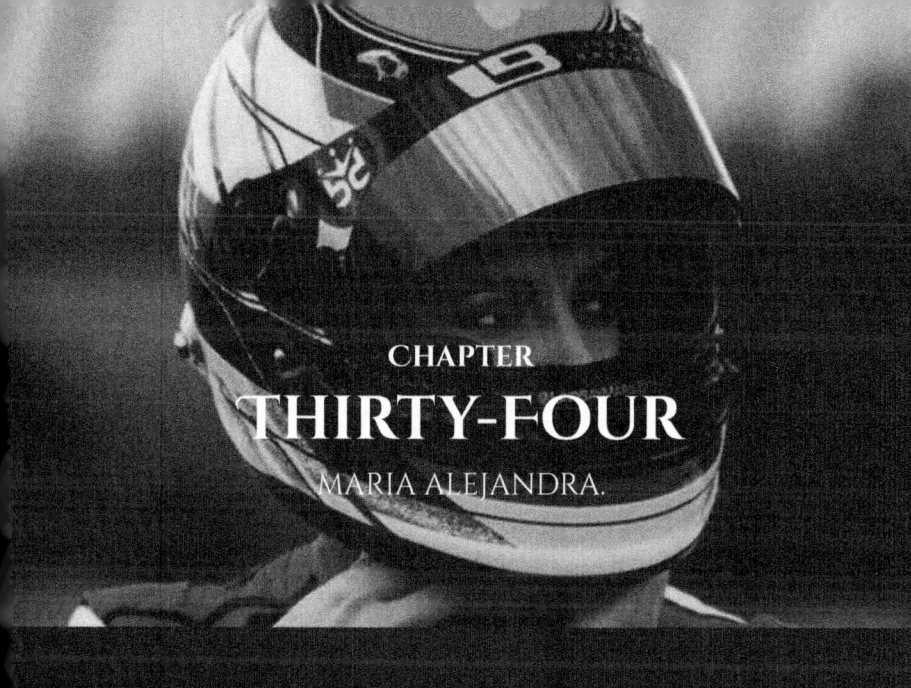

I wake up to a smell. It's smells like antiseptic and bleach. All my senses return to me and I hear arguing voices as they echo inside a small room with a blindingly bright light.

"Why do you think she crashed? It had to do with you, I know it. My sister is the strongest person I know, and when I had to drag her out of the dark room she had been crying in, it reminded me of something. Something I would love to murder someone for. Do you want to meet *Mictlan*, Mr. Donatello?"

"You think I'm not thinking the exact same thing you ar—"

I sit up with my elbows behind my back, holding my weight up. "I assume you're arguing in front of someone you think is unconscious," I interrupt them.

Luca's eyes widen before he rushes to my side. I look at León and his facial expressions soften when he sees me.

"Please don't do that again." I hear the Italian accent I love so much next to me.

"Something we can agree on," I hear *El Mictlan*, my brother, as he referred to himself earlier.

"Do what?" I question.

"I swear to god, Ale, if you lose your memory, I will kill you."

I laugh. "What if I said I don't remember you, how would you feel?" I ask him.

"Stabbed in the fucking chest."

I look over at him. *He's serious.*

"This is my cue to get the fuck out. I will talk to you later, *princessa*." León says.

"Okay, *Mi Rey*." He nods before walking through the white plastic curtain.

"You will not call him your king again," Luca tells me, his face taken over by jealousy. *I kinda love it.*

"You sure are in a bossy mood, aren't you?" I tell him.

He looks at me with a stoic expression. "Of course I am. You almost lost your life and that will never happen again."

I brush it off. "Every driver crashes at least once. Thankfully, technology has evolved to the point where a situation like Senna will never occur a second time."

"Still, you know that this isn't simply something you can walk away from. *Ragazza*, if you hadn't walked out of that car. I wouldn't be able to live with myself." He grabs my hand, squeezing it.

"Don't tell me that you would feel guilty just because you hate me. Forget it, Mr. Donatello, all is forgotten."

"Do you want me to get even angrier, Ale?"

"No, I don't, but I don't want you to feel the need to lie to me."

"I watched when you crashed, and I was there when I saw you fall onto the ground. They had to pull me off of you so they could get into the ambulance, and even then, I had to walk back to my post like nothing happened. I had to go to post-race interviews and answer questions I didn't even want to hear. When in reality, they didn't know that I saw my life with you flash before my eyes."

"Stop," I tell him.

"No, I'm not going to stop. I may not like the fact that your family life is everything I despise-"

"What a great start," I scoff.

"Listen to me. You may not be what I expected, but you are everything I dreamed of. You could kill every person in the world, including me, and I would still love you. Because the thought of losing you is worse than living without your snarky comments and overthinking. Even your family. None of that matters when I'm with you. Because, baby, I hate everyone except you."

I look up at him in shock. His words not processing in my brain.

"Did you just say love?"

"I'm tired of living in my past life. Why should I dwell?" He tells me, referring to Adèle.

"You said you love me." I'm absolutely paralyzed with shocked.

"Yes, I did. Because I do love you."

"I'm in the multiverse or some shit, I swear." I sigh.

"Baby, look at me." I turn towards him again, seeing tears in his eyes. I blink like fourteen thousand times and the image is as clear as day.

Luca Donatello is crying.

"I love you," he says again. To solidify the words coming from his mouth while they process in my brain, I pinch myself.

"Did you just pinch yourself?" He laughs, all his tears running down his face, contrasting with his smile.

"So, this is real. I'm not in a coma imagining this?"

He gives me an irritated look. "You don't have to say it back, but don't bl—" I cut him off and kiss the ever-living shit out of him. We part, and I whisper against his lips, "I love you too."

His grin widens then stretches into the smile that I never thought I would ever get the privilege to see all those months ago. That all disappears. "Now you're going to tell me about your family because I have questions." He crosses his arms and I laugh.

"You look like a ten-year-old pouting," I point out.

"Don't change the subject." I turn to him and chuckle.

"Okay, crack at it, big boy."

"Have you ever killed someone?" He starts asking.

"Not purposely."

"That doesn't answer my question."

"That's the honest answer." I shrug.

"Why does everyone think that your father and brother are the leading businessmen in Mexico?"

I sigh. This is going to be a long one.

"They bought a business prototype from a guy in the Netherlands. It would be able to sell millions a year. So, my dad bought it, and it did better than expected. My father needed a cover up, and the only way to do that was by hiding in plain sight. He has a guy in the countryside of Sinaloa who everyone thinks is the real Don, but that's not the case," I explain to him briefly.

"Why didn't your father just leave the cartel when he knew that the business cover up was doing so well?"

I chuckle. "Because he makes more in two months than that business makes in a year."

He stiffens. "What does his job entail exactly?"

"That's not a question for me. I knew from a young age I wanted to stay out of it. Why do you think I became an F1 driver? Had I wanted to, I could be the heir to the Castillo empire, but I gave it to my brother instead."

"Okay, one last question: what does *El Mictlan* mean?"

I inhale. "I don't think you want to know."

He looks at me, trying to get answers.

I speak, it's not like it's gonna scare me anyway.

"My brother has many names. *El Rey, el Rey del Hampa,*

asesino, heredero, etc. His god-given name, Mictlantecuhtli, the worst. Remember when I told you my father loved giving us mythological names?" He nods before I continue speaking. "Well, he gave me the Greek goddess of war and my brother, the Aztecan king of the underworld. You see, the Aztecans, culturally, weren't the nicest people. They worshiped the Sun God while fearing the God of Darkness. Mictlantecuhtli was the one they answered to in order to keep them safe, so they killed people as sacrifices. Meaning that when my brother is called that name, he becomes the judge of life and death, choosing the final exit of most people's souls." I grab a water bottle, uncap it, and take a sip while examining Luca's expressions.

"So, I'm guessing I shouldn't mess with him," he says nonchalantly.

"That would be a no."

He laughs. "The funny thing is that I always connected someone like your family to the worst parts of my life, but now it's given me the best."

I smile. "And what would that be, Mr. Donatello?"

"You."

CHAPTER THIRTY-FIVE

MARIA ALEJANDRA

The dry heat has never been my favorite, but at least there's no humidity. It makes you feel sticky, especially if you're in a place like Abu Dhabi. The car wasn't super hard to drive because of the weather; it was the track.

The track has some of the longest straights in Formula One, which makes the speed undeniable. I may dominate here, but sectors eleven to nineteen gave me a fucking whiplash.

I placed first, an amazing way to end the season. I had been fighting Ren by a point for third place in the championship. Xavier came first in Drivers'; Amir got second, and I got third. Being in the top three your rookie season is insane. Elektra won Constructors', leaving Dupuis in second and Sansui in third. Overall, it's been a great season for everyone and, beyond any doubt, an eventful one. My contract has already been renewed for next year, with Luca sitting by my side as team principal.

No one knows about us, but I know people are suspicious. Especially after he ran to my rescue after the crash. No team principal has ever done that before. Xavier obviously knows; it's almost impossible for him not to. His face when he found out was the smuggest shit I've ever seen.

"I can see into the future," he said when I told him. I laugh at the memory. That man is the funniest, most sarcastic person I've ever met, and he wears it well.

I feel like I'm floating outside my body.

They call my name. I yell out, cheering with the whole team below me. I look down to a smiling Luca.

"Thank you," I mouth towards him, and he winks. My eyes start watering.

Nope I am not crying.

There's a point in a person's life when they feel like everything is in its place, and at this moment, that's what I'm feeling. And I'm grabbing it by its throat.

I would be nothing without Formula One. I wouldn't belong anywhere. This is my dream and it's where I found the love of my life in a completely unexpected way. I don't know what's to come, but I know that Luca will be next to me.

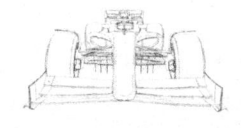

Walking towards my cool down room, I'm pulled by my arm into another room. I yelp. It's dark when the door is shut. All I can hear is breathing, desperate breaths.

"You know, *ragazza*, seeing you up there turns me on."

I immediately smile when I hear his accent fill the room. "Do you have a kink for my happiness, Mr. Donatello?"

"No, I have a kink for your success."

"World domination is the plan." I laugh as he leaves kisses down my neck.

Here we go.

I have my racing suit around my waist and the cool compression shirt on top. He shoves the suit down my legs, the material just like my shirt is apparent on my bottom half. Luckily, they're two pieces, so he rips them off easily. One thing about Luca is he takes what he wants when he wants it.

It's a blessing and a curse, but in this current situation, it's a god-given gift.

"You know, I've always wanted to fuck you in your suit."

"Is that so?"

He hums before shoving my spandex down. His hand immediately goes to my clothed pussy his mouth close to my ear. He has me against the wall of what I assume is a closet. What type of closet? I don't know, nor do I care.

"I'm going to have to make your congratulation orgasm quick. Okay, baby?"

I bite my lip and nod.

Shoving my panties down, he aligns his cock with my

entrance and slowly pushes in. I'm already wet from his voice, so it slides in perfectly. I hiss.

He starts moving, and it feels fucking incredible. I stabilize myself with my arms on his shoulders, throwing my head back. The rhythm is slow. I can tell he's trying to find my g-spot. When he finally hits it, I shriek. He covers my mouth with his hand.

"You know I love your screams, but not here. Try to keep quiet, okay?"

I try to say yes, but his hand blocks the words from materializing.

His pace starts going faster and my body starts tensing with every thrust. I can hear the slickness of us. He groans softly every time I tense around him. My sounds become more frantic underneath his hand.

I swear I'm trying not to make a sound, but when I tell you the dick is good, I mean every word.

He said quick and he meant it. I shake around him, seeing the galaxy he once promised I would see. Making sure I came first, his thrusts get sloppy before he unloads inside my cunt. Our breaths release in relief at how quick we can make each other reach our peaks.

Sexually compatible would be an understatement.

He kisses me passionately, and I moan against his mouth before he pulls back. I can feel the smile on his face. "I'm so proud of you, baby," he says. I touch his features with my fingers.

"And I'm so proud of you." Standing up and removing my arms from around his neck, he pulls me into him.

"Don't even think about wiping off my cum. The thought of it under that race suit for all your interviews will earn you a reward once we get back to the hotel." My breathing falters.

That means no peeing for me.

CHAPTER
THIRTY-SIX
MARIA ALEJANDRA

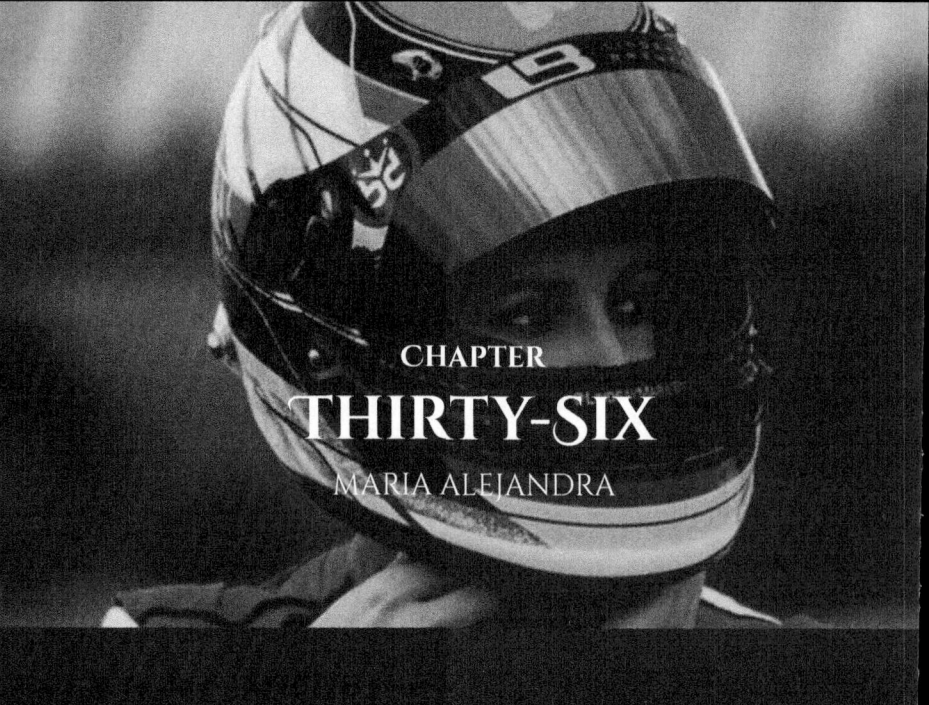

He wants to see where I grew up.

A place that I left and told myself I would never go back to. The place where my mother was killed along with hundreds of other people. But I'm taking him anyway. Only because he did a whole monologue on how he wanted to see where the love of his life grew up. I don't really believe that. He's more interested in what my family does. I don't blame him; the house is something else.

My family's eccentric. They have money, and even though they use it wisely, the family home is nowhere near humble.

Before we got in the car, I told him not to turn random corners and to follow me at all times. I don't want him to get lost, especially in my brother's man cave, aka torture chamber. He doesn't need to see what I'm sure he already has images of in his head.

I'm not ready for him to run away simply because my family is different. So, I plan on guarding him from every dirty secret possible.

"*Ya llegamos, señora,*" our driver announces. I look up to see the entrance way. The pathway to enter is dank and dark but has some classic aspects to it.

"*Gracias, José. No me digas señora, me siento vieja.*"

He chuckles before I climb out. Luca follows.

José pops the trunk open from the driver's seat and takes out our mini suitcases. We only plan to stay three days. Just enough time for Luca to get to know my family better. I can't be here for more than that and he knows it.

"Remember the rules we went over?" I question Luca again. He grabs me by the waist, bringing me closer to him. My hands move up to the center of his chest.

"Don't worry, *ragazza*, I know about all the skeletons you hide in this house." He kisses me softly, reassuring me.

"*Ya hermanita, no quiero ver eso.*" I hear León's sarcastic words boom through the driveway. I turn to see him shielding his eyes. I laugh before his blinding smile shows. Walking confidently towards us, he smothers me in a welcoming hug.

"Okay, I saw you three weeks ago. It's not like we're long-lost siblings." All the breath in my lungs almost disappears from his tight grip.

He lets go of me and turns to Luca, shaking his hand. Luca accepts without a fault. "It's nice to see you coming to your senses." Luca's stone-cold expression comes back as he looks at my brother.

"Well, I guess it's time for a tour of the Hacienda," León says, before Luca looks in my direction and squeezes my hand comfortingly.

Picking up my bag, I walk in behind my brother and feel the cold nature of the living room brushing past me. I get chills immediately, gulping and thinking about all that has happened here.

"Welcome to the home that my sister and I no longer live in, but I'm forced to visit every so often."

Luca walks past me, looking around. "It's nice," he says, but I know he hates it.

Another thing we agree on.

"The house, for the most part, is a normal modern take on Spanish architecture. As you know, my dad doesn't want people to assume that bad things happen here," I mutter the last part softly.

"The detail is nice. He knew what he was doing when it came to being incognito." He can say that again. Little does he know that in the closet next to the stairs sits a whole armory. The same closet where my father puts the coats of his guests.

"After we take your stuff upstairs, I'm sure Ale will show you around her favorite part of the Hacienda, the gardens."

I stiffen but nod after I regain some feeling. "Yep." I smile at Luca who looks down after meeting my gaze.

I start walking up the stairs and hear footsteps trailing behind me. Making my way up to my room, I set my things down. This place is basically a maze. Having different wings pretty much explains it all. There's another staircase next to the kitchen which leads to my father's part of the house, and on the other side is my mother's. León and I's wings are the steps off the primary entrance.

"I'll leave you both here. See you later for dinner." León walks out, shutting the door behind him. My room hasn't been touched since I left. The color is a bright purple, my favorite color at the time. I now despise the color. I'll leave purple for Vio to wear.

"Purple, a very scandalous decision," he tells me.

"I despise the color." I shudder at the thoughts of what happened on the bed he's sitting on.

"What's wrong? I wouldn't have come here if I knew you'd be so frightened." I look at him, putting my hand on his shoulder.

"I'm fine. It's just that this place brings back so many memories and I don't know how to process it all."

"You've never told me what your life was like when you were little."

I start playing with his shirt anxiously. "It's a thing I like to leave in the past. I ran as fast as I could when I had the chance. Never looked back and that's good enough for me."

"One day you'll tell me, and I'll be here to listen to every word that comes out of your mouth."

I smile and laugh softly. "It will come, but not here, not now."

"Okay." He nods, looking out the window. *He wants to see the gardens.* I walk towards the door and twist the knob slightly. I take a deep breath.

"Come on, we still have a whole garden to see."

He chuckles sadly. I know he wants to know about another part of me. I'll tell him soon. But the place and time must be right. Because my trauma is something that's better left unspoken.

I trust him, but how much?

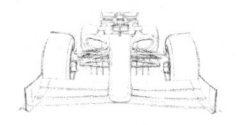

I see green on all sides of me. The vines, as always, are a plush pine color, bringing back an intense nostalgia. One that I'm fond of but also makes me nauseous. I know what Luca's thinking. My house is eerie, while his is nice and lively. The one thing they have in common is the likeness of abuse. His is mostly mental, while mine is taxing on both parts of myself.

"Where are you taking me, Ale?"

"The only place in this house where I felt safe." I take his hand, leading him out of the maze. I take the passageway that doesn't lead us to the center, but goes around it. Passing another set of steps, we reach my track, old and dusty. My karts sit on the side, rusting over the years that I haven't used them. He looks at me.

"I remember a time when you told me that having a butler was the height of wealth. And yet you have a track in your backyard." Letting go of his hand, I open the wire gate surrounding the drag strip.

"That was different. This was a gift for my eighth birthday. One thing you should know about Sinaloa is that there's a lot of untouched land. Why do you think it's the mecca for drug rings everywhere? Once my dad had a stable business, he knew that he wanted his house to have acres and acres of land. The gardens were already built before I was born, but part was untouched, so he built me this." I shrug, gesturing both my hands towards the circuit.

"A very dramatic present for an eight-year-old, don't you think?"

I look at him. "My dad always knew I was going to be a racer after I watched someone win a world championship on TV when I was six."

"And who would that racer be?" he mocks, but I think he already knows the answer.

"You." I close the gate and turn back around, walking towards the maze yet again. He catches up to my strides.

"So, you were obsessed with me before this all

happened, huh?" He gives me a cheeky smile and I stop in front of him.

"I was six and didn't even know who you were, only that you were fast."

"Were?" he challenges.

"Old man, you retired years ago. I don't think you could drive an F1 car again for the rest of your existence. Not to mention how out of race shape you are. Have you gained like thirty pounds in just pure muscle?"

"I could jump into any car and beat you, *ragazza*."

"Is that so? Last time I checked, I've beaten younger men at their own game for the last year or so." I look up at the sky, thinking to myself.

"Hmm. One day we're going to test that theory out, aren't we?" He smiles down at me, bringing my frame into his arms. Looking down at me, he kisses my lips softly.

Pulling back, I whisper softly, "In your dreams, old man." I take off running as he starts chasing me. I laugh with every stride I take. Finding the nearest entrance, I make my way through and start slowing down as he gets farther behind me. I would love to see him try to get through the maze by himself. It takes years of practice.

"I'm going to find you, little girl, and when I do, I might even fuck the life out of you."

I look down and wonder if I want to be caught or if my defiance is talking more than my vagina.

I think I'll go for the defiance option.

"I would love to see you try," I yell out. I find my way

through the maze with ease. I forgot how good I am at getting through this thing. Taking a sharp turn, I see that I've reached the middle square of the maze. Suddenly, feeling a chill run down my spine, my heart drops. I know where I'm at and this is the exact place I didn't want to see.

Looking around, the pain comes rushing back. I feel like I'm being pushed under water and drowning. Someone's holding my head down until I can't breathe anymore. I start hyperventilating at the sight in front of me. My mother's grave, the wall of flowers. All the white has gone to dust. Fading as the wind takes away the petals.

"You can't run from me, baby," I hear in the distance as his footsteps get closer. My eyes start throbbing, and my brain fades away from my body.

Everything goes black.

My eyes open, the black that once consumed me fading away as the sun burns into my skin. Looking up, I see blue. A crisp cerulean meets my gaze. No clouds, just the sun. My eyes shoot down and green consumes my whole body. The grass, a cold texture on my skin, collides against the heat my body is producing.

My hearing starts acting up and I hear nothing. Standing up, I wipe off all the dirt my clothes have accumulated.

I realize that I'm still in the maze.

The world around me is in complete silence until my ears start ringing.

A sudden sound explodes through my ear drums. I turn and see black chairs sitting adjacently with an array of people sitting in them. My father, brother, and Luca are sitting in the front. No emotion runs through their eyes. They look blank.

Ahead of them, vines tangle with each other. This looks familiar.

Black roses are scattered all around. It's a memorial service just like my mother's and grandmother's. I look to the right and see both their graves sitting in the midst of branches. Then I realize what this is.

It's my memorial.

I'm staring at my funeral, the black roses symbolizing my death. Just like all the women in my family. But the difference is that there is nothing in the middle, just a white skull. Not a black rose like the others, because my life is encompassed in the color black.

A chain reaction spreads through me as I fall to the ground, sensory overload hits. I hear children laughing. I turn to look at them.

They run past me like I'm not even there.

I am nothing. Just black ash blowing in the wind, just like my mother.

They sprint towards Luca, and a little girl jumps on him.

He reacts, a sad smile on his face. "Where's Mommy?" the girl speaks. He looks at the memorial.

"She's right there, sweetheart." He points to the flowers.

"No, Daddy. That's not her. Those are roses."

"Let me tell you something, *piccola mia*. Your mother loved the color black. She died in this world, but not in our hearts. We all turn into ash and her black roses. Because when we leave the people we love, when we finally reach the inevitable, we leave our black roses behind with all the color that surrounds them. The impact that we leave is the life that we lived."

I freeze. That's my daughter, and he just said exactly what my father said when we attended my grandmother's funeral.

This must be a sick joke.

The little boy who came in with my daughter runs towards León. He's sitting next to a woman with dark red locks. Her black hat is drooping over her eyes, so I can't see her face. The boy jumps into her grasp. Her hands are covered in black satin gloves, contrasting against her skin tone.

I just sit there looking at what's in front of me and I don't feel anything. No anguish. No frustration. No longing.

I hear cries; something you would hear a bird release. An owl flies overhead, diving for the ground and stopping in front of me. It lands, setting its gaze on mine. It's staring in my direction with its round eyes. Its feathers are obsidian mixed with a carob undertone. Mimicking my movements, I turn my head slightly as it follows.

Suddenly, it flies away, and a single feather blowing in the wind drops into my hands. I admire its softness before it soars away towards everyone. And when I look up, they're gone.

I wake up.

CHAPTER
THIRTY-SEVEN
MARIA ALEJANDRA

I woke up in my bed.

Luca was distraught after I passed out and forced me to tell him everything.

After I finished talking, he stayed calm before he said he would be back. Ten minutes later, I could hear the sound of punching.

I could tell he was upset. I just appreciated the space he gave me when he left the room. I didn't need to experience that again. Especially with him. He came back and said that he was sorry, which makes no sense to me. Why would he be sorry? It's not his fault. He kissed me, told me he loved me, and then we fell asleep. My brother came banging on the door saying dinner was in thirty minutes.

So, we got up and dressed.

Walking down through a dark Castillo house is not for

the faint-hearted. During the day it's fine, but at night. Not so much.

I lead him towards the dining room, which is on the other side of the house. Yes, the house is fucking huge.

We enter the black, dimly lit dining room. My father sits at the head, as always, with León right next to him. On the other side of him is Lillian. She's rocking her age in all white. Even though she technically took my mother's spot, I've always had an affinity for her.

Maybe it's because León is like my second father, but Lillian is genuinely the nicest. She treated me the same way she treated her son.

"*Mi niña.*" Lillian jumps out of her chair, running to hug me.

"*¿Lillian, como estas?*"

She smiles. "*Bien. Bien.*" She looks over to Luca at my side.

"*Esté debe ser tu hombre.*" She smirks and raises her eyebrows. I laugh, nodding. I see my father come up behind her. He nods in my direction as a greeting.

"Take a seat," *Papá* says, gesturing towards the table. León stays seated with a smile. We walk over to the other side of the table, so we're all sitting near each other. The dining room is huge, and there is an array of chairs still empty. But still, even when I was little, we always had dinner here, no matter what happened. It was the only constant I had, along with León.

"How are you both?" Lillian asks.

"Good," I say in a cryptic tone. I'm not in the mood to go on about my life right now.

"I see you took a walk around the gardens today," my father says right next to me.

"Yes, Luca enjoyed them. Didn't you?" I turn to look at him, his jaw clenches.

"They're okay."

"Just okay?" my father questions.

"I like the overall structure, but everything else is nothing I haven't seen before."

Way to make an impression on my father, Luca.

"I made those especially for Ale's mother. She always loved them and that seemed to rub off on my daughter." My hand clenches at the mention of my mother coming out of his mouth. We haven't talked about her since she died. Why would he be bringing her up now?

I hold my tongue, hoping Mauricio will shut up, but of course, he goes on. "That's why we buried her there; she loved it."

"She sure did," Lillian says quietly.

"Can we stop talking about her?" I feel Luca grab my hand, making it release all the tension I was balling up in my fist.

"Why would we? I mean, this is the first boy you've brought home. He should know about your mother."

"You mean the woman you killed? The woman who resented me my whole life because I was the product of her pain?" My father looks at me shocked.

"What do you mean who I killed?"

"You know what I'm talking about, so don't even start."

He slams his hand in front of me, and I flinch. I feel Luca about to jump up, but before he can, I stop him by putting my hand on his thigh.

"Watch how you speak to your father, *princessa*. Don't forget your place."

"I have loved you for so many years, but you have never been a father to me. Me leaving for Mexico City was a breath of fresh air for you, wasn't it? León is the only person who has single-handedly been a father figure to me my whole life."

His breathing is taking a toll on him now as he looks over at his only son and heir."Oh, you mean the boy that I crafted with my hands to become just like me?" he snarls, and León finally enters the conversation.

"Stop it, you two. *Papá*, you know that this is a hard topic for Ale. Just let it go."

His gaze darkens after León chips in. He looks over at me, his features overcome with malice.

"This is where you're wrong, *princessa*. The sweet boy that you love and adore was the one who actually killed her." The words don't process for a moment until finally it clicks.

"No," I say shakily. "That's not possible. Stop playing with my mind just like you've been doing to Lillian and León for years."

"Why do you think León killed her, huh?" He looks over

at Lillian, and she's already crying. León just looks at me with no emotion. Nothing to say. Not even defending himself. That's when I know. It's true.

"When León was young, he always hated your mother because she took over Lillian's spot. So, when I found this little boy with a knife covered in her blood, I knew that he was going to be my heir and he would be worse than I ever was. All this 'he was my only father figure' *mierda* is deception. It's all fake." My father smiles at me with zero remorse.

"How could you?! You knew! Every time I told you how I've resented him my whole life for what he did to her. I never would have expected this from you, of all people," I scream every single syllable in León's direction.

I continue, "You know, it's funny. I've condoned and set aside all the things that you do to people every day because I thought you treated me with the same kind of loyalty. But that was all a lie." I let out a breath and chuckle. I can feel the tears running down my cheek.

"No sabes toda la historia, Alejandra," are the only words I hear before I walk out.

CHAPTER THIRTY-EIGHT
MARIA ALEJANDRA.

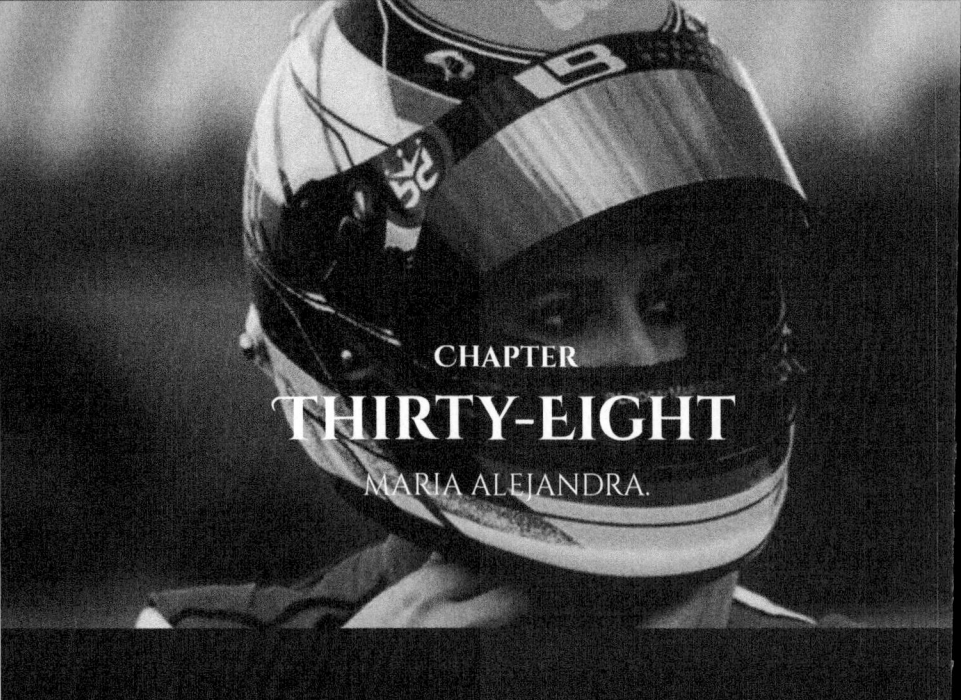

I'm broken. Even more broken than I was when Luca left me at Chapultepec. I feel anger and pain. In a way, maybe my dream was a sign. Letting me know that I would soon fall apart. It could be the years of not wanting to confront my mother's abrupt death or the mommy and daddy issues that I grasp onto but never address.

Everything I thought I knew was a lie.

I ran out of my house as soon as I heard those words come out of León's mouth. Grabbing my suitcase and Luca's in hand, I left and grabbed a taxi. I didn't care if we couldn't catch a flight. All I could do was run as far away as possible.

Luck was on my side, and we booked a flight to Mexico City within ten minutes of arriving at the airport. Ever since we arrived home, Luca and I haven't gotten out of my bed. I don't want to.

MORPHINE

We just lay here while he holds me. I have never loved a man more than I do him. I've concluded that he isn't real.

"*Ragazza,*" he says, against my hair that I haven't washed in five days.

"Hmm," I respond with my head up against my pillow.

"You have to take a shower. I'll help you if you want."

"Nope."

"Please, do this for me," he whispers, pleading. I take a breath and open my eyes, being greeted with darkness. Getting up slowly, my whole body aches.

"I'm only doing this because you asked me to." I can hear his smile as he walks up to turn the light on. I was hoping for a warning, but the bright bulbs flick on in seconds, and I cover my eyes dramatically. My eyes adapt to the light slowly until I see him reach his hand out. I take it and we walk into the bathroom together.

I turn towards the mirror, looking at an aged Ale. I don't even recognize myself. The young me who was full of life is drained.

"You look beautiful. Don't stare at yourself like that. I hate it." He comes up behind me, kissing my neck. Luca turns on the shower, and I thoughtlessly take my clothes off before I jump in.

Luca walks up behind me, still clad in his sweatpants, and grabs the shampoo, pouring it into his hands before massaging my scalp. I groan. *Why does this feel so good?* Pushing me gently under the water, the soap drips off me. He repeats this until I'm clean. Grabbing a towel, he wraps it around my body. He moves us towards the sink, reaching over to grab my toothbrush. He takes the toothpaste and preps it for me.

"Here." Handing me the toothbrush, I turn the sink on so I can coat the paste with water before I put it in my mouth.

He walks out, and I hear rustling before he comes back in. Spitting all the residue into the sink, I turn on the faucet again so that it can glide down the drain.

"I picked out some new clothes for you to wear." He drops them in front of me. I look at him and start tearing up.

"I love you," I say suddenly.

"I love you too, *ragazza*." His smile is somber but genuine as I hug him

"Why does this always happen to me?" I breathe out against his chest.

"I hate seeing you like this. It feels like someone has stabbed me in the chest."

I start bawling, and he holds me like I'm going to slip out of his arms.

After a few seconds, I see red and start screaming. My hands reciprocate my feelings. I don't want to, but I can't help it. I start hitting his chest, each swing getting more forceful. It's like I've been possessed. He takes them all, being my punching bag for a few minutes until I calm down. I stop, then fall down onto the floor. He follows me while holding me in his arms. Wiping away my tears, I look up at him.

"I'm sorry," I mutter.

"Why in the ever-loving fuck would you be sorry?" He brushes away a straggling tear running down my face.

"Because I just hit you." I hiccup, and he just stares at me.

"I would take all your pain. I would take it without a second thought. But that's not possible. All I can do is let you cry and scream. If that's directed at me, I'll accept it with welcoming arms. Your pain is my pain."

I get up and slip out of his arms, putting on the clothes he brought in for me. One of the articles of clothing is his hoodie, my favorite.

"I don't want to leave you like this. But I have something to do today," he tells me while I'm getting dressed, disrupting the silence around us.

"Don't worry. I know you have stuff to do; it's important."

He grabs my head with both hands on either side. "Hey, nothing is more important than you. But this is urgent for the team, which impacts you as well." I nod. "I'm going to take a shower and you're going to watch the next episodes of *The Circle* that you wanted to watch." He kisses my forehead.

"Okay." Walking towards the bed, I envelop myself in the covers after turning on Netflix. Luca appears, freshly showered, and comes over, pressing a final kiss on my lips before walking out.

After watching all eight episodes of *The Circle*, Luca isn't back yet. I don't mind it. I'm preoccupied trying to find out who gets eliminated in the latest episode.

While I'm going through every reality TV show spoiler website on the internet, I hear the front door open from downstairs, followed by rustling. He bought food. My stomach rumbles. Walking down the stairs, I make my way to the kitchen, and see Luca unpacking the groceries.

"Hi."

Turning around he sees me and smiles. "Look at you getting out of your room."

I'm about to respond when I see a thin plastic covering his neck. I rush up to him, looking straight at the material, making it known that I'm interested.

"Did you get a tattoo?" I ask him. He looks at me, quirking his eyebrow. Taking his shirt off, I see the tattoo in its entirety.

It's two roses with no color inside, just black. Ink is spilling out of them in a vine pattern. The roses are on his chest, and the ink trails up to his neck. It's amazing.

"When you told me about your dream, I knew I had to get this tattoo. I had it in my head and sent it over to my tattoo artist. He flew to Mexico just for me and did the whole thing in a day. That's why I said I had to go so soon." Running my hands over every inch, he hisses.

"Sorry, did it hurt when you got it?"

"No. I like having you inked on my skin, the burn felt good." I slap him, making sure I don't hit a part of the raw area before I smile up at him

"You're amazing. You know that, right?"

He grabs me by the waist, getting closer to me. "If you die, then I die with you."

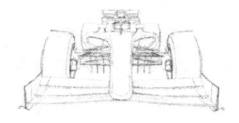

"Are you sure about this?" I question, making sure he knows that what we're about to announce to the world is a do or die situation. It's not like people aren't on to us, but this makes it official.

"I've never been more sure of anything."

"What if they fire us?"

"They can't do that, it's the first race and start of the new season. We'll explain, and if they don't like it, I'll take the fall."

"You won't be doing that," I tell him.

"Yes, I will, and if anyone questions it, I'll simply ignore them." He shrugs just as I hear the car squeal, signifying that we just pulled up to the paddock.

"Ready?" He smirks. I nod, opening the door. Feeling the

heat of Bahrain blow past me, I start walking as Luca comes up behind me, grabbing my hand.

The cameras click just as it happens. I take a deep breath before we walk into the paddock, hand in hand.

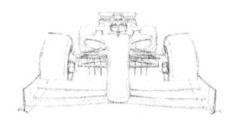

A few months later.

"We will be asking you an array of questions, just like always. You already know that this one will be a little more personal after the whole announcement. If you don't want to answer any of them, you can simply shut up." Lauren laughs, and I nod.

I sit down on the little black stool. Ring lights blaze onto me as a mic is placed overhead. A few months ago, I didn't even want to be interviewed. But here I am, facing the music and most likely answering the questions everyone wants to know. When Luca and I walked into the paddock that day, people immediately went crazy about the whole thing. I didn't care at the time, but once social media got a hold of the news, people were brutal. Of course, with me being the only female driver currently in the sport, the slut shaming was very real. It got better as time went on.

The hashtag #TeamAluca was everywhere. Corporate wasn't very happy, until Luca shut them up, fighting for both our positions, which we kept. Publicity ratings have gone up, and merch sales have gone through the roof.

Everyone loves a good love story, especially one that's unconventional.

"Okay, people. Season six of *Drive for Your Life*, take sixty-four in progress."

The interviewer goes straight in. "So, what were you and Luca like when you first met?"

I look up at the camera, staring straight into the lens, tilting my head.

I say, "We absolutely despised each other."

That's when I smiled.

LUCA'S EPILOGUE

Two years later

Being nervous is something I've never been fond of. But I've never been more anxious than I am right now. I acknowledge the fact that I'm a cold-type of guy, but this woman makes me different. I wasn't even this nervous when I was proposing to Adèle, who I thought was my soulmate.

This time is different. I'm proposing to my real soulmate.

I know she's going to say yes, but that doesn't necessarily mean I'm not afraid of the slim chance she isn't ready.

I'm older than her, and now that I am forty-one, her being in her twenties makes me feel like an old ass man. We've been together for almost three years, and I think it's time.

Also, it's the perfect occasion. I was going to propose

after one of her wins, but once I started tallying up her ranks, I knew she would become a world champion. I resigned last year because I knew it was time. The year after I decided to leave, she goes and wins everything. Ale is currently up on the podium, crying over her Drivers' Championship win. Xavier is at her side, looking at her in approval. I like that boy. He deserves everything he gets.

Standing here behind the curtain at the side of the podium, I breathe in before they start spraying champagne. My leg is twitching. I absolutely HATE this feeling. Jackson Owens stops them and says, "We have one more surprise for all of you and for one specific driver up here in particular. We have the honor of watching the living legend and previous Elektra team principal say a few words." Ale looks puzzled, looking out into the crowd, not seeing me anywhere. I shove the ring in my back pocket, grab the mic, and walk out. Her head turns.

"I just wanted to say a few words as the ex-boss of two of the drivers up here. They all did a great job today, especially my girl. Formula One is a sport where drivers risk their lives every day for your enjoyment and their own. I hope you all enjoyed the race today and let the celebrations begin." Xavier doesn't even flinch. He grabs the bottle and starts dousing me in champagne. I laugh once the cold liquid hits my face.

"Feeling good now, boss?" He smirks, looking at my back pocket.

"Yes." He looks at me with a skeptical expression. I want

to take a drink, but I don't let myself. I look over and see Ale gazing at me, interested in why I'm up here.

"You just had to take my shine away," she sings with a smile on her face.

"Always." I look down at her with a massive grin.

At this moment, it's as if everything around us has become background noise. Racing teams and fans cheer as Ren and Xavier start spraying champagne on them from the podium. The liquid flying everywhere. Ale's bottle is in her hand.

It's time. Grabbing the ring out of my back pocket as effortlessly as possible, I get down on one knee. Ale immediately reacts by taking a step back. I hold the black velvet box in front of me while I kneel, baring myself to her.

"From the moment I met you, I knew you were a fire no one could put out. A fire I didn't know would spread through my body and control my every emotion. I know we didn't get off to the best start. But that attitude, while needing some work, keeps me going. I love waking up to you every day, following you all around the world, seeing you in your element, doing what you were meant to do. Seeing you happy is my life's purpose. I know I may be a little old, but you make me feel young again. I'm the only person in this world who can keep up with you. Because you are a spark, one that no one can capture, only follow. I will love you and follow you for the rest of my days." My breath shudders before I say the words I've been nervous to say. "*Ragazza*, will you marry me?" The tears from earlier are streaming down her face. Her hands are still covering her mouth as she just stands there.

"Just say yes already, woman!" Xavier screams out from the side. Snapping out of her thoughts, she nods, and I stand up. The emerald ring, with diamonds all around the stone, adorns her tan skin beautifully as I slip it on her finger. I hear cheers and as I look out at the crowd, everyone is going crazy. I turn my head back around to see her with a smile on her face.

"Is that a, yes?" I ask quickly for confirmation.

"Of course, it is." She jumps on me, and I catch her. The champagne starts flying everywhere, and this time on top of us.

I kiss her softly before setting her down. Glancing down at her ring, I notice she's admiring it.

"I had to get you your favorite. Ever since you told me about Queen Victoria's tiara, I knew that your crown would be this ring. The one that you deserve to wear."

"I love you so much it hurts," she lets out.

"Ditto, *ragazza*."

ALE'S EPILOGUE

O*ne Year later*

"You look perfect," I hear Violetta say behind me. My custom Adèle wedding dress just got in today. The day of my wedding.

Yes. My fucking WEDDING.

I had a vision, and they executed it flawlessly. I wanted to go with a classic form with a twist. Having the chiffon ruffle in black and white was the perfect decision. It's so me, and I absolutely love it.

The bouquet is a mix of white lilies and black roses. I wanted a piece of my mother here today. Even though she wasn't the best to me or anyone else, I know that this was the right choice. I loathe her, but she was still my mom, and this will be my last reference to her in my life. A final goodbye.

Walking out onto the balcony, I take a deep breath of

fresh air, looking out at Florence. The place my future husband calls home.

The gardens were his suggestion when we first discussed a location for our wedding. I was adamant about staying somewhere in Mexico. We compromised and our honeymoon will be in Cancun. I can't wait to drag him around my home country yet again.

But for now, I look at the setup below me. The altar is right in front of the statue of Persephone, and the chairs line up adjacent to it.

The view is perfect. The red and the green contrast in such a way that it looks like a dream. One that I don't know if I'm living in.

Suddenly, I hear footsteps below me and chatter in Italian. Noticing who the voices belong to, I rush back inside.

"*Eso fue abrupto,*" Violetta chuckles as I run back in. "*Luca casi me acaba de ver.*" She looks at me in shock, her mouth full of the sandwich she just took a bite out of.

"*Tienes suerte de que no te haya visto. No queremos mala suerte aquí.*"

"*Ya, se.*" She nods, and I hear the door open.

"Rookie, you ready?" I see Xavier come in. I smile at him in his black suit. All my bridesmaids have all black attire, including my male bridesmaid, being the ray of sunshine he is. I happened to snag him before Luca could get him into his clutches. I even took a video of it, then I posted it, and of course, it went viral.

Let's just say, he went nuts and posted his own separate photo.

THEXAVIERVALENTE: *I knew this was coming, I can see the future. The rookie is getting married, and I am finally going to be her groomsman. Sry, @LucaDonetello she got to me first!*

Luca's groomsmen are what I expected from him, Amir, his brother, and Ren.

"Yep." He takes a full look at me.

"Ale, oh my God. Luca is going to cry when you walk down the aisle."

Violetta and I burst out laughing.

"What? I'm serious. The dress is so you, the ring looks amazing, and the hair with the makeup really helps with the whole—" His hands gesture up and down my appearance.

"Look," I finish his sentence for him.

"See, you know what I mean. Now let's get you downstairs so you can marry that man."

I look around, making sure I have everything. Violetta grabs the veil, fastening it in my hair before turning me around and hugging me. I hug her back with four times the force. *"No puedo creer que mi mejor amiga se va a casar,"* Vio says.

I laugh out, trying not to let my tears get the best of me.

"Estas lista?" she asks, retreating from the hug.

"Nunca he estado más preparada."

Grabbing my hand, she leads me out the door and down the stairs. The music starts as Xavier and Violetta walk down the aisle arm in arm. Next thing I know, I'm at the altar with my Luca.

The Luca I hated. The man I despised. And now, here I am getting married to him. He raises the veil that was preventing me from seeing him well, and I notice a tear run down his face.

"Are you crying?" I whisper. He shakes his head like there isn't any wetness around his eyes.

"I told you," I hear Xavier say behind me, everyone laughs in response to his single tear. *"State tutti zitti,"* he yells out at everyone. They go silent until the priest starts speaking. He goes through the whole 'this man and this woman are gathered here together' spiel.

Then he says, "Now it is time for you to say your vows." Reaching for my piece of paper from Vio, I open it up. I take a deep breath before I start speaking.

"Luca. I remember a time when I despised you, not only because of your egotistical personality, but because I thought you were a threat to my dream and my career." I pause and then continue, "It turns out, you were the best thing to have ever happened. I didn't know what it was like to be treated well by a man in my life. You showed me love, along with how to hold on to it. *Ti amo marito mio.*" I look up at him as he looks down at me with a smile across his face.

Reaching into his pants pocket, he takes out a piece of paper. He starts saying his vows.

"Let me tell you a story. My great-grandfather once loved a woman so much that he made these beautiful gardens for her. Her love for plants and flowers was the center of her universe. He dedicated his life to her purpose, starting a wine business in my family's name. The statue we're standing in front of is the epitome of his love. My great-grandfather saw his wife as his Aphrodite." He pauses. "Maria Alejandra Atena Castillo, you are my Athena. Strong, resilient, and beautiful. All these characteristics make me love you more every day. I may not have a decade old statue for you, but you have my heart, soul, and my entire being. Here we stand in front of a piece of a love story that decided my family's fate. You are my fate, my purpose, and I know I love you more than my great-grandfather loved his wife. Here, I give you my life in its entirety." I start bawling my eyes out.

And just to think that this man made me want to strangle him just years ago. "I now pronounce you man and wife; you may now kiss the bride." Luca darts for me, enveloping me in a kiss.

"I knew this was going to happen! You should thank me," Xavier shouts from the side. I laugh against Luca's lips, and he does the same.

Looking down at me, he says, "does this mean you're mine?" He gives me his signature smirk. I remember hating it for so many months, but in this moment, I realize how much I love it now.

"Yes, husband. This means we belong to each other."

What the fuck happened to Luca Donatello?

Me, that's what.

ACKNOWLEDGMENTS

When it comes to this book, I have a variety of people to show my gratitude towards. The first person I want to thank is YOU, the person reading my book. As my queen Lucia Franco says, "Readers make the world go round." That is my truth, as a reader and now published author. I put a part of myself into Ale and Luca's story, anywhere from personal experiences all the way to my favorite tropes. I wrote this manuscript for the reader in me. I want to thank you all for reading the words that I write at an ungodly hour.

My Parents: While I know you might not love what I wrote (especially you mom, pretend you never read the spicy scenes) your constant love and push for me to do what I love my whole life, has led me here. I wrote a whole book, and your unconditional support has helped me more then you know. I wouldn't be here without you and Morphine wouldn't be published if you love wasn't never-ending. I know I don't say this much but I appreciate and love you more than words can describe.

Jess: Thank you for listening to my five am voice messages thinking I'm crazy but telling me the opposite.

You've helped me grow as a writer and made me realize the things that I needed to fix. Your friendship and constructive criticism keeps me going. Can't wait to write some words with you one day.

Isa: Thank you for being the most positive and kind person in the world. You make me realize that genuinely pure souls exist on this planet. Not to mention you having to listen to my five am voice messages as well as Jess (I know you both love it.) Your grammar blows me away, so I thank you for everything you do.

TRC DESIGNS (Cat): We have been friends for a little bit, but my love for everything you do has driven it. I am proud to say that you designed my discreet cover and made it everything I wanted it to be. You are a true creative genius and I appreciate the love and heart you put in every single day for our community.

Thegraphicescapist: My first instinct when I realized I wanted a person cover is to have a woman on it. To me all my stories are driven by my MFC. When my friend Isa sent me this cover over dm, I knew that this was it. EVERYTHING about it fits who Ale is in this book. For that I thank you, my person cover is a fucking piece of art, and I am indebted to your creativeness for it.

Lucia Franco: Where do I even start with you? You are the most kindhearted and compassionate person I know. Pushing me to strive for more and get my book out there. Off-Balance is my favorite series ever and I am so proud to call you, my friend. Thank you.

Salma: Thank you for ripping this book apart while making me realize the things I needed to fix. I needed constructive criticism and you gave it to me at the max! Your comments and desire to help me, I will forever be grateful for. Our like-minded obsession for older men is the best thing that could have ever brought us together, thank you.

My Betas: Thank you for every single comment and criticism that you gave this book. Not only did it inspire me to keep going. But it made me want to release Morphine. Thank you.

Gaby: Your support as my aunt made me feel something that I can't even describe. You were excited from the start even though you didn't even read a word I wrote. You are one of the most influential people in my personal life to have led me to this point. Thank you.

Me: I am writing an acknowledgment to myself because I just wrote an entire book. A WHOLE BOOK. Sam, I know you feel weird that you are writing an acknowledgment to yourself, but you deserve it. After everything you have been through you are here doing better than anyone who has hurt you. Remember: your best revenge is success.

About the Author

Sam is trying to get through school and fulfill her dream of becoming a full-time author. Her Mexican heritage and obsession with F1 as well as age gap tropes has driven the inspiration for "The Rush World Series."

Having been a reader before writing her first story. She started this journey with her bookstagram page and podcast in hand. Now she is taking the final step to achieving her dream by releasing her first book Morphine.

Her life revolves around watching anything pertaining to Game Of Thrones, Formula One and fantasizing about her array of celebrity crushes. Reading and writing has empowered her to survive through tough times. A gift she hopes she is passing on to her readers through her writing.

If you want an author with too many plans and no genre to hold her down, make sure to check out her words she writes while delirious at 3am.

*If you want more of the author before the next book release, check out **@AUTHORSAMLYNN** on all the following platforms including her podcast **@THEBOOKISHBABES** and her book reviews **@SAMSIMPSFORSTORIES** all of which can be found on her website.*

https://www.authorsamlynn.com
Thank you for reading. Are you ready for the next book? Can you guess who the next hero and heroine is?

Printed in Great Britain
by Amazon